GREEN FIRE

In May 1981 a Turkish assassin, Mehmet Ali Agca, shot and seriously injured Pope John Paul II. On his South American trip of March 1983 a further attempt to kill the Pope was uncovered in Guatamala. *Green Fire* is based on an attempt to kill an earlier Pope, Paul VI, during his visit to South America in 1968. The result is a first novel of outstanding power and suspense, raising many issues only too topical today.

About the author

Frank Jameson was educated at Oxford University and spent many years working in Latin America, during which time he travelled extensively through Colombia before returning to England to become a history lecturer. Apart from his interest in politics and history, he is a devotee of horse racing and bridge, is an avid collector of classical music, and describes himself as a 'movie buff'. He is married and lives in London with his wife and daughter.

GREEN FIRE

Frank Jameson

CORONET BOOKS
Hodder and Stoughton

For P. and L.

Copyright © 1984 by Frank
Jameson

First published in Great Britain
in 1984 by Hodder and
Stoughton Ltd.

Coronet edition 1988

Printed and bound in Great Britain
for Hodder and Stoughton
Paperbacks, a division of Hodder
and Stoughton Ltd., Mill Road,
Dunton Green, Sevenoaks, Kent
TN13 2YA (Editorial Office: 47
Bedford Square, London WC1B
3DP) by Richard Clay Ltd.,
Bungay, Suffolk.

British Library C.I.P.

Jameson, Frank
  Green fire.
  I. Title
  823'.914[F]   PR6060.A/

ISBN 0-340-38082-9

One

March 1968. Colonel Durand was angry. No one had hinted to him until that very morning that the normally routine meeting of E.I./J committee at Sickle House would be called for six p.m. instead of the usual eleven a.m. It was just such inconveniences, he reflected grimly, that had plagued him all his professional life. The scandal, for example, over certain atrocities committed on the Japanese defenders at Ramree had happened to break on the very day before his first promotion board. As a result his career – the career of one who had previously been described as "possibly the most brilliant young officer of engineers in the field today" – had been brought to an abrupt close, and simply because of an unfortunate accident of geographical location. So that here he was, still only a colonel, fiddling his life away as military co-ordinator to a lot of cloak-and-dagger wallahs in their Northumberland Avenue think-tank.   ·

And now, with his evening ruined, explanations would be necessary to Marion. While generally tolerant of his job's vagaries, his wife would not take kindly to his non-appearance that evening: the cocktail party at Seringapatam, their expansive residence in Oxshott, had been planned for months and was to be one of the major events of the local social calendar. Should he, then, make his apologies to Sir Ian and absent himself? The temptation was considerable.

The advantages of membership on the steering committee of E.I./J were trivial, and his impressions of the new direction the committee was taking under Sir Ian Crombie were not favourable. Sir Alan Nottingham, Crombie's predecessor, had appealed to him as a man with a military turn of mind: his background as Chief Constable in two of Britain's largest cities had produced a certain bluff lucidity, an impatience with the convoluted traditions of the Foreign Office, and an ability to reduce complex issues to clear-cut matters of security. Sir Ian, on the other hand, coming from St Antony's College, Oxford, with doctorates in law and economics, represented all that Durand most disliked about the new bearings in the service.

Colonel Durand's irritation, aggravated by an acrimonious passage of arms over the phone with Marion, was not assuaged when, on entering the conference room on the fifth floor of Sickle House at six p.m. precisely, he found only one other person there: Philip Ledbury, a long-standing member of E.I./J, and a loyal Crombie man.

"Perhaps you could tell me, Ledbury, why this meeting has been called at this ungodly hour? And how long is it likely to go on, anyway?"

Ledbury shrugged discreetly. "Perhaps we are to be offered an item of unusual interest?"

"Interest as defined by Crombie, no doubt."

"Well . . ."

He was spared further hedging by the abrupt arrival of Sir Ian Crombie, flanked by Blakely and Cameron. Behind them, carrying a sheaf of documents, came Hammond, chief of support operations, political warfare.

Having stormed to his chair, Sir Ian opened the meeting in typical fashion. Slumped backward, his chin lowered on his chest – producing a doubled or tripled effect in that never prominent part of his face – he waited in silence for at least a minute, as if lost in private meditation. Only then did he gather himself and launch the heavy charm for which he was famous.

"Gentlemen, I must ask your forgiveness for calling you here at this hour, but when you have heard what Pug here has to say I think you will agree that it is in a worthwhile cause."

Turning in his best Claude Rains manner, he flashed a dazzling smile at "Pug" Hammond. Hammond, a forty-five-year-old ex-commando who had attracted the attention of the War Office in the Korean conflict by his outstanding administrative skills, gave with his seventeen-stone frame an impression of ponderousness which was always dispelled, however, the moment he spoke to his brief. Hammond was one of the few men who commanded the admiration of both the "ins" and the "outs" of the service – both those in Crombie's inner circle, for whom he was Pug, and those who, like Durand, hankered for the good old days of the Alan Nottingham regime and who called him, perhaps wishfully, the Gauleiter.

"Let me tell you a story," Hammond now began, "which really starts back in 1944. As you know, in that year the red armies started to sweep across Eastern Europe and to some people there the postwar pattern was already clear. In Budapest there were two brothers, both musicians of considerable talent. One of them saw the writing on the wall and got out once the Soviet war machine began to roll towards Hungary. He went to America and carved a comfortable niche for himself in Hollywood where, under the name of Tamás Kovaks, he is now well known as a composer of film scores. But it is with the second brother, whom we shall call Janos, that we here in this room are concerned. Janos stayed on in Hungary after the war and appeared to accept the 1948 revolution unreservedly. As a reward for throwing his lot in with the new regime he was quickly made a kind of cultural commissar. Later, as an official cultural attaché, he worked in many Western capitals including, most recently, Washington.

"Now, we know that some time in the 1950s Janos was made a colonel in the KGB, but what remains uncertain is where, if anywhere, his true loyalty lay – then, or later. According to our Washington section there is more than a little evidence that Janos from time to time passed information to the CIA. This raises the obvious question: was he agent-provocateur, double agent, triple agent, or even a 'don't know'? None of this might seem very important since, however one assesses Janos, his intelligence has always been what one might term 'medium level' . . . but something has happened recently which makes the case of Janos altogether more interesting."

Here Hammond paused for effect.

"During his Washington posting Janos struck up a friendship with an Englishman, Bertrand Andrews, who is – as some of you may know – the brother of the orchestral conductor Gavin Andrews, and who is himself a talented amateur musician. He and Janos, therefore, had immediate interests in common. Bertrand Andrews was at that time First Secretary to the British Ambassador on Massachusetts Avenue. I have here a detailed memorandum from him of his last meeting with Janos and the dramatic conclusion of their friendship, which I would like you all to read before this meeting proceeds any further.

"May I suggest that at this stage the best thing is for all of us to adjourn for a preliminary reading of Andrews' curious document? Our task then will be to consider what construction should be put on this whole business. I did not circulate this material before the meeting as, frankly, it contains information of a highly sensitive and potentially sensational nature. For the same reason I must ask all of you to return your copies to me at the end of the meeting."

"Gentlemen, let us resume in an hour," Crombie cut in. "By then we will have had time to digest this report. What I want from you is the fruit of your considerable collective experience. I have my own views, naturally, on the implications of this case, but I will welcome, as always, your expert advice."

Cursing inwardly that there was clearly no chance of an early end to the meeting, Colonel Durand removed himself to his favourite chair in the library adjoining the conference room, there to ponder Memorandum WA/DA/E.L./J/68/31, marked MOST SECRET.

He began to read, at first with irritation: ". . . I cannot pretend that I was pleased with the Washington posting . . . my background and interests centre on Eastern Europe and . . . it did seem to me in many ways typical of the Service that . . ."

Scanning rapidly, Durand stopped at the point, several pages into the memorandum, where the real story began, and read on: " . . . yet it was through this assignment that I met [here a name on the original typescript had been blacked out and the word 'Janos' superimposed in the

8

familiar departmental boldface type] surely the most remarkable man I have ever encountered. We first met in 1966 at a reception for the new Romanian ambassador, when my knowledge of Hungarian surprised and delighted him. Although contact on both sides was wary at first, since we each suspected the other of being a member of the intelligence community (a suspicion in my mind later borne out by events) our common love of things Slavonic and Magyar, especially the music of Bartok and Kodaly, gradually drew us close. I frequently entertained Janos at our house in Georgetown (my wife liked him too). We also liked to spend cold winter evenings at José's bar, just off Dupont Circle. Despite our friendship there was always something withdrawn about Janos and I gained the impression not only that his day-to-day life was an affair of considerable tension for him but also that he was hard pressed by circumstances that he could not – or dared not – divulge."

Durand paused to write in a firm hand on his notepad: "Check Andrews for possible homosexual or bisexual tendencies? Tenor of relationship seems overintense."

He returned to Andrews' narrative. "One incident in particular impressed me – and I may say depressed me as well. One evening in José's we were discussing the fashionable theories of convergence between the USA and the USSR, and the conversation strayed to a consideration of whether there was any difference between the CIA and the KGB – and indeed whether intelligence services served any real purpose in the great affairs of state. I put it to him that both the CIA and the KGB were 'services' only in the sense of being self-serving monoliths, and that their true impact on government policies was negligible. Janos looked pained, anguished even, as if I had touched on an exposed nerve. 'If you knew all, my friend,' he replied, 'you would not talk like that.' And soon afterwards he cut short the evening, saying he did not feel well.

"Though this incident was disturbing from a personal point of view I did not connect it with any particular aspect of Janos' situation until a little later. Another night, this time in my apartment, we were discussing Conrad's *Heart of Darkness*. Janos suddenly burst out, and I believe I quote

9

him accurately, though from memory: 'One does not need the solitude of the Congo to come face to face with evil as a living force. It is with us every day, on these very streets. Let me tell you that Hannah Arendt was never more accurate than when she used that phrase *the banality of evil*. In my youth in Szarvas our parish priest used to tell us that the envoys of Lucifer whom we were most likely to encounter were the lesser demons, the most stupid ones. I know that evil *is* stupid, and I know that because I am close to it. But one must not make the terrible mistake committed by many of your Western intellectuals who think that the stupidity of evil makes it a matter for laughter. Let me tell you that it is the lesser minions of Satan who are the most dangerous of all.'

"This was quite an outburst, and it made both my wife and myself wonder whether Janos might not be heading for some kind of nervous breakdown. And our forebodings were very shortly proved to be justified, though not at all in the manner that either of us had expected. Only a few nights later, at 1.30 in the morning of the first of February, we were wakened by the sound of our doorbell ringing and a desperate pounding on the door. Opening it, we found Janos outside – he had sustained two serious gunshot wounds, one in the neck, the other in the chest. We got him on to a couch in the living room and there, before the doctor I had sent for could reach our apartment, I watched my good friend die. He was only partially conscious, but kept repeating: 'You will soon see it, my friend . . . This year, remember . . . You will see the darkness . . . They are going to do it . . . You must warn him . . .' These five statements were reiterated, gradually becoming garbled. When I asked him who was going to do what, and to whom, he became curiously secretive, as if he feared being overheard, and pointed urgently to the breast pocket of his jacket.

"After Janos had died I investigated the pocket and found a letter addressed to Cardinal Rósza, the Hungarian Primate. Fortunately the Cardinal's name was typed on the envelope, so I was able to make some quick calculations: if I was justified in reading the letter, as I believed I was in such a vital matter, I could open it and reseal it afterwards in another envelope, simply retyping the addressee's name.

On reading the contents I took it upon myself to make a translation, which is now appended to this report. Shortly afterwards the doctor arrived, but he could do no more than confirm that Janos was dead. We did not search Janos' other pockets.

"When the police arrived I quickly became convinced that I had taken the right course of action. The officer in charge of the investigation, understandably wary since he was handling a homicide case that involved a foreign diplomat, became more thoughtful than ever once he had examined the papers on Janos' body. He spoke privately with the doctor, I heard him make a couple of phone calls in the next room, and after no more than half an hour three burly individuals arrived who were improbably introduced to me as representing respectively the State Department, the Immigration Service, and the Office of Cultural Affairs. My scepticism about their status was increased with the arrival of further personnel some twenty minutes later, two of whom were identified as FBI men. It was noticeable that between them and the first three there was a distinct coolness. Areas of jurisdiction, it seemed, were being contested. I was enjoined to say nothing about the case, pending further instructions from my ambassador, with whom the authorities would now be dealing. It was unlikely, I was told, that I would be called upon to testify in any court of law.

"The sequel to all this was that a few days later I was requested to attend a meeting at the State Department. HE agreed that I should co-operate with the authorities in any way that seemed fitting for a representative of an allied nation. I was to be accompanied to the interview by the Head of Chancery. It was also agreed that I should say nothing at this stage about Janos' last words, nor about my reading of the message to Cardinal Rósza. If, after consultations with London, it seemed suitable that this information be passed on to our American allies, my ambassador would handle the matter. The interview accordingly was a routine affair. I was, however, asked several times to recall anything Janos might have said to reveal a closeness to high-level decision-making centres in

11

Eastern Europe. It was hard for me to explain the truth, which was that Janos had always seemed to my wife and myself to be more a metaphysician manqué than a covert politician.

"This, then, is a summary of my dealings with, and my knowledge of, Janos."

That was the end of the relevant part of Andrews' memorandum. The rest of the document consisted of a pathetic plea to the Civil Service Commissioners that the writer's association with the dead Hungarian should not be held against him, nor act as a bar to advancement. Andrews spoke of "a web of unavoidable circumstances that had extended beyond the compass of a normal career officer". Durand reflected contemptuously that this claim did not bear out the cultured and sensitive self-image that Andrews had been at pains to present in his account of his relationship with the dead man. Conning this part of the dossier with the swift dismissiveness that Durand's critics would have said was at once his strength and his greatest weakness, he came finally to the translation of the letter from Janos to Cardinal Rósza.

Washington, 30 January 1968

Your Eminence,

Time does not permit me to explain why I approach you now, but let me urge you to use your undoubted influence in the Holy See to urge His Holiness to turn away from the path he has marked out for this year. If I say that an Apocalypse is at hand you may understand the danger in which we all stand from the actions of those who know no law, natural or civil, no morality, and no humanity. Let the Pope return to the example of Pius XII in immobility.

Sir Ian Crombie reconvened the meeting at a few minutes short of half past seven. "Your comments, gentlemen, please?"

"If you ask me," Colin Blakely remarked, "this whole thing sounds like a gloss on the old saying that if you've got a Hungarian for a friend you don't need enemies."

The others braced themselves. From a career-oriented man like Blakely this was a *faux pas* of the first order. Crombie's dislike of facetiousness was notorious.

Sure enough, the response came short and sharp. "I would have thought that this was neither the time nor the place to exercise a dubious penchant for levity. Can we please have some more valuable comments?"

"The only note I have made here can have little real significance," Ledbury offered, warily anticipating Crombie's likely reaction. "But it does seem curious to me that Janos, although presumably a communist, should have been so committed to a Catholic view of evil, and then should have died on a date with a special significance in the occult calendar."

"What significance is that?" asked Durand, unashamed of seeming a simple soldier.

"February the first is Candlemas Eve. A time of traditional evil, like Hallowe'en or Walpurgisnacht."

Crombie's temperature seemed to be rising. "I bow to no one in my admiration of your erudition, Philip, but is this really the sum total of your insights? I hardly think we are dealing with an episode in black magic. Really, gentlemen, I am astonished at you. Can we now have some serious professional perceptions?"

There was a short silence, broken eventually by Alan Cameron, one of the men generally regarded in the Service as a key figure in Crombie's "Scottish Mafia". "What amazes me is Janos' failure to use any form of cipher in his bizarre message to the Cardinal. Even allowing for difficulties of decipherment, I cannot believe that any top-ranking agent would ever communicate material of this alleged sensitivity totally *en clair*. I think that what we have here is simply a case of abnormal psychopathology . . . there's something morbid and lugubrious about the man Andrews portrays, don't you think?"

"Judging by this memorandum alone," Crombie said briskly, "I would be inclined to agree with you. But the other information we have on Janos builds into a more solid picture. Would you care to elaborate, Pug?"

Hammond took up his cue. "According to Pete Rhodes,

13

our man now in Washington, there is reason to believe that since 1948 Janos has been a colonel in the KGB. But the American sources go further – Rhodes' contacts hint that at some stage in the fifties Janos became what the Yanks call a 'walk-in'. As you know, Washington is always suspicious of these Greeks bearing gifts, so they adopted the usual tactic of using him as a double and testing the reliability of his information. His forecasts of Russian intervention in Hungary in 1956 apparently convinced most of the waverers that they had indeed struck gold."

Sir Ian sat back, beamed seraphically round the table. "An undervalued gentleman, our Janos – a man in fact who I believe cultivated a middle-range reputation as the best possible cover for his real and outstanding abilities. After all, in every line of work – but perhaps most particularly in our own – there's nothing more boring than the known quantity, the reliable hack. This garbled message to Andrews, therefore, together with the oracular letter to Cardinal Rósza – allowing always for the unfortunate *mittel-Europäische* leaning towards melodrama – surely deserves our most serious attention. And especially since we must not forget that Janos died delivering them . . ."

He paused, his elbows on his chair arms, resting what there was of his chin on the backs of his linked fingers. "And what does that suggest? If we accept that Janos was indeed a top-grade operator, then for either side to eliminate a man of such stature is almost unprecedented. Clearly he had become the possessor of information so delicate that he simply *had* to be silenced . . . As for your point, Alan, about the lack of cipher, I think our difficulties here at this meeting answer that. Janos obviously understood that signs and symbols can be a better code than anything dreamed of in the cybernetic philosophy. And if he seems in this case to have overdone his obliqueness, then I for one am willing to take that merely as a sign of our own stupidity. The truth, I suspect, gentlemen, is staring us in the face, but we're too blind to see it."

"Has anyone been able to discover," Ledbury murmured drily, "what the good Cardinal makes of the message?"

"Hardly," Crombie pointed out with some acerbity.

"Always remembering that we have not even admitted to knowing of the thing's existence . . . But I doubt if he makes very much of it. A man in his position must receive such apparently deranged exhortations by the dozen."

Colin Blakely, the more usual target for Sir Ian's sarcasm, cleared his throat. "Surely what is crucial here is the relationship between Janos and Rósza. Janos hints at an acquaintance. If so, then the letter might be taken seriously. Do we know if such an acquaintance existed?"

Hammond sorted through his notes. "Apparently Janos and the Cardinal grew up together in Szarvas and attended the same elementary schools. They both fought as guerillas against the Germans in the war, though not in the same units. Thereafter, when in 1948 Janos accepted wholeheartedly – or seemed to – the communist takeover, their paths diverged and it seems that they never saw one another again. Rósza quickly attracted the attention of his ecclesiastical superiors. He was one of the youngest bishops in the country's history, and was given his cardinal's hat two years ago – when he was still only forty-eight."

Ledbury fingered his copy of Andrews' memorandum. "I notice that the translation of Janos' letter remains unsigned. Presumably, however, Janos would in fact have signed it in a manner that the Cardinal might have recognised?"

Hammond frowned. "After so many years? It's possible, of course. But – "

"But anyway quite irrelevant." Crombie leaned forward abruptly, cutting him short. "We are here to decide on our own course of action, not to speculate on the Cardinal's . . ."

It was eleven p.m. before the meeting broke up. By then a consensus had been reached that Sir Ian Crombie should ask the Political Analysis people for their views before proceeding any further, and also that Hammond, through Peter Rhodes in Washington, should very discreetly sound out the Americans. Colonel Durand supported this, on the principle that any delay in actually committing men to the field on such flimsy evidence was better than none. He was well aware, however, that – no matter what Political

15

Analysis came up with – Crombie would press on regardless. Once Sir Ian had made up his labyrinthine mind – as he clearly had now – nothing short of a threatened cut in Civil Service pay scales would make him change it.

The steering committee was to reconvene the following day, after both Crombie and Hammond had completed their researches. This would mean, Durand realised, another evening meeting, and Marion to be placated once again. He calculated his years until a peaceful golf retirement, and shuddered.

Two

On the evening of 29 March 1968 the lights on the twenty-first floor of the twenty-two-storey office block known as Sickle House once more burned on into the night. The excitement had begun there in the early afternoon when Crombie's most faithful disciple, Alan Cameron, had arrived with a mandate for an immediate Grade-One contingency activation. So unprecedented was this that even the senior personnel in Service Conditions Department had immediately had to take out and dust down the book of rules relating to a Grade One: the little-used file quickly became dog-eared as SCD was plagued from all quarters to rehearse the requirements expected of them in such a situation.

The steering committee meeting called by Sir Ian the previous day did not in fact convene until seven. Colonel Durand, who had spent the day on routine paperwork in his office two floors down, followed by a more than usually unpalatable Civil Service canteen dinner, arrived at the meeting in a thoroughly negative frame of mind, determined to say nothing that might interfere with what Sir Ian must by now have decided. His prime consideration was to get home to Oxshott, and Marion, as soon as possible.

Sir Ian opened the proceedings with his usual vigour. "Well, gentlemen, now that we have decided to take effective action on the basis of the information we discussed yesterday, the question before us is what that action should be."

Durand smiled to himself, but kept his own counsel. The protest, when it came, was Colin Blakely's. "Excuse me, Sir Ian, but I'm not aware that any such decision was taken. I

17

cannot appeal to the records on this as yesterday's discussion, unlike today's, was unminuted, but I recall most clearly that our only conclusion was that the warning emanating from source Janos – for all its obscurity – was probably genuine. That and no more."

"But surely, my dear Colin," Crombie replied, ominously smooth, "you are not suggesting that on the one hand we treat this information as high grade and authentic, and yet on the other hand we do nothing about it?"

"If Colin will not suggest that, then I will," Ledbury put in. As an old stager, from the Sir Alan Nottingham days, he seemed to believe that he had both a duty and a right to restrain his new chief's worst excesses. "If a 'best-case' scenario applies and we are indeed with what Janos terms an apocalyptic event, then it seems to me that we are utterly out of our depth. Our intelligence service would need to be on a Russian or American scale to deal with the possible implications. If we were to act upon this matter we would need the kind of worldwide operation we cannot conceivably, as a second-class power, afford. I would also point out that I don't think we dare risk another public fiasco, with the Commander Crabbe case still so alive in the media's memory – particularly as we all know the present Prime Minister isn't exactly the Service's best friend."

Crombie, however, was ready for that. "The PM need know nothing of our actions. National security, per se, is not involved. If anything comes of our enterprise, we can present him with a highly agreeable fait accompli. If not, then our hands are clean and he need never know. I hardly have to remind you that a success would be good for the morale of the Service, and would add weight to our request for an increased supplementary estimate this year. The talk in Whitehall is all of cutting defence subheads – obviously the PM has to throw a few scraps to his backbenchers, but I aim to see that our budget is not affected, or die in the attempt."

Again Durand held his peace. It was hardly unknown for men in the field to die in the pursuit of a defence subhead.

Ledbury too, his duty at least notionally done, remained silent. And Blakely, unwilling to see too dangerous a

18

gulf open between himself and the man to whom he ultimately owed his job, suppressed his doubts. That left only Hammond, the military man, who to Durand's relief was clearly behind Crombie all the way. But then, since the Janos affair seemed to have been his baby from the start, that was only to be expected.

The meeting turned therefore, without further argument, to the consideration of future actions. And in that connection, as might also be expected, Crombie's brief was detailed and impressive.

"Political Analysis has worked all day on this one. An opinion is forming that the warning given by Janos must refer to a threat to an individual rather than directly to institutions or a regime, and that, because of the scale of his other, more general remarks, the threat is unlikely to emanate from some terrorist group or minor world power. Two central problems remain, therefore. The first is that we cannot know for certain which side Janos was primarily working on – and that means, put baldly, that we cannot know whether the event referred to is a coup projected by the CIA or the KGB. Both, I fear, are capable. The second problem is that the world we live in is complex, and the number of countries that could be dangerously affected by some sensational action – an assassination, for example – is depressingly large, so that our logistic, administrative and support difficulties in this operation will be formidable. Frankly, Pug Hammond here is not confident that we still have enough field agents of the right calibre . . . Perhaps you would like to talk to this, Pug?"

Hammond poured himself water from the carafe in front of him. "The question is entirely one of numbers – identify the most sensitive world areas, keep their number to around twenty, and we can cope. But that won't be easy . . . Vietnam is one obvious candidate, the Middle East another, especially after last year's war. The Nigerian civil war is another possibility, though in my view a remote one. Rhodesia and South Africa must merit close attention. And already, as you see, the list is lengthening. Our Eastern Europe desk says the situation there is highly unstable – and then of course there's the United States."

Not even Durand could let that one go. "Are we seriously contemplating a major operation within the USA? Even apart from the agreement, which we share with all our Western allies, never to operate on each other's territory without consultation and approval, surely the numbers required for even minimum coverage there make the whole thing out of the question?"

Hammond frowned. "Assuming we waive our operation agreements, an American venture would require at least a dozen extra operatives. And at least, as far as cover is concerned, we do have an American election year as an excuse to accredit any number of additional 'journalists'. Party conventions in Miami and Chicago, the list is endless . . . but it could be managed, I believe."

At this point Colin Blakely, career or no career, could contain himself no longer. "Am I really in a minority of one when I say that I can hardly believe my ears? Surely what is being proposed here is not only an outrageous breach of trust between allies but also something that, if it were ever widely known, would lead to the most appalling political repercussions?"

Durand sighed. "I have to say, sir, that I think you are being a little naive about the Yanks. Have you forgotten the Ivens case in sixty-five, when our Special Branch caught the CIA in London with its pants down? That was hushed up by the FO – 'in the interests of the alliance', I believe they called it. And what's sauce for the goose, sir, is surely sauce for the gander?"

"My feelings exactly," put in Crombie. "Which is not to say that we should not make every effort to avoid, as the Colonel here so vividly puts it, being 'caught with our pants down'. And it is for that reason that nobody outside this room, absolutely nobody at all, must know the full scale of this operation. We – "

"But Sir Ian – " only Ledbury, out of them all, had the seniority to dare to interrupt his chief " – are we not all neglecting the very real possibility that this coup, or assassination, or whatever, might take place right here, in the UK? Should not MI5 be put in the picture – and the Special Branch too?"

20

Crombie eyed him unfavourably. "My words, Philip, were 'the full scale of the operation'. Naturally our people will be alerted, but in limited terms. The same will apply to departments even closer to home, in this very building."

He leaned forward. Durand saw that the time for discussion, if there had ever been one, was over. They were to be told now what was going to happen. So that there was a fair chance, he thought thankfully, that they would all be out of the place before midnight.

Crombie cleared his throat. "As far as areas of prime risk are concerned, an enterprise of international significance, whether it comes from the left or the right, can be considered unlikely this year in Africa – except possibly on the southern rim, where the leaders of South Africa and rebel Rhodesia can always be said to be at risk."

Durand averted his gaze. The reference to "rebels" in Rhodesia offended him – in general he supported Ian Smith, falling back on the "kith and kin" argument. But he knew better than to say so.

"I have decided to rule out Nigeria," Crombie went on, "civil war notwithstanding. But in Asia there are many possibilities: Indonesia, the Philippines, India, Pakistan, Japan, and, most obviously, Vietnam, where assassination was used to get rid of Diem in 1963, with far-reaching results. The Iron Curtain countries I think we can leave to the undeniable efficiency of their own security services. In Western Europe all political leaders are potentially at risk, but an assassination there would be unlikely seriously to damage the stability of the area. So now we come to the area where I believe the maximum deployment of personnel will be needed – the Americas, North and South. The United States we have already considered, while in Latin America the tradition of political assassination is well-established and capable of producing profound political and social disruptions. We know that attempts have already been made by the CIA to eliminate Castro, but it is my impression that this is no longer Washington's policy. Nevertheless, both Washington and Moscow have much to gain – and much to lose – in this area.

"On the basis of these few humble thoughts of mine – "

here Sir Ian paused to glare round, daring anyone to challenge his humility " – Pug Hammond has already drawn up a list of those twenty nations most at risk, and it will be circulated to you all in due course. Agents will be dispatched as soon as time permits. We're calling Peter Rhodes back from Washington to handle the London end of this. Of necessity he already knows so much of the circumstances leading up to this operation that he is virtually one of us. But I must repeat that no one else, positively no one, is to know its full scale . . . Philip here will cover our tracks with the FO hierarchy and with MI5. Colin and Pug will act with me as an inner sub-committee. Clandestine Ops will be given orders on an ad hoc contingency basis. Political Analysis will be asked for a country-by-country breakdown of potential destabilisation points, plus a list of any events of international significance taking place in them. I personally will square things with Sir Wilfred, but only in the most general way, since on no account must any word of this come to the ears of the outside world, or of the PM. I do not exaggerate when I say that our future credibility as a department may depend on this."

Crombie sat back. Waited. "Any questions, gentlemen?"

Colonel Durand shot his cuffs, covertly glanced at his watch, and suppressed the question uppermost in his thoughts: namely, whether Sir Ian had recently been tested for the correct balance of his mind.

Three

Prevailing wind conditions had enabled the Iberia Boeing 727 to take off from Madrid airport and climb steadily without having to bank and turn north over the city. Seated near the rear of the plane, David Lancaster noted with satisfaction that there were few passengers aboard for the two-hour flight to London. In the normal cramped circumstances of tourist class he yearned for the comfort of the first-class section, from which his travel and subsistence allowance debarred him, even when responding, as now, to an Adlon 6 – the Service jargon for a sudden transfer on a red alert basis.

Today, however, he was lucky and could spread himself out, and maybe it was a good omen. Since the Montevideo office had closed in 1964 he had been at the Madrid post, where embassy policies did not need or encourage the kind of expertise he could provide. Nevertheless, even as a virtual supernumerary, he had managed one or two successful coups through his cover identity as special correspondent for an international newspaper consortium: an interview with a Spanish communist leader in exile, another with a leading light in the Basque separatist movement, and many lesser contacts. All these had led to a voluminous file now being stored in the British Embassy, one which contained the most detailed projections on the possible future of Spain after Franco. His more secret SIS work, on the other hand, had not yielded anything very spectacular. Indeed, in order to safeguard his own career, he had had to cover his own tracks in the biggest project he had undertaken. His attempt to "run" Diego Portales inside the Spanish Ministry of Defence had gone badly wrong, and he had had his work cut out to prevent the debacle from seeping back to London. But it had only been when Portales had asked him for £5000 for an unspecified purpose, that Lancaster had finally called a halt, realising that even the most boneheaded official in the Ministry of Defence would be able to work out that on his salary Portales could not afford to run a motor boat at Malaga.

Lancaster reflected that for him the time was out of joint. His ambition had been to specialise in Latin American affairs, but no sooner had he joined the Service than this area of its work had been virtually eliminated. Perhaps it was peculiarly unfortunate that he had been recruited in the aftermath of Suez. The bitter lessons of 1956 had determined all but the purblind to turn their backs on the British imperial past. The obvious first candidate for administrative cutbacks had been South America, generally regarded anyway as a fief of the American cousins. In the River Plate the Service lingered a little longer, out of homage to the Argentine connection, but by the time Lancaster set his sights on a foreign service career, Perón had already cut the lifeline between London and the "sixth dominion". He just squeezed into the last phase of Montevideo office operations, where all his professional skills save his reputation as the best Spanish speaker in the Service were learned. Ever since he had entered that grubby little government building by Westminster Bridge to pass the Foreign Office language test with the highest percentile of any candidate in years, the linguistic promise there revealed had flowered, and he was sure it was this factor that lay behind his sudden present recall.

At thirty-two, Lancaster was in many ways typical of Service personnel in class and educational background, relying on his brain rather than his good looks or charm. In one area, though, he was different. His disenchantment with conventional academia had led him to question the standard political values of a man of his status and class. For this reason he had examined as an undergraduate the political philosophies of both the far right and the far left, and had conceived a strong dislike for all forms of political liberalism, which seemed to him always to will the ends without ever willing the socio-economic means. It was his contempt for cosy Western middle-class sensibility that had first attracted him to the world of political intelligence, where the individual could be outside the normal laws of bourgeois society. So it was that when in his last year at Oxford he was approached by his tutor to discover if he would be interested in a job in government service, requiring "high intellectual gifts, imagination and linguistic talents", he already half knew what he was being offered, and realised too that he was keen to accept. His political extremism, being as yet only a principle and unfocused either upon left or right, he kept to himself. And now, nearly ten years later, he still maintained a watchful respect for both: neither might be likeable but both – when well-administered – got things done.

"So you think the old man's gaga, eh? You could be right. Mind you, Janos was a pretty big fish – big enough to have made a splash in some very high places . . ."

Peter Rhodes, now Lancaster's case officer in London, had a considerable opinion of his own ability to run a security network, and bitterly resented the way in which Sir Ian Crombie kept him mostly away at arm's length, in a post at Washington. In consequence he maintained a conscious and vigorous policy of contempt for Sir Ian, and disobeyed his rulings whenever he dared.

Thus, when Rhodes discovered that he was in London to brief agents going out separately to twenty different countries, he took advantage of his position to disregard completely Crombie's instruction that the wider implications of Operation Janos should not be divulged to them. He felt, in general terms, that the more an agent knew of the operation in which he was engaged, the better he performed.

So he had told Lancaster everything that Crombie had told him, together with some mildly facetious speculations of his own.

"But how could Janos have access to this kind of information?" Lancaster now asked.

"Don't let that Magyar spirituality fool you. I dare say

Janos was a sensitive flower and some even say he was a more than passable musician but the side Andrews saw is only half the story, if that."

Lancaster was becoming steadily more irritated. According to Peter Rhodes, Sir Ian was involved in a madcap scheme and had simply picked the names of countries to be included in Operation Janos out of a hat. Why Colombia? Lancaster wanted to know. If there had to be a shortlist of twenty, why was that republic chosen? All he could get out of Rhodes was a series of gratuitous sideswipes at Crombie's competence.

"What was this other side Janos had, and how come you're such an expert on it?" persisted Lancaster.

Rhodes eyed him speculatively, head on one side. "Do you know anything about three-dimensional cartooning? No, I suppose not. It's geological in a way, overlaying one image with another to build up an impression in depth. And Janos was the most difficult character I ever worked on. I admit he became something of an obsession with me – I still can't believe he's dead. I feel he's going to pop up somewhere and confound us all. It's almost as if my entire *raison d'être* in the Service has vanished with him."

"Would it be too much to ask what you know in hard terms?" Lancaster's courtesy towards a superior was wearing decidedly thin.

"Well, it's clear to me that Janos was a highly accomplished double agent. What I never found out was where his true loyalty lay. The CIA claimed to have turned him, and every test they set him he passed with flying colours. But he was content to stay where he was and, I ask you, have you ever heard of a walk-in that big who doesn't sooner or later ask to be brought in for good? If I had to put money on it I'd bet that Janos was still working for his old Russian masters, though I sometimes wonder if by the end even *he* knew who he was working for, or why. And what I *will* put money on here and now is that he was on to something big, so big he had to go, for all his usefulness to the reds. The one thing you can be certain of in this crazy business is that his information is genuine. Someone somewhere in the world this year will be in the sights of an assassin's rifle . . . It's just the way Crombie's going off at half cock that I can't stand. He's playing politics with your hide, you and the others. He badly needs a success to blow the Treasury out of the water. A pre-emptive strike like this would provide enough ammunition to keep the SIS out of trouble with select committees and snoopers from the Treasury for a decade."

Lancaster sighed. It made sense. "So we're going to bat for an appropriation. Who was it said those who create wars never fight them?"

"Cheer up, old chap. Between you and me the chances of the blow landing where you're going must be next to nil. All you've got to do is lie low until this mess gets sorted out one way or the other. Get yourself some girl or some drink, paint a masterpiece, take up yoga. I envy you, I really do."

"This cover as Second Secretary, Technical Assistance – is it really going to work? I mean, what happens to the existing Second Sec?"

"All taken care of. There's a locally appointed vice-consul who's just being put out to grass. Parker, the real technical assistance expert, will move up – ostensibly to fill the post of vice-consul, but he'll continue to do all the paperwork on the technical programme. The most you might have to do is take a plane now and then to visit some expatriate hack in heavy engineering or whatever."

"So all I do is keep tabs on the American station officer and his minions? And on the communist guerillas and whatever Russians I can get close to?"

"That's about it. Listen to people – look and listen . . . There's only one possible target where you're going, and that's the Pope. Strictly off the record, Colombia nearly wasn't included in Operation Janos but one of the research chappies came up with this papal visit. As far as I'm concerned you can discount that possibility. It doesn't make sense for either side to make a move against the Pope, even given how crazy both the superpowers can sometimes be. Anyone who'd bet on you would be putting money on a thousand to one shot in a class field. And I'm a gambling man."

Four

Later that week David Lancaster's BOAC VC-10 touched down at Eldorado airport, just five minutes late, after the one stop at Antigua for refuelling. For the last hour of the journey, over Colombian soil, Lancaster had systematically called to mind everything he knew about this strange and beautiful land. Somewhere down among those green mountains life-and-death struggles were going on which were as remote from the normal European experience and sensibility as the invasion of the Spanish Armada. At a time when the civil rights movement in the USA engaged the world's attention no one took any notice of the wretched of the earth in Latin America, by comparison with whose sufferings most minorities in the USA lived a halcyon existence. It was typical of Western liberalism, thought Lancaster, to concentrate on a fashionable form of protest, where the tide was running in its favour anyway, and largely ignore the more inconvenient problems of the truly underprivileged.

In Colombia relationships between man and man and between man and woman were still, in European terms, feudal. The merciless brutality of the coffee plantation overseer and the use of murder and intimidation as a means of social control were routine. Then there was the *machismo* which meant that rape was an act applicable only to middle and upper-class Colombian women – the rest of woman-kind was there for the taking. But all these evils were eclipsed by the remorseless savagery of a social system that left tens of thousands of children to die of starvation in the streets of Bogotá, Medellín and Calí, so that the privileges of the oligarchy might remain intact.

All this Lancaster knew, but it bred in him more contempt for the elite than pity for the oppressed, and an obsession with the stupidity of the Colombian leadership.

But now it was time to put aside such reflections – heretical in a defender of the Western capitalist way of life – for the plane was ten minutes out of Eldorado airport, descending through the nil visibility and lurching with the air turbulence common over the Andes.

The Head of Chancery at the British Embassy, Richard Miller, was a bespectacled, prematurely balding career officer, who fancied himself as an academic but who had never been able to square his financial greed with the poor material expectations in Academe. His rise in the Foreign Service, however, had hardly been meteoric, and he now betrayed towards Lancaster the sort of resentment that career diplomats so often entertain towards members of the SIS: that feigned superiority that barely masks a suspicion of having missed the boat.

"Of course," said Miller, "we are under orders from the Foreign Office to afford you such co-operation and facilities as you may require, but it would help me to know your exact purpose in being here. HE is very much *au dessus de la mêlée*; Oldham takes the line that he just doesn't want to know what you chaps are up to, so long as you don't get in the way of normal routines. There is even a standing order from him that in cases like this I should assume full responsibility. Mr Oldham would prefer not even to know that you people are operating in his territory. I can't afford to be so complaisant, and I may as well tell you that I find your presence here quite extraordinary. What possible interest your section can have in a backwater like Colombia escapes me. And this cover as Technical Assistance Secretary. What's behind that?"

Lancaster could see across the wide Carrera Décima to the offices on the other side of the street at the same level, seven floors up. The Caja de Ahorros S A seemed to be in the process of moving offices, whether in or out he could not tell. He watched as half a dozen men wrestled with a filing cabinet. Without taking his eye from the scene and barely troubling to disguise the learned-by-rote explanation he had prepared for the occasion he replied: "Latin America desk wishes to carry out an evaluation of the US Public Safety Programme to gauge the extent to which it is used as a Trojan horse for the U S armaments and allied industries. There is a suspicion that international trading agreements are being undermined by the covert use of, shall we say, blandishments and incentives to would-be or potential importers. If we established the truth of this, we could then decide our own strategy, whether to fight fire with fire, or possibly to implement this kind of OD programme in Africa."

Miller sighed. "I sometimes think the whole of our work has been overtaken by economics now. I joined the FO because of an interest in international politics, yet I find myself overwhelmingly concerned with trade statistics. Now it seems even your branch has been sucked into the economic vortex. I feel my last illusions have gone."

"How do you assess political stability here?"

"Well, I'm a great admirer of this president, Carlos Lleras, and I feel he's doing a good job."

Lancaster was unsurprised by this reaction. "What about the guerillas?"

Miller shrugged. "They get publicity out of all proportion to their real importance. If you came back here in ten years, they'd still be stuck in the cul-de-sac they're in now. In a way the *violencia* put paid to their chances in advance. People here yearn for a period of peace and quiet, and that's what Lleras and the National Front are giving them."

Lancaster allowed Miller to drone on for a while, occasionally asking bored questions which were answered in the same manner, before he slipped in the one that really interested him. "How do you see the Pope's visit?"

"Strictly speaking, we don't know there *is* a visit. The public announcement won't be made until the beginning of May. But of course we've known about it since last month and I imagine your people earlier. Naturally, we've done some homework."

"And your conclusions?"

"Have you seen our résumé on it?" Miller asked, passing him a green folder with pink and orange flags sprouting from the pages. Lancaster flipped through the neatly but arbitrarily paragraphed typed sheets which seemed to contain entirely banal and anodyne information – Pope's sixth journey outside Italy – opened another Eucharistic Congress in Bombay, December 1964 – first visit to Latin America by a reigning pope – he had been in South America before when Archbishop of Milan – Pius XII visited Buenos Aires in 1934 for Eucharistic Congress before he was Pope – fears about Paul VI's health – there was nothing that was not perfectly well known to any informed observer of the international scene.

"It doesn't say here what your reading of his true purpose is."

"So that's one of the attributes they look for, is it? Your reading speed I mean. I take my hat off to you if you've really already digested all that guff."

"It's true, though, isn't it?" insisted Lancaster. "There's no appraisal, for example, of the political significance of the visit."

"What you have in your hands is simply the first draft done by the Third Secretary. The political analysis will now be added by me."

"Is this a significant trip or is it simply internal church politicking?"

"Both, I think." Miller had resumed his official, patronising tone. "The Pope is travelling to open up his power base, in a sense. If he wants to push ahead with the Vatican Council innovations he's got to break out of the straitjacket of the Roman curia. On the other hand, he has to try to put a spoke in the wheel of the theology of liberation over here. Things are going too fast on this continent, so he's trying to co-opt change. The international synod approach, when the bishops go to him in Rome, isn't enough. Basically, he's got to come here and really become involved in the Latin American bishops' attempt to head off the left within the Church. It's a shrewd move, really. In European terms this is a distant part of the globe, but from where the Pope

31

stands it's the region most in need of his guidance. If he can make a successful appearance here he's killed a number of birds with one stone. He's escaped from the clutches of the Curia and the isolation of the Vatican, and so has thrown a sop to liberal Catholics. He's improved his image as a 'pilgrim Pope', not a remote and immobile figure. And, most important of all, he'll have put the brakes on a runaway Church in Latin America, combating its Marxist element and so giving comfort to the Catholic conservatives. He'll have strengthened his own authority while steering a middle path and not siding with any faction."

Miller swivelled back in his chair, well pleased with himself. "You've just had in effect a sneak preview of what will be in my report to London, less the obligatory grovel."

"So it's possible the local left might see his visit as a reactionary move?"

"Not only possible; they *do* see it that way. Some of his own priests openly oppose the visit on the ground that it will shore up Lleras and Co."

"Would there be any reason why the Colombian right might not like it? "Lancaster asked.

"None that I can think of. From their point of view it's all gain and no loss. Unless the Pope were suddenly to call for social reform in specific terms, naming men and institutions, which no Pope would ever do, and least of all this one."

"So the Pope's visit should go off without a hitch?"

Miller smiled. "I can't see anything to suggest otherwise. Certainly the left, however antagonistic they may be, will never risk their already slender power base among the peasantry with an open move against His Holiness."

Two weeks later, as he sat in the Anglo-American club in downtown Bogotá chewing a pepper steak, Lancaster tried to take stock of his situation and put together his impressions of the "Athens of the Andes". The ambience of Bogotá had left him with conflicting sensations. Considered purely as a model city, outside of space and time, it was a great improvement on the tawdriness of Montevideo, his only previous Latin American posting. The ubiquitous sellers of lottery tickets seemed to typify the land itself, combining a primal innocence with a shrewdness in bargaining that would have done credit to an Ernest Bevin. Foreign Office reports made the point that this was a land of "two nations", divided between a small coterie of highly intelligent and well-educated people and a great rump of illiterate marginals. It was, Lancaster had noted sourly, typical of the "neutrality" of the FO that this split was presented minus its social and economic causes, while the presence of a ruthless oligarchy was tactfully glossed over.

Representatives of the "two nations" had been parading past the restaurant window ever since Lancaster sat down. As if in obedience to some unwritten law, the working women and girls of the city, the maids, typists and secretaries, displayed an overwhelming preference for reds, greens and, especially, yellows. The pampered beauties from the wealthy suburbs of El Chicó and Antiguo by contrast went in mainly for blacks, whites and the subtler shades of green.

It seemed to Lancaster that the most telling image of the arrogance and insensitivity of the elite was that of the *oligarqua* sauntering down the Carrera Séptima, sunglasses perched atop their heads in the St Tropez manner, while the wretched refuse of the earth thronged the other streets of the city, spiralling out from their slums and *villas miserias* in the south to beg and implore a living as far north as Calle 30, where the no-man's land between downtown and the Chapinero quarter began.

One obvious target for Lancaster's professional attention was the American diplomatic community in Bogotá. Simply on the basis of probability a fair sprinkling of the large US contingent, consisting of embassy officials, cultural affairs officers in the USIS, Ford Foundation men, Peace Corps officials and the rest, had to be at any rate minor intelligence operatives. It was his introduction to the aforesaid Anglo-American club by the British vice-consul that had first narrowed the field. One lunchtime, as he sat in the club bar, gazing at Bogotá's solitary civic fountain outside, dwarfed by the monolithic skyscraper of the Banco de la República, he had struck up a desultory conversation with the No. 2 man at the Centro Colombo–Americano, Ed Summerby.

Summerby seemed to want to interest him in something he called the "Society for the Promotion of Democratic Values", apparently an Anglo–American cultural organisation, dedicated to preaching the virtues of free enterprise and representative institutions to the benighted Latins. Summerby seemed to be the typical hectoring conservative republican and had obviously identified Lancaster as a potential sympathiser.

"Like I told you, Dave, Colombia is important to us. It's one of the few countries south of the Rio Grande that haven't succumbed to the military. Things have gone real well for us here in the last ten years. If you'd seen our reports in the mid-fifties you'd know how goddamn worried we were then. The *violencia* was providing a classic breeding ground for communism. I'm sure I don't have to teach you your recent history – think how often the reds have stepped in to fill a vacuum caused by persistent violence and dislocation. China, Korea, Laos, Vietnam, you name it. Sure they've had their failures – we fixed 'em good in Indonesia a while back – but the odds are always on their side in a chaotic situation. The Colombian National Front idea was a stroke of genius, and just in time too. Just think, Dave – barely a year after they patched up their differences Castro appeared on the scene. Now imagine the pickings he'd have had here if he'd been around this neck of the woods in the mid-fifties!"

"What about Gaitán's followers? There are a lot of people like them who aren't too keen on your compatriots."

"Sure we've got guys, even in the Front, like López Michelsen, that we could do without. But the overall picture is breezy. The only slight worry we got now is Núñez and his guerillas. You can never be one hundred per cent sure this kind of thing won't catch on big with students and intellectuals."

Núñez: that was a name Lancaster had encountered in London – the leader of the Castroist ELN (*Ejército de Liberación Nacional*) as differentiated – however infinitesimally – from the "freedom fighters", the Maoist FARC

(*Fuerzas Armadas Revolucionarias Colombianas*) and the ELP (*Ejército de Liberación Popular*). But better not let Summerby know that he was so well informed. He said: "But surely the key is the peasantry. So long as they remain docile, Núñez can stay up in the mountains till kingdom come. He won't achieve anything without them."

"Yeah, but that's what I don't like. Núñez and his men have played one very clever line with the peasants. They talk to them gently, try to convert them; there's no rough stuff, no forcing them into the guerilla army. If any of his men gets out of line, steals from one of the villages or rapes one of their women, Núñez puts the guy on trial. And there's only one way his trial ends. We could learn from Núñez back in the States. I tell you, I'd quite like to set him up in one of our federal courts for a six-month spell. He'd knock the shit out of the bleeding-heart liberals."

"You seem to have a sneaking admiration for him, then?"

"Hell, the guy's a red and that makes him Public Enemy Number One in my book. But at least he's got guts and he really stands for something. You're either for free enterprise or against it, right? That's what burns me up about these middle-class bums we've got in the States. Everything's wrong, according to them. The FBI, the CIA, the Pentagon, the multinationals. But where else do they get their fancy middle-class standard of living? Are they willing to give up their second car, their summer homes on Cape Cod, their trips to Europe, their kids' college education, and give it all to their starving brothers in the Third World? Are they shit! Yes sir, I'd like to let a few killers like Núñez loose among those hypocritical sons of bitches."

Summerby's outburst disturbed Lancaster, putting forward as it did the same basic contempt for so-called "moderates" that he himself held. Perhaps he could assuage the awkward twinges of his own conscience by proving to himself that Summerby was a genuine fanatic.

"What changes would you like to see in Colombia, Mr Summerby?"

"Hell, call me Ed. You reserved Britishers. Well, I'd like to see the place run much more closely from Washington. I don't see any point in pouring in millions of dollars of

American money if we don't have a say in how the money's spent. You know there's no proper check on the aid resources that come in here. I'd like to see our boys here in strength seeing that the money gets spent properly."

"But wouldn't that be regarded as intervention in the sovereign affairs of an independent state? Yankee imperialism?"

"Nuts. I'd give 'em a straight choice. Do you want the money or not? If you do, you can have it on our terms. If you don't want us here, you can't have the aid dollar either, so go screw yourselves."

"On that basis there soon wouldn't be any international aid."

"So be it. Who was it said that aid was taking from the poor in the rich countries and giving it to the rich in the poor countries? I reckon he got it about right. Now you take this Núñez business. Lleras should give us a free hand to mop up. There're squads in Florida trained for this sort of thing. Why, with some of these new helicopter gunships we're using in Vietnam we could flush the reds out of the hills in no time."

It was the tenor of this somewhat inebriated lunchtime conversation that led Lancaster, in his initial report to London, to describe Summerby as a harmless right-wing loudmouth. London . . . how far away it seemed to him now, sitting in the restaurant of the Anglo–American club, staring out at the Carrera Séptima. Already Lancaster felt himself hemmed in by the saucer-like layout of Bogotá nine thousand feet up, surrounded on all sides by the Andes. Where the only way out to the external world was by plane, there came upon him a genuine sense of isolation, even when he was one of over two million souls in the city. And in this vale of tears, what was his role? The very uncertainty of his mission seemed to fit with the unreal quality of the city. It was as if Crombie, in pursuit of a mirage, had deliberately sent him to a land of illusion.

Five

May 1968. Ed Summerby watched as the Avianca 707 travelled almost the entire length of the enormous runway at Eldorado airport before lifting off and gaining height rapidly. Confident that his departing boss would not see him, he gave the plane an ironic finger.

Everything was working out well. The ex-CIA supremo in Colombia, a stickler for the spirit as well as the letter of Washington directives, was now on his way to New York, then H Q, then transfer. The new director would not be in post till September, which left Ed as Acting Director for four full months. The Washington end had run as smoothly as J. J. Johnson had assured him it would. With the cat away the mice could play. Now it was time to call in Jim Everett from Caracas.

After making his way inside the airport building Summerby located the international phone desk. He was motioned without delay into a booth and the Caracas number was obtained for him with surprising ease – considering this was Colombia. He spoke into the mouthpiece slowly and without waiting for a reply: "The collection is now ready for your immediate inspection." He paid the fifty pesos to the girl at the desk, who rewarded him with an all-purpose airline smile. He glanced at his watch. If the Viasa flight was on time Everett's ETA in Bogotá would be four p.m. That left four hours to kill. Since it took the best part of an hour to drive from Eldorado to downtown, Summerby decided to pass the time at the airport.

He ran over the plans again in his mind. It had been astute of J. J. to arrange unofficially to get hold of Everett for the duration, but was it really more cunning than his own decision to use Efraim Hernández as decoy? Old station hands had clucked sceptically when he first broached the idea of putting Hernández on the payroll, but Summerby had backed his political acumen against theirs and J. J. had supported him. Hernández was perfect on a number of counts. The DAS, the Colombian secret police, would undoubtedly rise to the bait. The story of how Hernández, "the beast of Arbango", the lion of the *violencia*, had been trapped in an apartment block in Bogotá in 1959 but had managed to shoot his way out, leaving three policemen dead and several wounded, had already passed into folklore. His continued survival was still regarded as a blot on the Colombian security services' much-trumpeted efficiency record.

Nevertheless, as far as Hernández was concerned, the time for him to throw in his lot with anyone who would actually pay him had come. The conservative-liberal electoral alliance, designed to end the *violencia*, had left gangs like Hernández' more and more isolated. No more could he pose as a standard-bearer for the conservatives against the *liberales salvajes*. The once-proud "Army of the South", under his leadership, had dwindled both through desertions by demoralised fighters and by several bruising encounters with the military. So the moment was ripe for the kind of overture Summerby had made. Through intermediaries in Pereira Hernández had accepted the offer from the detested *yanquis* and was even then on his way to Bogotá.

Summerby and Everett greeted each other warmly. It was five years since they had last worked together on a J. J. "special". Everett, however, seemed doubtful of the operation and got down to business as soon as they were in the car.

"How reliable is this Hernández?"

"For what we want him for, the best there is."

"Will he be able to work with Frias's Cuban mob?"

"There will be very little overlap. Don't forget that it's the Cuban who does the wet job. Hernández is there as bait."

"Even more to the point," continued Everett, "how good is Frias?"

"Good enough to have had Fidel himself staked out before Kennedy blew the whistle."

Everett made an approving noise before wincing as Summerby blindly swung the car into the left lane, to avoid being carried on to the Avenida de las Americas. "I didn't join Donovan's raiders just to sit on my ass in Caracas."

"That's why J. J. selected you for this enterprise, Jim. Let's face it, you and I are both too good for the horseshit we're given to do. We know it, J. J. knows it and goddamit, I reckon even Arlington knows it. That's why J. J. arranged for your leave to begin in mid-July. Only instead of vacationing in the US of A that's when you move in here. But I thought you ought to come over for a preliminary rap and meet the team. I particularly want you to get to know Hernández. You'll be handling his end in August."

"I've never worked in Bogotá before," Everett said after a moment or two. "Why should the D A S rise to Hernández? I'm sure you're right when you say they will, but just satisfy the curiosity of an old trooper, will you?"

"I wouldn't be telling you anything that everyone here doesn't already know. When the cops nearly cornered him on Calle Octava in fifty-nine, Hernández swore vengeance. A few months later a patrol car was ambushed near Honda down on the Magdalena, a long way from Hernández' base of operations. Hernández left his calling card: five men were killed by the monkey's cut."

"What the hell's that?"

"*Corte de mica*. It's an old *violencia* trick. First you cut someone's head off, and then you put the head on the chest of the stiff. It's a symbolic gesture."

"Hmmm."

"Left beside the corpses were five combat jackets bearing the legend *Dios y madre* on the cross-over-heart insignia peculiar to Hernández's band. Besides on each of the jackets were the *noms de guerre* of Hernández and his four chief lieutenants – *Sangre Negra*, *Media Via*, *Venganza* and *Tiro Fijo*."

"Jesus, I guess the Cubans will meet their match here."

"But there's a twist to the tale," Summerby continued. "The five cops butchered turned out to be DAS agents operating under police cover. Colonel Acosta has sworn a personal vengeance on Hernández and his henchmen."

"How do these guys get like this? I mean, there are some strange tales coming out of Nam but this beats anything I've ever heard."

"Look at it this way. Hernández was fifteen when the *violencia* blew wide open. Rumour has it that he saw his father castrated by a band of commie–liberal marauders. His younger sister was raped and murdered. If all that's true you don't need to look any farther for the explanation. Our man in Pereira, who set this deal up with Hernández, says he's definitely got a screw loose somewhere. The same goes for his men."

Everett shook his head. "The guerillas I was dealing with in Venezuela were small fry compared with this lot. *Politicos* I can understand. I know where a communist is coming from, but I can't get behind the breed you've got here."

"Like the man said, desperate times call for desperate remedies. With any luck Colonel Acosta and Hernández and the whole goddamn shooting match will cancel out and leave us ahead of the game with the big one in the pot."

"*Ojalá*, as they say," murmured Everett, staring out at the approaching tenements of the city.

Still on the lookout for the CIA presence in Bogotá, David Lancaster was quickly able to extend his watch beyond the Anglo–American club. *Listen*, Peter Rhodes had advised him. Look and listen . . .

From the very beginning of his tour as Second Secretary, Technical Assistance, he had had to work closely on his official assignment with members of the British Council. The two London-based members of the Council, whose offices were situated a few floors above those of the Embassy, presented so odd a couple that it almost seemed as though they had been hand-picked to demonstrate the British tradition of professional eccentricity. The younger man, the No. 2, was scrupulous, efficient, introverted and self-effacing, almost a caricature of the genus Civil Servant.

But the senior official, curiously known as the "Representative" (an obvious echo of the great days of the Raj, thought Lancaster) was transparently self-serving. And it was he who provided Lancaster with his first foothold on the ledges of Colombia's official intelligence subculture.

It was at one of Paul Fitch's expense-account cocktail parties that Lancaster had his best opportunity to look and listen. To celebrate a joint Anglo–American English-teaching project Fitch had invited his opposite number from the US Embassy, the cultural attaché, and his deputy, Josh Brown, who ran the English-teaching courses. The latter, a beaten and pathetic individual, was notorious in local diplomatic circles for his social gaffes and general ineptitude. Brown's overlord, Mike Dawson, the cultural attaché, however, was an altogether different proposition. Gaunt, steely-eyed and humourless as only a successful North American bureaucrat can be, he immediately conveyed to Lancaster the odour of the "Company". The wonder of it was that he continued to tolerate the hapless Josh Brown without writing to Washington the kind of report that would immediately have ended Brown's days as a foreign service officer. But, just as Goebbels conveyed his humanity in one area alone, that of concern for his children, so perhaps Dawson's weak spot was the spaniel-like Brown.

Lancaster decided to play a hunch. If Dawson really was a Company man it was just possible that he had leads to important contacts who in turn might have links with the guerillas. It was an obvious first precaution on assignments like Lancaster's to sound out the intentions of the far left and to learn what its leaders proposed in the near future. If the CIA had penetrated their ranks or those of their sympathisers there was an outside chance he might pick up a useful lead.

Opening with "You're just the man who might be able to help me", he outlined a scheme for bringing highly trained young British volunteers of the VSO into the Santander and Tolima peasant communities as part of a literacy campaign which the British government would subsidise through the Ministry of Overseas Development. Dawson predictably took this solemn bait and offered to introduce him to the Ford Foundation team, who were in Colombia working on the feasibility of just such a scheme themselves.

A few nights later he sat in an apartment in the smart Chicó area with two young sons of the American mid-West, Peter Heyck from Ann Arbor and Daniel Green from the University of Illinois. As with Dawson, everything about these two bright young things, their recruitment, social background, and the vagueness of the information they provided on the literacy programme they were supposed to be working on, seemed strongly redolent of the Company.

"What do you know about the peasant communities of Tolima and Santander?" Lancaster began, after the small talk had ceased.

"E L P groups have clashed with Núñez there as a result of intra-party factionalism," said Green, speaking as though reading a computer print-out.

"How's that again?" said Lancaster, warily slipping into mid-Atlantic idiom.

"Why those two regions?" Heyck asked, moving in to protect his partner's flank, clearly aware that Green had been indiscreet.

Lancaster had his answer ready. "Because they seem to offer the greatest challenge for our volunteer effort. The British VSO wants to collaborate with the ECLA literacy campaign and at the same time to appeal to truly motivated young people. The Ministry wants to promote a genuine pioneering scheme to tap the real idealism of our young, and also to blunt the cutting edge of our critics. We're attacked from the right for giving charity to beggars who don't need it and from the left for propping up the status quo."

"You realise of course that these two areas contain the biggest concentration of guerilla strength in the country," said Green.

"I had heard something of the sort," Lancaster replied. "But it would follow, wouldn't it, that the areas most in need of aid would be most susceptible to the guerilias?"

"Mm" was the only answer from Green. Heyck grunted

antiphonally. After appearing to ponder his response most carefully, Heyck spoke again.

"We do have an adviser in Barranquilla who might be able to help you – Julio Roca of *El Espectador*. Before he became a journalist he did a doctorate on peasant societies in the Andes at the Nacional. He was there with Fabio Núñez, I believe."

"Who?" queried Lancaster, spotting the trap.

"Núñez is the guerilla leader of the ELN."

"Oh. I didn't know. You seem very interested in these guerillas, if you don't mind my saying so."

"We have to have our ear to the ground for anything that might affect the Foundation's work. Those guys in Cuba were badly caught out in fifty-nine through treating the Sierra Maestra as an unimportant side show."

"True. This Roca – could he really help me plan a feasibility study on this project?"

"I'm sure you wouldn't find your journey a waste of time. He's been very valuable to us."

"But *you've* never thought it worth while to work around Barranquilla, in Tolima or Santander?"

Heyck and Green exchanged glances. "They're both such sensitive locales," replied Green. "Anti-*gringo* feeling runs high. You might just get away with it, being British 'n' all, if you can persuade them that's somehow not being Yankee – but such fine distinctions often mean little in rural communities."

Lancaster smiled. "Perhaps that's a job for my vice-consul." He had no wish to appear overeager. "I think I'll ask Mr Parker to go up and talk to Roca. I'd love to go myself, of course, but *very* unfortunately I've got a series of visits and conferences planned in Calí next week."

His irony was unmistakable. The two young Americans laughed dutifully, and Lancaster brought the meeting to a rapid end.

A few days later Paul Fitch once again provided an opening for Lancaster. Parker's visit to Barranquilla had paid off. He had sounded out Julio Roca and found him to be of a distinctly left-wing persuasion. When the possibility of acting as a contact for British journalists writing in-depth pieces about Colombia was mentioned, Roca had sounded enthusiastic, especially when the possibility of a fee was raised. Immediately after the debriefing with Parker, Lancaster had written to Roca under the name of Frank Pearce, stating that he was a freelance newspaperman with a commission from a syndicate of European left-wing journals to write about the revolutionary potential of Colombia. Roca had replied by return of post to the Bogotá Apartado Aereo number, expressing himself keen to meet Pearce. A meeting had been arranged for the first week of June. Moreover, Roca had hinted that he had unimpeachable credentials to act as an intermediary with the Castroite guerillas and might even be able to arrange a meeting in the mountains with Fabio Núñez.

Now Fitch and Lancaster were crossing the Avenida Décima at lunchtime, discussing Technical Assistance problems. A wretched Colombian boy of nine or so, ragged and bedraggled, his eye sockets blanched with malnutrition, held out his hand pathetically.

"Regáleme diez, Señor."

"Fuck off, you little bastard!" Fitch knocked the boy aside. "These fucking little *chinos* – if you give one of them anything, you have the whole city trailing after you."

There were times when Lancaster found it hard to control himself in Fitch's presence. This was one, but he managed to restrict his outward disapproval simply to handing the wretched *muchacho* a twenty-centavo coin.

"As I was saying," Fitch murmured, lowering his voice as they entered the foyer of the Hotel Bacatá, "if you know anyone going up to Barranquilla in the next few days who'd be interested in driving back you could do me a favour. Damn nuisance about the timing of Parker's visit up there. I got the customs release on Niven's car – he's our AV man hereabouts – the day after Parker got back. Now the car's up there and Niven's bellyaching, saying that the terms of his contract as an AV officer with CETO specify that a car would be waiting for him when he got here. These little farts I have to administer don't seem to realise that this is Colombia. Goods get shipped in to the most god-awful

44

places, and die there. I've got the equipment for my engineers still lying up there in the customs shed at Cartagena two years after it arrived. Some swine hasn't had his palm greased. Shit to the lot of 'em, I say."

"What kind of car is it?" asked Lancaster.

"A white Ford Diplomat. That bugger Niven'll make a fortune on it when he flogs it at the end of his contract. Of course, I'm only the co-ordinator of his programme, so it stands to reason I can't afford a fancy car like that."

Lancaster thought quickly. "There's a sort of friend of mine, a journalist, who's flying in to Barranquilla next week and is coming down here afterwards. He's doing a few pieces on the new Colombia and I imagine he'd jump at the chance of driving where no white man has been before."

Fitch missed the attempt at humour. "Hardly that, old man . . . but they do say the road between Medellín and the coast is pretty hairy. And the other way, through Bucaramanga, is completely kaput."

"I'm sure if you had the documentation waiting for him in Barranquilla, he'd be very interested."

"Okay. Why not? What's his name?"

"Frank Pearce."

"Never heard of him. Is he one of these lefty bullshit artists?"

Lancaster shrugged. "Aren't they all?"

He could afford to be generous. His plans were going better than he could ever have expected.

Six

In *La Casa Linda* in Barranquilla a man could act out the kind of fantasies usually seen only in the pages of western *macho* novels. As Lancaster lay in his foam bath, flanked by two of the highest-priced girls the coast could offer, he reflected with amusement on the fury that would erupt in Westminster or Fleet Street if some of the uses to which taxpayers' money was put in the foreign services were ever fully realised. Still, a night like this, with *Mesdames* Esperanza and Socorro included, cost only a thousand pesos Colombian, and that was small beer, even by Fitch's standards of larceny.

Lancaster's sensual pleasures on this occasion were reinforced by reflecting on a deception successfully practised, and on a series of interviews that had borne spectacular fruit. His conversations (as Frank Pearce) with Julio Roca of *El Espectador* had led eventually to an arrangement whereby he was actually to meet Fabio Núñez. Armed with any good operator's detailed knowledge of Marxist–Leninism, Lancaster had been able to convince Roca that he might become in some small way a Debray to Núñez's Guevara. Roca seemed genuinely surprised at the effortless command of the Spanish language possessed by this journeyman political journalist, and gradually warmed to him, no doubt culturally flattered. Lancaster had produced his old war-horse, the folder of cuttings from obscure leftist journals in Europe that he always used when operating under journalistic cover, and they had spent an afternoon discussing some technical questions of Marxism in the work of Lukács.

Finally Roca, convinced of the authenticity of his political credentials, had made the contact. And here Lancaster found that his luck was even greater than he could have dared hope. The Núñez ELN front of the Castroite guerillas, having split with the Peking-oriented ELP, was now operating in Antioquia province. The arrangement made by Roca was that Núñez' men would contact him somewhere on the road south, before Yarumal. This solved the problem of how Lancaster could ever have got close to the ELN if they had still been in Santander, where the dirt road was up. Having presented himself at the British consulate in Barranquilla with the necessary papers in the name of Frank Pearce, he took possession of Niven's white Ford, still dusty from its stay in the customs shed.

His reception at the first *retén* or police checkpoint, just outside Cartagena, at least reassured him that there would be no embarrassing questions from the many provincial authorities he would be encountering. The paperwork satisfied even the punctilious *agente*, and he appended his signature of *paz y salvo* in an impressive multi-looped hand. Lancaster then drove on to his overnight stopping place at Sincelejo. The road there, across flat green terrain, impressed him: a good-quality paved highway ran south from Cartagena. This was far more than he had expected, since even an hour's drive out of Bogotá could take one on to mud tracks or pot-holed gravel roads.

Sincelejo was reached by nightfall. It proved to be what Colombians call a *pueblo triste*. There was just one hotel that Lancaster cared to consider. This possessed one room only with its own bath, available for the princely sum (in local terms) of forty pesos. Apparently it was always vacant, as no moneyed Colombian capable of paying that price would dare travel overland by this route.

At the desk the clerk offered him, with that mixture of deference and arch prurience common in Colombian innkeepers off the international circuit, a personally recommended woman for the night, "*o dos o tres, puede ser, caballero*", but Lancaster declined, leaving instructions that he was to be awakened at five the next morning.

He hoped to cover the entire stretch to his rendezvous with the guerillas outside Yarumal on the following day.

That evening, after dining on steak served in the *campesino* manner with *yucca* and *plátano*, Lancaster went to bed.

At five a.m. sharp a feeble pummelling on his hotel door aroused him. Opening the door, he saw that his caller was a little bent old man, looking at least ninety but perhaps, like all non-oligarch Colombians, in fact a good thirty years younger. After quickly dressing and packing, Lancaster descended to the foyer, which was still and deserted except for the *viejo* who had woken him. Motioning him to come with him by the back door, the old man conducted him to a car park at the rear, newly cemented. Lancaster checked the car, switched on and the engine roared into life – all was well. The clerk had warned him the night before that any car not left in this particular place, where it would be guarded by the hotel staff, would be stripped bare. Lancaster reckoned that preservation from such a fate merited a tip of ten pesos. To the old man such a *propina* was as the wealth of Croesus, and he grovelled pathetically, muttering over and over, "*Muchissimas gracias, Señor. Que Dios le ampare.*"

Only half an hour out of Sincelejo Lancaster realised that he had been lulled into a false optimism by the modern highway from Cartagena. The way south from Sincelejo was little more than a widened mule track, surfaced with mud, clay or sandstone; pocked and pitted with deep gashes, some of them holes three feet wide and six inches deep. As he slowed and listened to the pounding of the Ford's overworked suspension Lancaster realised that a new hazard was brewing up: the elements. About 5.45 rain began to cascade down until even the two-velocity wind-screen wiper failed to deal with the onslaught. Visibility came down almost to zero, and Lancaster was forced to cut the car to a crawl. When he finally reached Las Culebras, perhaps five miles on, dawn was breaking in a town that would have contrived to be dispiriting in a golden sunset. The small area of paved road around the dingy main plaza afforded some relief, however, and he stopped to enquire about the road ahead.

As he feared, the intelligence he got from the pinched, ill-nourished locals concerning the route to Yarumal was unencouraging. Early morning *aguardiente* drinkers shook their heads in disbelief at the idiocy of this *gringo* attempting to get through to Antioquia in such a vehicle. *"No pasará este carro"* was the usual expression, and the opinion was voiced that even a four-wheel drive automobile would experience grave problems with the mud slides on the hills of Antioquia.

Was there someone who could transport the Ford? The *aguardiente* drinkers looked doubtful. There was much scratching of heads until finally one of the ancients mentioned Diego Pérez. This was the signal for a universal clamour of approbation. Yes, Diego Pérez was the man – he was the owner of a powerful truck that regularly made the trip to Medellín.

Where was Pérez to be found? In the Bar Azul, which incidentally he also owned, came the reply. Don Diego always arrived at his office at seven a.m. to keep his drivers on their toes. And he regularly spent the hour between eight and nine having a leisurely breakfast in the bar.

After crossing the plaza to the Bar Azul, the best in Las Culebras, and appalling, Lancaster at once identified his man from the unmistakable air of *patrón* that Pérez exuded. There sat the truck owner, sipping *tinto* at a centre table as he condescendingly played draughts with one of his workmen and treated the audience to his views on politics. Lancaster came to the point quickly and the predictable bartering took place. Lancaster's opening bid of 1000 pesos· for a truck to carry the Ford Diplomat to Yarumal was countered by one of 2000. Eventually they settled for 1600 pesos – in local terms a huge sum – for an estimated eighteen hours of work at most.

The *patrón* took a spur-of-the-moment decision that he would make the trip in person, and instantly assigned his draughts partner as his co-driver. Lancaster was to remain inside the Ford, firmly secured on the back of Pérez's most powerful truck.

As the truck moved off Lancaster wondered if he had made the right decision. His guerilla contact was to locate him on the basis of a distinctive white English car, and would not be looking for a mud-drenched Volvo truck. On the other hand, to leave the Ford in Las Culebras would mean failing to make the contact in time, to say nothing of the huge costs which would be incurred recovering the car later for Fitch's man.

The country through which they now passed was unlike anything that Lancaster had seen in South America before. The subdued foliage of the Colombian uplands and the mists of the sierras were totally different from the open lushness of this tropical country, the vivid yellows and greens of the lowlands. Lancaster seldom descended from the back of the lorry, however, even when his drivers got out of their cab for a *gaseosa* in one of the tawdry bars on the Yarumal road. He had the pathological European fear of dysentery: he drank only the mineral water he had brought with him from Barranquilla and ate a supply of *tamales*, fruit and *empanadas*, also from the coast.

As the day slipped away and the rains ceased, he wondered if he had not perhaps panicked needlessly before Las Culebras. The condition of the highway seemed much improved. But such doubts were dispelled when, at about four that afternoon, they crossed the swollen River Cauca. The ferry, little more than a glorified raft, made the difficult crossing against a strong current. And on the other side of the river, as they began to climb the foothills of the western cordillera of the Andes, the combination of unpaved roads, mud, landslides and intermittent tropical deluges began to tax the powers even of the six-gear truck. Now, too, army patrols began to make an appearance, inspired not by a possible guerilla presence but rather by the need to clear a road for the traffic to Medellín. At about 5.30, just as dusk was falling, an hour's halt was called by a military detachment at the approach to a winding, single-track uphill stretch of road, blocked by a landslide, while their caterpillar tractor slowly pushed tons of mud and rocks over the nearly sheer drop. Then an army sergeant ostentatiously motioned the vehicles to proceed with care over the unblocked track. Some of the trucks in the line, being already on an ascending incline, found great difficulty in starting, having only conquered the treacherous surfaces hitherto by sheer forward momentum. The luckless army privates in the company were ordered to shore up the spinning wheels with planks, and to lend their weight to the efforts of the straining engines. Bespattered by mud as the trucks churned up the yielding surface, they managed to get all the vehicles in front of Lancaster's truck under way. Demonstrating their previously boasted expertise, his hosts were able to start their conveyance without assistance by some split-second technique of almost simultaneous use of reverse and forward gears.

Once past this obstruction, and having negotiated a further precipitous ascent half an hour later, the tropical night descended, and the *patrón* called a second and final halt. A line of trucks stretched ahead of them into the gloom. Pérez got out and came round to the back to tell Lancaster that they would have to shift for themselves as best they could that night. There was another landslip about half a mile ahead and the army would not be able to clear it until morning.

Seven

Lancaster finished his last rations of food and water and took an evening stroll along the line of stranded drivers. They were swapping travellers' tales of similar delays in the past. One would tell how on one occasion he had waited in a similar situation for twenty-five hours. Somebody else would tell a similar story of a nightmare delay on the execrable Colombian railway, and so it went on. Satisfied that there was indeed no hope of movement until daybreak, Lancaster retired to his post in the Ford, curled up on the back seat and was soon asleep.

He was roused by a soft click. Looking up, he saw staring at him from the front seat of the car a powerfully built man in his early twenties, well above normal height for a Colombian, and with a thick black beard.

"*Ni una palabra, Señor.* You are Señor Pearce? You are the English journalist who wishes to interview Fabio Núñez, yes? That interview can take place only if you come with me now. No, ask me no questions. Be assured, Señor, that my credentials are impeccable and that I have been sent here by Comrade Fabio himself. If you truly want to bring your project to success, you must trust and follow me."

Bleary-eyed, Lancaster stumbled from the car, stopping only to bring his coat and a small knapsack of personal effects – including his Colt .38 revolver – and dropped to the ground. There'd be a row over the abandoned Ford, he knew, but he'd face that when it came.

This was the darkest hour of the night, and the long line of vehicles stood silent, the earlier babel of voices, the smells of cooking, the sensation of vibrant life vanished, almost as if spirited away. If this was indeed an abduction planned by Núñez then it was done by someone who knew the Colombian people and their folkways intimately and was able to choose the precise moment – the story-telling over and the dawn still an hour distant – to enter the convoy unobserved.

During the next two hours Lancaster had occasion to be grateful that he had kept himself physically fit. Striking away from the "highway" he immediately faced an arduous battle with the steep gradients on the trackless hills surrounding the Yarumal road. By the time the first streaks of dawn had shown in a cobalt sky Lancaster estimated that he and his guide had ascended some 3000 feet. The man was dour and taciturn, only breaking the silence to point out when it was absolutely necessary the best way up some of the vertiginous slopes they climbed. As the morning wore on and they penetrated higher and higher into the western cordillera Lancaster began to feel his European sea-level lungs, not yet fully accustomed to the altitude at Bogotá, protesting at the rate of this rapid transit from plain to mountain. Just as he was about to demand that a halt be made, or that he be given an oxygen mask, his companion turned to him and said: "We will pause now, Señor, and take some food and drink. We are to wait here until the comrades come for us."

Sitting on an outcrop of rock, the guerilla, in the daylight revealed as even taller than Lancaster had thought, broke open his marching rations from a knapsack and produced a water bottle.

"My compliments, Señor. You have done well. I did not imagine a *gringo* could acquit himself so honourably in our mountains."

Thus did Daniel – for so the man introduced himself – break the ice. Clearly he had decided that the *inglés* was a good sort, *un buen tipo*. As they waited after their scanty meal, he questioned Lancaster laughingly about the car and what it was doing on the hump of the truck. "I confess, Señor, I nearly failed to find you. I was looking for a foreign car, of course, and went the length of the convoy without finding it. Only the second time along did my eye pick up your car in its peculiar position."

The afternoon was drawing to a close before Daniel's comrades made their appearance. By then conversation between the two of them had long petered out. Lancaster had discovered that, his affability notwithstanding, Daniel was unwilling to give even the simplest details concerning Núñez's "army" or the personalities in the *Frente Fabio*. Lancaster contented himself, therefore, with the surrounding beauty of the Andes. Their stopping place having been chosen so that no one could approach them unperceived, afforded spectacular views, and from its vantage point Lancaster was able to reflect that it was almost as though such beauty had been juxtaposed with the extraordinary inhumanity of man to man in this country as some form of black cosmic joke . . . Was it Einstein who had said God did not play games? He should have come to Colombia.

Lancaster was aroused from his reverie by the same sharp clicking that had woken him that morning. Looking across to Daniel, he saw his companion stiffen and loosen the catch on his M-I rifle. Lancaster had his Colt .38 revolver in his shoulder bag: this was not a gun he normally used, but rather the sort of weapon he had judged a nervous *gringo* might be expected to carry after hearing horror stories about lawless Colombia. He reached into the bag, drew out the gun, and began to feed bullets into its chamber. Then he observed Daniel relax and smile as a group of about a dozen green-jacketed irregulars came into view.

Moving rapidly but in good order, the detachment looked impressive as they came up to the bluff where Lancaster and Daniel were positioned. None of them was over thirty and all seemed men of determination and commitment. There was a vigour and ingenuousness about their faces that recommended itself at once. And their leader turned out to be none other than Antonio Penata, one-time anthropologist, second-in-command in the *Frente Fabio*, his background already known to Lancaster from his reading of the British Embassy files. Having heard that a strict hierarchy was enforced in the E L N, a corps of fighting men largely recruited from the social science department of the National University, he was surprised at the informality with which Daniel and Antonio greeted each other:

bear-hugs, the clapping of hands on shoulders, and jovial cries of "*carajo*".

When the members of the group had been introduced to Lancaster – "this is Comrade Camilo, this Comrade Gonzalo" – Penata informed him that Comrade Fabio was particularly looking forward to meeting him and had prepared a surprise in his honour. No, he would say no more for the present; Lancaster must hear the details from their leader, back at the camp.

By now partly inured to the tough trekking involved, and rested after his time spent admiring the mountains, Lancaster was almost looking forward to another few hours among the rock faces of the cordilleras. During the return to the guerilla encampment he received further compliments on his ability to sustain physical hardship, and also for his command of Spanish.

They reached the ELN encampment a couple of hours after dusk had fallen. Having been told that Fabio Núñez would receive him the next morning, Lancaster was taken to a tent, which in the equipment and the comforts of life it provided was little inferior to standard US army issue. By now totally exhausted, he threw himself on the truckle bed and was asleep almost immediately.

"Well, what do you think of our camp?" Núñez asked coldly after their tour of inspection. In the brief time Lancaster spent in his company this morning the guerilla leader had already struck him as a man one would respond to with fear and respect, but never with any warm emotion.

"I'm very impressed," said Lancaster. And he spoke the truth, since the organisation of the guerilla camp suggested to him a military intelligence of the highest order. A defensive perimeter had been designed in case of surprise attack, two barricades of solid rock, protected on either side by an abrupt and jagged scarp which extended for half a mile or so, forming a narrow canyon along which any attackers would have to come. The huge boulders that had been placed at each end, where the defile opened out briefly, and where the camp had been pitched, were crenellated into pillboxes and drilled to provide embrasures for the defenders. Núñez pointed out the pneumatic drills brought in from Bucaramanga and praised the ingenuity with which his men had dismantled these tools and reassembled them when his group moved into Antioquia in 1967. Separate loopholes had been provided in the sentry boxes for those with automatic weapons, to form a two-tier defence in the event of assault.

At both the eastern and western ends of this fortress there were only two approaches. At the eastern end there was a track through the canyon and another trail along the top of the bluffs, so rough and ill-defined that only the defenders could know about it. On the western side the two paths were narrow and wound away rapidly into the mountains. Each of these two tracks was designated as either an entry or exit point for those manning the observation towers. The efficiency of the defence arrangements was matched by the infrastructure of the camp itself. There was a fully-equipped infirmary, complete with doctor, also an excellent water supply, ovens for bread, and an impressive array of armaments and radio equipment.

"Now you will be able to report to our friends and sympathisers in Europe that we are no mere band of putschists but a true revolutionary army," Núñez asserted proudly. "What is our current standing in European eyes anyway, Comrade Pearce?"

"I am afraid to say, Comrade Fabio, that our friends in Europe as yet know little of the ELN. Of course there are a few who know Colombian affairs well, but, as you can imagine, recent events in Bolivia have tended to monopolise their attention."

"Naturally," said Núñez, "Comrade Guevara was a truly great man – but he was a fool to trust himself to those damned Bolivians."

"Also," continued Lancaster, "we hear that Fidel has hitherto concentrated most of his efforts across the border in Venezuela. Besides, there are some who worry that the split between you and the ELP and FARC will not help the cause of liberation, even though, you understand, I personally concede absolutely that your position is dialectically sound." Lancaster, when posing as a Marxist, always made a point of using the word "dialectical" at some point in the discussion. It had a circumstantial authenticity hard for non-Marxists to appreciate.

Núñez pondered this answer for a moment. Then he squared his shoulders and expanded his chest. "I promise you, Senõr Pearce, that before you leave us I will have given you ample proof that we in Colombia are no revolutionary beginners. We will give the *izquierdistas* of London and Paris something to cheer for, and they will know that the lamp of liberation burns brightly here. It is my hope that the one hundred and fiftieth anniversary of the bourgeois revolution that freed Colombia from Spain may at least see the dawning of our true liberty, when we will be free from our Yankee oppressors and the jackals in the oligarchy in Bogotá who snap at their heels."

Lancaster had already noted that this orotund mode of address was common currency among the ELN. Even simple administrative orders tended to bear a burden of ideological uplift, as if the guerillas felt the need constantly to impress one another with the political significance of what they were doing. Yet while it was easy to sneer, Lancaster's root emotion was one of reluctant sympathy for his hosts. Two men who had been close to the renowned Camilo Torres particularly impressed him: the camp doctor Luis Andrade and the priest Domingo Lacán. Father Lacán it was who took him aside after his tour with Núñez and spoke to him at length about the need for a new Catholicism, one in which the reflex action of the Vatican to do political deals with unsavoury regimes, as with Mussolini and the Concordat, would be replaced by a new commitment to universal human Christian values, even if this meant standing up to the men of power in the world. If only there could ever be a Pope who would denounce the exploitations of capitalism from the throne of St Peter.

"But does not the Church maintain that the kingdom of God is not of this world, that we must suffer meekly in this life to earn our entry into the everlasting joy of the next? The first shall be last and the last first, and all that."

"Ah, my friend, I see you are well versed in the art of trading scriptural quotations." Lacán looked at once animated and grave. "But why did Christ come into the world at all, if the kingdom of heaven and the earthly life are so utterly distinct? Surely the fact that He entered space and time indicates that this world is no mere shadow of the hereafter, and that there is an intimate connection between what happens in this world and the next. If historical evidence means anything, the fact that immediately after Jesus Christ's ascension his disciples practised a primitive form of communism is surely decisive. I agree entirely with Dostoevsky that the greatest sinner is the man who makes children suffer for his ideals and beliefs, and I believe that such men will be called to judgment. And what else are Carlos Lleras and that miserable pack that surrounds him but evil men, judged in this light. For it's by their consent and say-so that thousands of innocent children die each year in the gutters of Bogotá and the *barrios* of Calí."

Lancaster noticed the peculiar hatred in the priest's voice when he referred to the Colombian president. The small, bald chief executive seemed to be cordially detested by everyone in Colombia except the foreign diplomats. Even his own colleagues referred to him scathingly as "*el enanito*" – the dwarf.

Lancaster and Father Domingo continued in this way for upwards of an hour, until Núñez's aide-de-camp came with word that Comrade-General Fabio Núñez was now ready for his formal interview with the British journalist. To go from the fervent idealism of Lacán to the dour *Realpolitik* of Núñez was, for Lancaster, to experience clearly the Janus face of the ELN. The juxtaposition of the man of thought with the man of action was revealing.

All went well to begin with. Núñez explained the achievements of his guerillas in the past four years, the progress they had made among the peasantry, the establishment of revolutionary *focos*, and the encouraging recruitment of young intellectuals . . .

The problems started when Lancaster questioned Guevara's "many Vietnams" thesis: "Would you not agree, Comrade Fabio, that the death of Comrade Che poses questions for your own operation? After all, Latin America is not Vietnam. The liberation fighters there are being sustained and supplied by a powerful neighbour in the north and there are two great powers in reasonable proximity. The USA, on the other hand, has to operate far from its own hemisphere. And Vietnam is inured to warfare by three decades of struggle, against Japanese, French and now the Americans. In a word, are the objective conditions for a similiar revolution present in Colombia?"

"Such a view is typical of the do-nothing armchair intellectuals of Europe. All they ever do is talk. Is this all these socialists of the mouth can do for me, to send me a reporter full of defeatism? You are a true Menshevik, Señor."

"With the greatest respect, Comrade Fabio, I did not in the least wish to disparage your revolutionary struggle, for which I have the highest regard. I am simply asking the questions your critics might ask, critics who are to be found as much in the Soviet Union as in the West."

"You are right about the Soviet Union," Núñez replied, slightly mollified. "They are the betrayers of the people who cry out to them for vengeance on their oppressors. It is they who caused the death of Comrade Ernesto in Bolivia."

"The Soviets say that you and I and all who sympathise with you have misunderstood the experience of Fidel. They say that the myth of the Sierra Maestra has led us to overrate guerilla warfare and the subjective conditions."

Núñez grew angry again. "When will you Europeans learn to be true revolutionaries? Why must you always propagate the counter-revolutionary views of our enemies? It is easy to theorise in your Paris boulevards and your Left Bank cafés. Here we prefer to act – and if necessary to die for our beliefs."

Lancaster replied that the events of May in Paris showed that perhaps the young were prepared to do more than talk. Núñez asked for details of what had happened, having heard nothing of these matters in his mountain fastness. He became animated at the thought that the *bogotano* students might be able to follow the example of their Parisian counterparts. Lancaster then tactlessly mentioned that the level of police repression in Bogotá was immeasurably greater.

"Again you annoy me. It seems to me, Señor *gringo*, that

you are deliberately setting out to try my patience. The greater the repression, the greater the courage it engenders . . . But wait, we will see what you are really made of. I have a surprise in store for you. Come with me and let us see if you are anything more than a dilettante scribbler."

Emerging into the sunlight, Núñez rapped out a series of orders to his lieutenants. A shooting target was produced and a prewar model of pistol that Lancaster did not recognise was handed to him. Núñez turned to him contemptuously. "Let us see whether you are as inaccurate with the barrel of a gun as you are lacking in political consciousness." Motioning to Daniel, Antonio Penata and a couple of others, he bade them demonstrate their talents as marksmen. After two or three rounds had been fired by each man, it was plain to Lancaster that, although they were all competent, Antonio Penata was exceptional. The card bearing Antonio's grouping, when brought back to the firing line for Núñez' inspection, showed holes geometrically spaced with amazing precision. The competitive spirit rose up in Lancaster. He wanted to test himself against Penata, but he had to be careful. A left-wing journalist could not plausibly have attained his degree of skill. He decided to play-act a little to defuse such suspicion as might arise.

"Comrade Fabio, whenever I shot a gun in the course of my military training I used ear muffs so as not to be deafened by the report. Do you have any such earplugs I can use?"

Núñez exploded in laughter. "Comrades, here we have a man who presumes to advise me on guerilla warfare, yet cannot use a gun without protection for his precious sense-organs. No, Señor, you must show us what you can do in an emergency. The enemy will not do you the courtesy of lending you a hearing aid while it waits for you to fire on its soldiers. Imagine that that target is some boneheaded army private, recruited from the slums of Bogotá. He is going to shoot you if you do not shoot him first. Now – what do you do?"

Lancaster pumped three bullets into the target. Deliberately aiming fractionally lower than he would have done normally, his automatic responses still prevented him from spreading them as erratically as a true tyro would have done.

"Our guest is off target but his grouping is good," Daniel called out. He brought back the card. Núñez inspected it. "Indeed, Señor, either this is beginner's luck or your army training was not in vain. This is better than I could have hoped for. Tonight at a meeting of the full council I will tell you why. We will talk again, Señor Pearce."

That night in Núñez's quarters a meeting was called, attended by all members of the *Frente Fabio* group except those on guard duty. Núñez began, for once, without any empty phrases. "Comrades, I have decided to extend our operations. In a few days a trainload of *carabineros* will pass by the Amarilla and Roja rivers. I intend to ambush that train. Comrade Pearce will accompany us and report to the world the fighting calibre of the National Liberation Army," Núñez continued. "This will be a great propaganda exercise for us and will demonstrate to the peasantry that we do not fear the army. I intend to take only volunteers, so if any man dissents from the staging of this operation let him speak out now without prejudice and let him stay behind with full honour."

No one did object and all volunteered, but some questions were asked about the other column of the ELN, now operating some two hundred miles away.

"Will Parada's men be with us?" asked Victor Medina, who not long before had been a law student in Calí.

"No, it is not necessary," said Núñez. "The *carabineros* are not in sufficient strength, and anyway they are cowards who are good at grinding the peasants under their heel but will run rather than face us."

Next Andrés Valencia, an ex-seminarist, entered the debate: "Comrade Fabio, I say this not out of fear but out of prudence. Is there any possibility that the army might be setting a trap for us?"

"You do right to ask that, Comrade Andrés, but the answer is no. Our intelligence source in the Sixth Brigade at Medellín assures me that Colonel Tobón is convinced we would not dare to attack in the plain, and certainly not a full trainload of *carabineros*."

Lancaster listened as the various tasks involved were assigned. There were to be three assault groups, constantly in radio contact with each other. Mines would be laid in the chosen defile between the rails of the track the previous day and checked shortly before the train's arrival. He, Lancaster, would be an armed member of the assault, which it was assumed would be successful, and afterwards would take a series of photographs – the camera to be provided by Núñez – to be syndicated to left-wing journals and periodicals in Europe.

Lancaster listened in subdued mood. This was worse than he had feared. Technically, no doubt, he was up to what Núñez was demanding of him. It was the moral dimension that worried him. He baulked at taking an active part in the assault. But he salved his conscience with the thought that the squeamishness he felt could have only one end if indulged – a place of honour in front of Núñez's firing squad. And he could probably avoid any personal involvement in the killing during the actual attack.

While the details of the assault were being worked out, a guard entered the commandant's quarters to announce the arrival of a messenger from Parada, operating with the ELN's second column. The courier was introduced, saluted and handed a letter to Núñez. Núñez tore open the envelope, read rapidly and impatiently, then smiled.

"Good news from our comrades Juan and Alberto," he exclaimed. "They have claimed another village." He then read out Parada's dispatch. Lancaster found it instructive at many levels, not least in indicating the *modus operandi* of the ELN and the relationships between its senior officers.

Núñez' powerful voice, produced theatrically from the diaphragm, dwelt lovingly on Parada's words: "'Comrade Commander of the National Liberation Army, Fabio Núñez Camargo. The general staff of the Camilo Torres Restrepo guerilla front takes great pleasure in informing you that our operation Diego executed last Tuesday has been successful on the politico-military level required by the people's war.'"

Parada's letter went on to explain that his men had been engaged in the political education of a village. Leaving their camp at two p.m. Parada's group arrived outside the target village by ten p.m. At five the following morning operations commenced. While the main force waited some two hundred yards outside the village the assault group, using only small arms, moved in. Resistance was negligible, so that by the time the main column had responded to the first shots and come running up to support their comrades the latter were already masters of the situation. Parada reported that his group remained in the village just eighty minutes, during which time they assembled a crowd of about two hundred people and explained the purpose of their struggle. This was greeted with applause and cheering, after which the guerillas fired off volleys into the air to cow any civil defence units that might be thinking of regrouping. "We made an immediate appeal to the people," Parada continued, "using these slogans: 'Long Live the National Liberation Army' and 'Long Live Fabio Núñez'. I believe it is a victory when a revoluntionary guerilla band takes a conservative village and destroys the conservative myth that all revolutionaries are their enemies." Parada concluded by listing the casualties: five *guardia civil* of the village dead and two wounded, as against just one flesh wound sustained by the guerillas.

This good news made a profound impression on Núñez's men, on which he was not slow to capitalise. "Comrades, this is a good omen for our own operation. Tomorrow we march to the Rio Amarillo. Some time this week the troop train for Medellín must pass, and when it does it will be ours. Come, Comrades, let us prepare. Not a step backwards! Liberation or Death!"

Eight

Three days later Lancaster sat in a jungle clearing. Not the thick, luxuriant jungle of popular imagination, but a sparser, drier habitat. This particular clump of vegetation was about a kilometre distant from the Amarillo river. With Lancaster was an angry Núñez. Although the guerillas' explosives experts, Victor Medina and Gregorio Vásquez, had laid the mines between the rails on the Sunday afternoon, Núñez' main force had not reached the agreed spot for the ambush until 8.45 on the Monday morning – in time, as they thought, to intercept the train from Santa Marta to Medellín. But the chosen mail train, carrying the *carabineros*, their weapons and a payroll of over 300,000 pesos, had sped by the astonished Medina and Vásquez just after eight. Núñez was now more than ever determined to press home an attack. The next military train was due to pass from Medellín to the coast at about four p.m. and it occurred to Lancaster once again that Núñez was a shrewd tactician.

The spot selected for ambush was a small rocky gorge, with step-like ledges of earth some three metres apart running along the sides. The guerillas in the *Frente Fabio*'s task force were divided into four groups. One would be posted with Lancaster and Núñez on the western side of the railway line; another, under Victor Medina, on the eastern; two men would lie hidden in the jungle close to the Zaragoza bridge, just before the entry into the gorge, while a reserve would remain in the jungle clearing where they now conferred, ready to reinforce either the western or eastern assault force, as necessary. Ten men were kept back to form the reserve, and the western and eastern groups would comprise twenty men each (including Lancaster and the commandant).

Each of these four groups was carrying up-to-date radio equipment. Núñez gave his men precise instructions on how to use their transmitters and underlined the need for constant liaison. "HK-22" was the codeword for the approach of the train. Daniel and another would send this message through from their jungle vantage point on the far side of the bridge.

Also in Lancaster's group were Padre Domingo Lacán and Dr Andrade. Together they moved from the cover of the thick vegetation to their assault position in the thin screen of foliage along the side of the gorge and waited. The time was one o'clock in the afternoon. Lancaster, one of the chosen few, had been given a San Cristóbal automatic rifle. This particular carbine, then in common use among the soldiers of the Colombian army, was an elite weapon among the guerillas. It had been imported by the US Public Safety Programme from the Dominican Republic, its place of manufacture.

At around two o'clock Núñez decided to check that all was still well with the two mines, which were attached to the rails with parallel circuits. The detonator was to be handled by the experienced Gregorio Vásquez, who had given detailed advice on the likely force and direction of the explosion. Victor Medina, one of the youngest of the guerilla band but already with a reputation as an explosives genius, was sent down to make sure that they would still do their job. After clambering back up and replying in the affirmative, Medina rejoined the waiting men.

As the hot, steamy afternoon wore on, Lancaster reflected on the curious pass he had come to. That a member of the SIS should now be waiting to assault a regular army unit of a member of the "free world" was bizarre enough. More immediately disquieting was the thought that before the day was out he might well be personally involved in armed conflict. Despite his skills on the shooting range he had never tested himself in actual combat. It was one thing to hit a target as part of a scientific exercise in marksmanship; it was quite another to have to shoot to kill or be killed.

What Lancaster felt was not so much cowardice as a moral squeamishness. He resented having to make the absolute judgment involved in killing a man. The great point about his life in the SIS was that normally he did not have to ask himself whether what he did was "right". He was a technician and a good one, but a craftsman removed from the immediate impact of his work. Now he might have to cross the divide between theory and practice.

Occupied with such thoughts, Lancaster was jolted into immediacy by the crackling of the commandant's radio. It was Daniel from the Zaragoza bridge: "HK-22, HK-22, good luck." Immediately guerilla radios burst into life, keeping in constant touch with each other now that the ambush was imminent. The whistling and tooting of the train could be heard as it approached the bridge.

Then the roar of the locomotive as it entered the gorge, bouncing its echoes off the grim walls, was merged into a greater sound as Gregorio Vásquez pushed down the handle of the detonator and the explosion hurled stones and fragments of boulder into the air. For a moment nothing could be seen through the cloud of dust. As this cleared Lancaster could see that the train had careered off the rails. There came a burst of fire from the end carriages, obviously the location of the *carabineros*, and a flurry of bullets smashed into the ground uncomfortably close to Núñez's group. They opened fire immediately, while from the far side of the gorge a deadly crackle of rifle fire was heard from the other band. Most amazing to Lancaster was the way Lacán and Andrade warmed to their task. Andrade seemed like a man possessed. His carbine rained bullets down on the train while he bellowed above the din of his rifle, "*Long Live Camilo Torres. Down with the Mongols.*" Lacán's face was contorted in unpriestly hatred as he too joined in the frenzy that the presence of the Colombian soldiery seemed to inspire in his fellow guerillas. Both of them, Lancaster knew, were almost saintly in their idealism, but once in action it seemed to be the demons of hell who drove them.

A shout came from Medina's group across the gorge: "Be careful! There are civilians on board!"

Núñez and his men clambered warily down to the track to investigate. From a carriage window the face of a frightened child looked out. "Get down, get down, all of you, we don't want to kill civilians," yelled Núñez. At that moment, with Núñez, a recognisable figure from "wanted" posters, now an easy target out in the open, a *carabinero* leaned out of a window and aimed his gun at him. Lancaster, standing some four yards behind the guerilla leader, was the only one in the guerilla group who saw the danger. Without thinking, he raised his rifle and pulled the trigger. The soldier slumped forward, his head trailing out of the window, pouring blood. Núñez saw what had happened and without saying anything, he stepped back and slapped Lancaster on the shoulder appreciatively.

By now some of the *carabineros*, realising that they were outnumbered, had passed inside the train to the carriages where the civilians were located, and were attempting to use them as shields. Half a dozen women emerged into the sunlight, with the troops' automatics prodded in their backs.

As Núñez called, "Cease fire," Andrade made a run for the door at the other end of the carriage, hoping to take his foes from behind. Momentarily distracted, the *carabineros* turned to face this new threat. In that split second some of the hostages made a bid for freedom. Seeing their opportunity, the guerillas opened fire. Two of the *carabineros*, robbed of their protective human barricade, were killed outright, collapsing under a hail of bullets. Two more, bent on vengeance rather than self-preservation, opened up with their automatics into the backs of their shields and when the latter fell they in turn were riddled with bullets. The other two *carabineros* in this group managed to get back inside the train with their hostages, but almost immediately shooting was heard from within. A few seconds later Andrade emerged: "Viva Fabio!" he shouted. Disappearing for a moment, he re-emerged with the bodies of the two luckless soldiers, which he kicked brutally and contemptuously out of the door.

It was time to call up the reserve, for the remaining five

carabineros were still holed up in the end carriage with two Madsen sub-machine guns. These five were fighting a bitter rearguard action against the men on the eastern side of the gorge. As Victor Medina and his men edged along the ridge two of them had been picked off by a soldier firing from the back door of the train.

Meanwhile Núñez's group, running along the tracks, were fired on by the engine driver. But when he jumped out of his cab and ran round to the first carriage adjoining the engine, he met a hail of bullets from the reserve group as it came down off the ridge. Núñez' men then threaded their way to the front of the train from inside, overturning carriage seats as they hunted for any remaining soldiers. By the time all three bands – Medina's, Núñez's and the guerilla reserve – were assembled outside the end carriage, the desperate *carabineros* inside had torn up the carriage seats and erected them into a bulletproof barricade, from behind which the Madsens would deal death to anyone approaching their compartment door.

A quick conference was held. The guerillas had no more dynamite. Núñez could not be certain that there was not a powerful army detachment nearby, and had to act quickly. He could not afford the indignity of retreat before he had settled accounts with the *carabineros*. The only way out was to take the carriage by storm. While a fusillade was directed into the compartment from both sides a small group would force its way in by the door, while another would jump on to the roof from the next carriage and fire down through it. Caught between four fires, the defenders might become confused. It was a chance worth taking.

Medina, Lacán and Vásquez volunteered to form the assault wave by the door. Núñez raised his arm to give the order and for the next minute all hell broke loose. Wilting under the onslaught from all directions, the defenders became disoriented and in that instant Vásquez, Lacán and Medina burst in on them and did their deadly work. Suddenly silence fell. It was all over. Núñez had gained a victory but, with four of his assault team badly wounded, it was an expensive one.

Three sets of orders were issued immediately. The reserve

was to help Dr Andrade with the civilian and guerilla wounded. The other two sections were to collect the soldiers' weapons, ammunition, uniforms and packs. Lancaster was given ten minutes in which to take as many pictures as he could for his putative European journal. Daniel meanwhile was instructed to keep the strictest watch from the bridge for any sign of army reinforcements.

As Lancaster walked through the train he was appalled at the carnage. Fifteen minutes only had elapsed since the train entered the gorge, yet here was blood and devastation on a scale he could scarcely credit. Most terrible of all was the end carriage, scene of the army's last stand. The seats used as a barricade by the *carabineros* were shredded, and the defenders themselves had been virtually eviscerated by the lead that had poured in on them. And himself? Could it be that just a few minutes ago he had shot a man dead?

The harsh voice of Núñez ordering the retreat cut short any further introspection. Completing his journalistic pretence, Lancaster then climbed out and fell back along the railway track with the others. Even with forty guerillas still able-bodied, the haul of automatics, Madsens and revolvers with shells and round-clips, plus the boots and uniforms they had to carry, seriously impeded their progress as they melted away into the jungle. Lancaster's last glimpse of the railway struck him poignantly. Standing at the rear of the disabled train, a small peasant child, its fingers stuck in its mouth, watched half in fear and half incredulously as the *gringo* vanished.

Suddenly the political significance of the picture struck him. If a foreigner was reported working with the guerillas this could lead to big trouble in Bogotá. Perhaps Summerby might even get his wish, and Uncle Sam would intervene openly.

In an artificially darkened bar on the Avenida Séptima one afternoon early in June a man, an ex-right wing terrorist now in the pay of the Americans, could have been seen worriedly drumming his fingers on a table and looking occasionally through the green-shaded window at the northbound traffic, already building up to the rush-hour peak at six p.m. The rendezvous had been set for five, but ever since his narrow escape from a set-up in Calí in 1959 Efraim Hernández made it a rule to arrive an hour early at agreed locations. In the briefcase in front of him, neatly enholstered, was a Colt .38. On his person was an Astra revolver. Briefcase or no, few would have taken him for a businessman. In the eyes of many corrupt men there can still be seen the scintilla of their innocent youth, but in Hernández's eyes, such a divine spark was absent. This was a man who had never been innocent.

Some such understanding had already been arrived at by the waiter. The bar had a rule that glasses had to be re-plenished every half hour. When Hernández's beer and time had first run out together, the *camarero* had made so bold as to venture, "Another drink, Señor?" There had been something, however, about the way the man had fixed him with his reptilian eyes and answered, "*Nada, pues, nada*" that had made the waiter back off quickly, with the silent resolve that as far as this individual was concerned the half-hour rule and all other house regulations would be waived.

The hum of the traffic on the Avenida Séptima mingled with the shouts of the lottery vendors and the peal of taxi horns and honking *colectivos*. From somewhere nearby a record of "Sergeant Pepper" blared. The buses, building up in number on the northward run as the afternoon wore on, spewed out diesel fumes as they passed, some of them so bedecked with religious insignia, statuary and miniature lighted altars as to suggest more the procession of the Holy Grail than a mode of public transport.

The entry of a *gringo* at five minutes to five triggered in Efraim Hernández some ancient racial antagonism. *Gringos* he hated only slightly less than communists, as the hidden hand manipulating the oligarchs who had persecuted him throughout his life. Yet it was for *gringo* money that he was here. It was either that or humiliating poverty. He would have to take care to conceal his true attitude towards the *norteamericanos*.

After a few minutes the new arrival came across to him

and spoke in a heavy North-American accent, using the agreed codewords: "You're not Señor Fulano, by any chance?"

Three days later, in an obscure office of the USIS building on the corner of 20th Street and Carrera Tercera, away from the inquisitive eyes of embassy personnel and embassy-watchers, Summerby held a conference. Following Everett's contact with Hernández in the Carrera Séptima bar, the Cuban hit-man, Luis Frias, had also flown in and all the four principals of Operation Toro were therefore together for the first time: Summerby's right-hand man, Jim Everett, Efraim Hernández, Luis Frias, and Summerby himself.

News Summerby had received that morning made him realise that he was now more than ever engaged in a last-ditch enterprise. The pink-coloured report copied to him from Washington spoke of imminent cutbacks in the Company: from the first of January 1969 mergers would take place between certain national desks in Washington in the Area Divisions, and also between field operations and station case officers. Two of the candidates being considered for a merger were the Colombia desk of the Western Hemisphere Area Division and the Colombian operations conducted under diplomatic cover in Bogotá. The proposal was that a new area, roughly equivalent to the old vice-royalty of Nueva Granada, be created in northern South America, to be run and directed from Caracas. This proposal came with supporting documentation to suggest that the guerilla movement in Colombia had failed to catch fire and that Castroite forces operating there were no more than a paper tiger. In the first place, the non-co-operation of the FARC and the Soviet Union, the success of the military campaign against the rebels and the comparative political stability of the country all worked against the guerillas. And secondly, the death of Che Guevara had dealt a crippling blow to those who asserted that revolutionary willpower could convert the most unpromising situation into victory.

The covering note from J. J. Johnson explained that, since

the decision had been taken at directorate level, he was powerless to prevent it – "as yet, though circumstances may change, as you well know". It was as well, then, that J. J. had planned operation Toro for August. This, thought Summerby, was the prescience of a true winner, and he had decided to bring forward to mid-June the meeting in which the operation's principals would thrash out tactics. Only Everett, himself and J. J. knew the full scope and range of the plan. Luis Frias, the expert "mechanic" hired for the hit, would only be told the target at the last moment, while Hernández was to be used simply as bait to draw away the DAS – the Colombian secret police – and the security forces.

Now Hernández and Frias faced each other warily across the table. As a hobby Summerby had at one time in his life kept tropical fish, and he had often observed that for as long as a member of a dominant species of fish shared a tank with lesser breeds it was relaxed and contented, but that if one of its own kind was introduced it immediately felt threatened. And so it was with Hernández and Frias. Each tried to get the measure of the other, and each sensed the association of the other with violent death.

"Señores," began Summerby, "I wanted each of you to meet your partner in this operation. It is unlikely that you will ever meet again but it is just possible that emergencies will arise so that I would have to call on you to work together. In that case I would not want suspicion to arise between you. In this operation I intend for security reasons to use as few people as possible, and therefore, in case of some last-minute contingency, I want to lay the ground-work for your possible collaboration."

Hernández said nothing but stared unblinkingly across at his Cuban "partner". Frias met his gaze with thinly-veiled hostility.

"As you know, *Don* Efraim," continued Summerby, playing up to Hernández' notorious vanity, "I want you to stage a diversion in Bogotá on a day late in August this year while I and my associates carry out an operation elsewhere in the city. Our work will also be covered by the presence of the Pope in Bogotá on that day. Good security demands that I tell you very little about our end of the project. Just to assure you, however, that you will be on the side of right and justice I *can* tell you that our mission will be aimed at communist subversion and the enemies of Christianity."

Summerby's way of speaking fitted well with his corpulent physique. The orotundity of his speech seemed as flabby as his two-hundred pound frame. He continued: "Colonel Acosta has sworn to take you dead or alive should he ever find you in Bogotá again, and thus there is no doubt that he and the DAS will rise to the bait. You will be expected to hold them off for one full hour with your men."

"Señor Summerby," Hernández replied, lazily and somewhat contemptuously, "you will know that I have made fools of those *pendejos* in the DAS before and I can do it again. Acosta is nothing. He would not have lasted five minutes in the days when I ruled Cauca. No doubt if he called in the army with tanks he could blast us out eventually, but our agreement specifies a diversion for just one hour, *no cierto?*"

"Right," said Summerby. He turned to his colleague. "Explain the set-up, Jim."

Everett found Hernández as formidable in the flesh as by reputation. He began hesitantly. "I have, that is *we* have, the Company, that is, taken out a lease in the name of Esmeraldas Internacionales SA at the north end of Calle 23 on Carrera Segunda. The house we've rented there has a special significance. Plans that we have obtained show that ten years ago a tunnel was built between the University of the Andes and the Avenida Jorge Gaitán as a pilot project to test the feasibility of an urban subway system – the scheme was abandoned, it seems, because the National Front caucus leaders were unable to agree on how to float a public issue to finance it. The initial stretch of tunnel still remains, but is inaccessible at the terminal points. However, the sewer running along Carrera Segunda is separated from the unused tunnel by just one thickness of wall. Our intention is to drill a hole in the wall of the sewer and install a screw-action circular trap door linking the two tunnels."

"Let me understand this," said Hernández. "Your plan is that I should stand off Acosta in the house you have leased. The getaway route is through the sewers into this subway tunnel. Where are the entrance and exit points?"

"There is an entrance to the sewer at the back of the house in Calle 23. That's why we chose it, of course. As far as I can make out, it's the one place in the city that gives access into the drainage system and lies across the line of the abandoned subway. I don't mind telling you I had to do some arm-twisting to get this lease."

"And the way out? You said the terminals are inaccessible."

"As a means of entrance, yes. There are emergency stairs leading up from the subway system, but they give out on to the gardens of the Quinta Bolívar. If you went in that way and you were spotted, you'd have the army swarming round you in no time at all. But as an escape route it's more than adequate. We'll have a man posted there to open up the hatch. It's not ideal, as the place will be overrun with tourists at that time of day, but that shouldn't worry you. Nobody's going to oppose an armed posse."

"And I have your absolute assurance, Señor, that I and my men can get out that way?"

"I give you my personal guarantee," Summerby interposed.

"How did you come by all this information?" asked Hernández, still suspicious.

"The city architect's deputy and the second-in-command at the Departamento de Planeación are on our payroll," Summerby explained.

Reassured, Hernández gestured scornfully towards Frias. "And this Señor, what is he to do?"

Summerby took it upon himself to answer, in carefully chosen words, for the Cuban. "Luis is our principal agent in the destruction of the communist cell we are planning for this coming August."

Frias confirmed this with a supercilious nod. His complacency annoyed Hernández. "It seems strange that a Cuban should need a *norteamericano* to speak for him in the company of a man of his own race."

Luis continued to smile disdainfully. Summerby quickly intervened. "It is my sincere hope that you will find it possible to work together if the need arises. Señor Frias is a sworn enemy of that anti-Christ Fidel Castro, who expelled him and his family from Havana in fifty-nine. You should be united at least in your common opposition to these godless tyrants."

"*Como no*," said Hernández, shrugging blandly. "Of course."

For several days there had been jubilation in Núñez's camp. The attack on the train was generally considered to have been a great triumph. Gregorio Vásquez had even begun to compose a ballad, with spirited guitar accompaniment, celebrating the exploit.

Now, after something over a week with them, Lancaster was preparing to leave. He had told Núñez that it was his intention to make contact with the Moscow-led FARC in the south, and the commander had given him the name of a civilian liaison officer, a professor of sociology at the National University. If any significant stroke was being attempted by the left in Colombia, Lancaster concluded, it was not being planned by the ELN. His forecast for their political future was not bright. It seemed to him that they were drunk with the elixir of Cuba and that the myth of the Sierra Maestra weighed more heavily with them than a sober and judicious assessment of political reality in Colombia in the late 1960s. For all that he thought them engaged on a forlorn quest, in the short time Lancaster had spent with the guerillas he had learned to respect them. There was not one of them who could not have made a comfortable living in the middle echelons of Colombian society, yet in pursuit of revolutionary ideals they daily faced privation and often death. Even against the interests of the Western alliance he was officially in business to protect he could not but wish them well.

After a night of farewell carousing Lancaster quitted the guerilla camp next morning and set off back towards "civilisation". Núñez had arranged that Daniel and Gabriel García, an ex-philosophy teacher, should accompany him to the outskirts of Yarumal. Lancaster could then walk the last couple of miles into town and make his own excuses to the authorities for his absence. On a bright, blue morning Lancaster and his comrades began to descend the rocky screes of the Andes towards the heartland of Antioquia. Looking back, he caught his last glimpse of Núñez and Father Lacán standing on a high rock bluff, watching him go.

Nine

"So where the hell is the car?" Fitch demanded angrily.

"I've told you all that happened, Paul. There's nothing to add."

"And I'm supposed just to let it go at that? You don't have to deal with that prick Niven, complaining all day long that he can't do his job without a car. Can you imagine his reaction when I tell him his precious Ford arrived at Barranquilla but has simply disappeared *en route*? I can't even give a convincing story to the insurance people, for God's sake."

Lancaster had got in from Medellín the night before. In Yarumal he had hired a *carro particular* for the run to Medellín and had caught the last plane to Bogotá at 5.30 that evening. Enquiries with the British consul in Medellín had failed to disclose the whereabouts of an English car either abandoned, wrecked or eviscerated. Lancaster wondered what the sequel to his disappearance had been, and what the swarthy *patrón* and his sidekick had done with their charge.

Naturally he could not tell Fitch anything approaching the truth. Instead he had made up a tale that the journalist Pearce had let him down at the last minute, and that he had decided to drive the car down from the coast himself. His version of how he came to lose the vehicle was that he had been stopped for questioning by a suspicious army patrol. On his return to the car park from the checkpoint, the vehicle was missing.

Fitch had been unimpressed. He still was. "And what's more, I don't know what the hell kind of an operation you're running here. We're supposed to liaise with you but

77

you suddenly disappear for almost two weeks. Parker says you're on a field trip, but then clams up when I press him for details. What is your status in the Embassy anyway? I asked the Ambassador about you the other night and he referred me to Youngson. Youngson referred me to Miller. Miller, the so-called Head of Chancery, tells me you work directly to HE, yet *he* claims to know nothing about you. What are you, some kind of Mata Hari, that you've got them all creeping round on tiptoe whenever your name's mentioned?"

"I accept that you have a right to ask questions about the car and you've every reason to be annoyed about it. I accept this and I've already apologised and said I'll write a report . . ."

Fitch interrupted him. "But what were you doing swanning round in Antioquia anyway? I've been here three years and I've never had the time to travel overland. You've only just got here and you're off gallivanting round the wilds of Colombia."

Lancaster took a deep breath and tried to answer calmly. "What I was going on to say was that what I do and the interpretation I put on my duties is no concern of yours. I have to answer to HE and the Foreign Office – not, thank God, to the British Council."

This roused Fitch to new heights of fury. "Typical fucking Oxbridge arrogance. Just because I didn't read Greats at Balliol I'm of no account in your eyes. I've seen the same look on Miller's face. Well, I didn't start with a silver spoon in my mouth. I first decided to go into the Foreign Service when I bicycled all the way down to Greece before the War."

Lancaster stood up firmly. Fitch's bicycle journey to Greece was part of the lore of the Bogotá diplomatic circuit, and was often referred to in the Embassy with derisive laughter. Whenever Fitch grew more than usually tiresome, abusive or inebriated, he would revert to the tale of his conversion on the road to Thessalonica.

"Is there any point in continuing this conversation? The only substantive issue is to do with Niven's car. I'll have a word with him myself and see what I can do to

78

help him over his problems until a new car can be got out to him."

"But can you guarantee that he won't pester me in the interim?" Fitch persisted. "Or is it all right if I send him down to you when he comes in with that whining bitch of a wife of his? There's a first-class cow for you. A good cocking's what she needs, but looking at her face I wonder who'd ever have the guts to give it to her."

"Look," replied Lancaster, who was starting to lose patience, "I've done all I can to help you over this problem. I've offered to conciliate all necessary parties but you seem only interested in making difficulties."

"That's rich. You lose a car in the middle of a joyride and I'*m* making difficulties. Well, let me tell you, the matter is not resting here. I'm putting in a formal complaint about this incident and about your attitude in general. Express to Latin America division with copies to HE and the ODM."

"Please yourself. But don't start anything you can't finish. You'd better be damn sure you're not in a greenhouse before you start throwing stones. I'm not sure your subheads would bear much looking into."

"Damn cheek. My hands are clean. The auditor has given me the A-okay three years on the trot."

"The auditor, as you well know, sees what he wants to see. But perhaps Diana might be interested to know about your evenings at the 'Film Society'. How is expensive Lucia of the laughing eyes, by the way?"

"You bastard. Who the fucking hell are you anyway? Some shit from security or MI6? My god, if it wasn't for the pension I'd have chucked this god-awful job years ago. They're crawling out of the woodwork on all sides now."

After Fitch had stormed out, angry but badly shaken, Lancaster cursed himself for the lack of self-control that had led him to reveal all he knew about the egregious British Council representative. Well, he'd blown it now. The sooner contact was made with the FARC and his operation was wound up, the better.

But this Friday was destined to be a black one. Scarcely an hour after the tempestuous meeting with Fitch, he was buzzed from the central switchboard.

"Major Watkins, diplomatic courier, to see you urgently, Señor Lancaster."

Watkins, a red-faced, archetypal ex-army officer in his fifties, entered Lancaster's office in a state of agitation, seemingly untempered by his fourteen-hour flight from London via New York. He still had on the officerly camelhair coat he had worn when boarding at Heathrow the day before. He sat down briskly, lit up a cheroot, and addressed himself to Lancaster.

"Is it safe to talk here?"

"Safe enough."

"Well, the long and the short of it is that Operation Janos is off. You will be recalled through normal channels in a few days' time but as this whole affair now threatens to become a *cause célèbre* all our field agents are being notified personally of the background before they return to the UK."

"What's gone wrong, then?"

"I don't know how much you know about the scope of this operation, but I must admit that when I first learned what had been attempted I was shocked. Did you know that Crombie has deployed operatives in sixty-three different countries?"

"I know nothing except the orders relating specifically to me and Colombia." This of course was not true, but Watkins was an intelligence man, though Lancaster knew nothing of his role beyond the obvious fact that he was operating behind courier cover.

"The word is that Crombie has fallen victim to some form of delusional mania," continued Watkins. "He has always detested Harvester, you know, and sees the recent rumblings from the PM and the Select Committee as part of a Harvester-inspired plot to reduce the Service to a cipher. It seems that Harvester has argued at the highest level in Whitehall that if retrenchment has to come Six is the obvious area for cuts. The argument was cunningly slanted in the direction of government policy. Harvester maintained that if we are pulling out of a global role, withdrawing east of Suez and all that, then it's nonsense to try to match ourselves against the CIA or KGB. Resources should go into Five and we should concentrate on counter-espionage."

"I'm aware of some of the undercurrents. But what have they to do with my assignment in Colombia?" Which, incidentally, he had believed to be one of twenty, not sixty-three.

"Well, put the case that Crombie believes there is a conspiracy against him and that the PM and the Select Committee are colluding with Harvester and MI5. What does he do? His response is to prepare a coup of such dimensions as will flatten the opposition once and for all. Now this is where the plot thickens to the point where people like me are no longer able – or allowed – to follow it. Anyway, Harvester's men got wind of something. Who knows all the ins and outs of it? Maybe the Russians were on to Crombie and tipped off Five. Who knows?"

"So Harvester blew the gaff to Number Ten?"

"Not quite," Watkins went on. "If he had maybe the damage could have been contained. As it is, all hell's broken loose. You may know that within Five there is a faction that has little time for either Harvester or Crombie, and even less for the PM, whom they suspect of selling the country down the drain. The 'Young Turks', we call them. These Young Turks argued strongly to Harvester that if he should *not* inform Number Ten of MI5's suspicions there was possibly a golden chance of discrediting Crombie, snubbing the PM, and drawing in a netful of sleepers or doubles at the same time."

"How were they going to pull that off?" Lancaster made a mental note to check Watkins out in the Service Yearbook.

"The idea was that a number of controlled feeds would be put out as bait inside Five. If there were sleepers, this kind of material would have to be relayed to Moscow, and we would then expect a significant reshuffling of their KGB manpower under diplomatic cover. The net could be tightened and the list of suspects gradually whittled down."

"And Crombie? How were they going to spring the trap on him?"

"They were giving him enough rope to hang himself with. Then all would be revealed and the illustrious

Sir Ian would be caught well and truly with his trousers down. Knowing how the PM reacts to Crombie at the best of times, the drama could then have only one ending."

"But doesn't all this assume that Crombie's coup was bogus? Suppose he really was on to something?"

"Rumour has it that the Young Turks had a source close to Crombie, and his information was that Crombie's intelligence was flimsy and far-fetched."

"So what's the upshot of all this?"

"Somehow the best laid plans of mice and men etc. The PM got wind that something big in the intelligence world has been kept from him. He didn't take kindly to the thought, I can tell you. Both Harvester and Crombie, the two supremos, have been told to suspend all operations except those personally vetted by Number Ten, on pain of dire sanctions. He and the Defence Secretary are meeting with the top intelligence brass in a few days for a top-level review of all activities undertaken for 1968. It's predicted that there's going to be the most almighty shake-up in both Five and Six and that many heads will roll. Anyway, as far as you're concerned it's bag-packing time. As I say, I'm just the bearer of news, but you'll get it officially over the wires in a few days."

"Incidentally, who is your superior, Major Watkins? Who do you report to on Operation Janos?"

"Colonel Jack Durand. I served with him in Burma, you know, and you might say he handed me in after the war. He's not everybody's cup of tea, but I swear by him."

"How long are you going to be with us, Major?"

"Just overnight, I'm afraid. It's Lima tomorrow, Quito on Monday and I'll be talking to Hedley in Caracas on Tuesday before I fly out to Mexico City. Hedley was in London a few weeks ago, you know. Something to do with the American, Everett, I believe, and things not being as they seem. Anyway, your name came up. He remembers you. I believe you did firearms training together. He says you're quite an ace with sidearms."

"You've been in this business long enough not to believe

all you hear, Major. Can I buy you dinner tonight at the Anglo–American?"

"Offer gratefully accepted, old boy."

Lancaster swung the car sharply on to the airport road before veering right into the campus of the National University. His mind was made up. He would not sit meekly in his office waiting for the cable with his recall. Watkins' visit was unofficial and unminuted, and he could always claim justifiable misunderstanding later if his conduct was queried. But while he was here he was more than ever determined to make contact with the FARC group. An eyewitness report on the two principal guerilla bands in Colombia would surely place him high among the contenders for the next senior Latin America position to come up. Besides, with any luck he would be able to establish once and for all that CIA information was ideologically coloured and that programmes of assassination, abduction or hijacking did not feature among the objectives of the left, whether Castroist or Moscow-directed.

The FARC contact recommended by Núñez, Ernesto Cárdenas, professor of social theory at the National, proved to be a slender, vague, but very affable man. In his mid-forties, well known for his seminal work on peasant society in the Andes, he was acknowledged to have leftist views, but perhaps no more so than those in the radical wing of the governing Liberal Party itself. Lancaster had therefore been greatly surprised when Núñez had given him his name as civilian co-ordinator in Bogotá. Looking at him now, Lancaster wondered how long he could endure the rigours of the *picana eléctrica* if ever the DAS got their hands on him. In another time, at another place and on a different operation, Lancaster might well have been collaborating with the Americans on intelligence, and then what price Cárdenas? As it was, on this job the CIA were the last people who should know, so Cárdenas was safe.

"I had been told by mutual friends to expect you, Señor Pearce," said Cárdenas, ushering him into his spacious office.

"Then you know why I am here. That is good, for, with

respect, I did not want to waste time with Colombian formalities. Time is short and the contact must be made in days rather than weeks."

"Not so fast, Señor. I am but a humble courier. The contact you seek requires a procedure that must be strictly adhered to. In short, I will not know who the true contact is, nor his liaison group nor even the reason for which you meet him. The procedure is that I hold a cocktail party in my apartment to which fifty people are invited. The fifty names I have here with their Apartado Aereo numbers. It is to be assumed that some of the names are false and their post boxes merely a type of poste restante. Some time during the party the contact will be made but by whom I cannot say."

"How soon can you arrange the party?"

"Let me see. Today is Friday – I could do it by next Thursday."

"Much too late. How about Monday?"

"Señor, impossible. This is Colombia. With great luck I could manage next Tuesday evening, perhaps."

"Tuesday it is then. My compliments to you, Dr Cárdenas. Maybe while I wait for the mysterious stranger we could talk about your latest book, which I profited from."

"With the greatest of pleasure, Señor."

"I know how you feel, Paul. State has been leaning on us hard recently. A lot of times I feel the Foundation's going to hell in a basket. Here, let me fill you up." Heyck refilled Fitch's glass with Glenlivet malt.

"But can you imagine the arrogance of the bastard, warning me off after he had ballsed up the whole thing and lost our car? A brand new Ford, I ask you."

"And you say he knows details of your private life too," said Heyck.

"The bastard threatened me." Fitch repeated the phrase as if he couldn't believe it himself. "Threatened me, can you credit that?"

"How long has he been here, did you say, Paul?" asked Green.

"That's the thing of it," moaned Fitch. "He's only been here five minutes before he's off, giving out some cock and bull story about investigating peasant communities for the volunteer programme and leaving that poor sod Parker to do the work. 'Course, I blame our Labour government. They've had it in for the Council since the earliest days. Cultural imperialism, I heard that twat Hambleton call it."

The names of British backbench MPs were not part of Heyck and Green's briefing, so they let Fitch's sally go by without remark.

"Whereabouts exactly was he when this incident took place?" asked Heyck.

"Somewhere in Antioquia. Don't ask me more. Antioquia to me means Medellín pure and simple. I work too damn hard to be able to spare the time exploring the highways and byways of the Andes."

"And you say his entries in the Foreign Office Yearbook are sketchy and vague?" queried Green.

"I spent the afternoon trying to find out what I could about him, because by God I mean to nail the bastard. All I could find is that he's spent time in Madrid and Montevideo on Technical Assistance programmes."

"Certainly a slippery customer, the way you describe him. If we hear anything from our sources we'll let you know." There was the ghost of a wink in Green's eye as it met Heyck's.

"What about fluttering Hernández?" asked Everett.

"There's no point," replied Summerby. "There's only any percentage in using the polygraph on long-term employees. Their lies are deep and really ring the bell. Take Frias. His scores came out positive on his last grading but that's not exactly surprising, I guess. He's hardly in a position to offer his services elsewhere."

"Just what I mean. It's conceivable that Hernández could be a plant."

"Are you serious, Jim? You saw him at that meeting with Frias. It only needed something to set him off and he'd have been blazing away at anything in sight. No one would ever use a wild animal like that for undercover ops.

Anyway, he didn't know till a month or so ago that we'd offer him this contract."

"But he's had time to put out feelers to the opposition since then."

"In theory, yes. But with his record do you really think the Soviets are going to want to play ball? All our back-up data and all known profiles place him as a fanatical anti-communist."

"All the same," said Everett, "I'd be happier with a polygraph flutter."

"You're still playing it by the book, Jim. This whole op. comes from a book that nobody's written yet. You can't expect orthodoxy in our position. Besides, Hernández is a tricky customer. A maverick. A polygraph test could be all he needs to push him over the edge. The last thing we want at this stage is a rogue steer on the rampage."

Everett looked up from his heavily cluttered desk. In front of him were two files. One was the "lynx" list. The other was a copiously flagged print-out from the International Communism division of Counter-Intelligence, Washington, headed "Smoth".

"Anyway, Jim, right now we've got bigger fish to catch. You're worrying about a minnow and here we are with a barracuda loose in our fish tank."

Ten

Somewhat to David Lancaster's surprise, when he contacted Cárdenas' office on Monday, he learned that the party had been arranged satisfactorily and would take place the following night as promised. On arriving in his hired Thunderbird at the professor's apartment in the Chapinero district on Tuesday evening he was introduced to a few of the more extrovert members of the gathering. Perhaps they were harmlessly extrovert, but Lancaster thought there seemed little point in going through the elaborate charade of preparing aliases and phony addresses for people whom Cárdenas appeared to know personally anyway. Once more he reflected that he would not give much for the chances of this urban network if the professor were ever put under torture.

At first natural caution kept him close to his host. In the first half hour with Cárdenas he learned more than he cared to know about the many infinitesimal theoretical shadings that differentiated the Castroist E L N from the Maoist E L P and from his immediate target the Soviet-backed F A R C, especially since all three groupings apparently had vociferous representatives present this evening. Yet it was soon clear to him that, so far as Núñez and his band were concerned, he already knew more than anyone at this gathering. Growing bored with the esoteric and highly technical discussion, he drifted into the next room where dancing was taking place. His attention was immediately attracted by one of the women. Petite and graceful, she wore a cream mini-dress and, round her neck, a striking gold medallion which from a distance resembled one of the Chibcha artefacts he had seen in Bogotá's gold museum.

Lancaster was struck by the paleness of her skin and her lustrous brown eyes.

She was clearly an excellent dancer. The grace of her rhythm and the economy of her movements reminded him of some svelte jungle creature. Her black hair was long and straight, yet she had no Indian blood, he was sure. Even as she smiled at her partner Lancaster detected the slight reserve that often denoted a daughter of the Colombian aristocracy. The woman fascinated him and he gazed at her for several minutes until she caught his eye. He looked away quickly, embarrassed. How was it that beautiful women often knew, as if by some kind of internal radar, when they were being scrutinised?

He soon found a corner of the room from which he could view her less conspicuously. All his intuitions told him that this was someone who put only a small part of her personality on display at any one moment. Yet, in his primitive classification of female types, only Nordic blondes were supposed to be like this. Latin women were supposed to be more obvious.

There came a moment when the object of his admiration began to pick up radar vibrations even from his hidden vantage point in the corner of the room. Half turning, she caught his eye again. This time he would have to act decisively, or else bow out.

Lancaster elbowed his way into the middle of the room, mulling over as he went the many introductory lines he had used before in such circumstances. He discarded them all as inappropriate. There was something about the atmosphere of this particular party that inhibited his usual mock-serious banter.

Falteringly he began: "Señorita, I was wondering if . . .?"

"Yes, I could see you were," she cut in, smiling gently.

Lancaster was disconcerted. "Perhaps you misunderstand me. I only meant that – "

She waved his explanations aside. "You are no Colombian, Señor. If you were, you would know the saying, *los ojos dicen que sí, aunque la boca no.*"

Lancaster had not heard the saying, but he translated it

roughly in his head as *the eyes have it*. Certainly her meaning was clear enough.

As he danced with her the amused by-play continued. Her sense of humour was different from his. He realised how badly he would have put his foot in it if he had used any of his stock flirtatious openers. She for her part seemed genuinely interested in his work as a journalist and went out of her way to compliment him on his Spanish.

He felt a twinge of disappointment when she left him after about ten minutes. She claimed to have revolutionary business to discuss, but Lancaster wondered if her going was not some firm signal for him not to read too much into their initial easy companionship. He took the opportunity to slip into the other room, intending to ask Cárdenas about this elusive Cristina – by now he at least knew her name, if little else.

His host was in good humour. He slapped Lancaster on the shoulder and smiled when he heard the question, as though it were not the first time he had been asked it.

"Cristina Amaya, always Cristina Amaya! In this city the men *hacen cola* – you know, they form a line to get to know her. There was a time when I considered getting jealous. There I would be, at a party – like this one, say – and some plausible type would get talking to me about my work. Like a fool I'd be flattered. Then, pretty soon, all he wants to do is ask me about Cristina."

"So she's one of the 'new women', is she?"

"I am told she has had many lovers," Cárdenas replied neutrally, watching the Englishman for his reaction.

"Unmarried, you say?"

Cárdenas smiled again. "Cristina is the kind of girl you are probably more familiar with in Europe or North America. She is twenty-five, and the daughter of Don Diego Amaya, but all the things inculcated into ordinary Colombian women – marriage, children, all the traditional aims – for her these are things for the future. Right now she lives for her work, in the university and in the movement. Men she takes for her pleasure, I think . . . But for all that I admire her and, yes, love her in my own way."

Lancaster nodded politely and decided he would make

any further overtures to Cristina Amaya without the dubious mediation of his host. His journey back through the press of earnestly-talking people and out into the room where Cristina was dancing was interrupted, however.

"You are the English journalist who is a friend of Ernesto, no?" The speaker, from his coal-black visage, was clearly a *costeño*, contrasting strongly with the *mestizo* and *criollo* coffee colour of his companions.

"Hardly a friend. I scarcely know him. Just a journalistic contact."

"And you are a correspondent for the *European Left Review*?"

"That's right."

"And is the British Embassy the usual venue for a reporter from a Marxist journal?"

Lancaster breathed in deeply and tried to slow his quickening heartbeat. "Why do you say that?"

"I saw you emerging from the Embassy only yesterday, Señor. I do business with your English Stuart Insurance Company on the third floor of the *edificio*. As I was entering the elevator on the ground floor yesterday afternoon I saw you come out, obviously on your way down from the Embassy."

"Have you ever worked abroad as a correspondent, Señor – ?"

"Calderón. Diego Calderón. No – Why do you ask?"

"Well, it's simply that if you had you would understand that the embassy representing one's own country is a fertile source of information. Diplomats are often bored and homesick and frequently careless when meeting their own nationals. A visitor from England reminds most of them of what they are missing. They relax their guard and provide information to a bird of passage they would never give to a permanent resident. For example, I managed to get an interview with the Head of Chancery yesterday that was most revealing. I've a pretty good idea now how the guerillas of both north and south are viewed by the diplomatic community, and most important of all by the Americans. I think you'll agree that was not time wasted."

"You believe it is good to know your enemy?"

"Certainly. Don't you?"

"It is good to know him – if you know who he is. Most of our opponents do not advertise themselves so clearly as your Head of Chancery. You must forgive me, Señor, but it is conceivable that you are a British agent or are in the pay of the *norteamericanos*."

"You must ask the highest authorities on the Colombian left as to my credentials. Men much more powerful than Professor Cárdenas can vouch for me. I understand your suspicions and can applaud them. But if I tell you that he who endures till death has given me his personal seal of approval, you will perhaps understand."

The effect of these words was quite the opposite of what Lancaster had intended. Feeling certain from the astute cross-questioning that this was the link man, he had intended merely to put him at ease and show him that he could now with confidence go ahead and set up the contact. Father Lacán had told him that only a hand-picked few outside the ELN knew the codeword used by the guerillas for Fabio Núñez, and that if he ever wished to test the calibre of a civilian supporter he should refer to the slogan, a none-too-subtle amendment of Camilo Torres' "*hasta la muerte*". But Calderón drew back now, clearly impressed but confused, as if he had been bitten by a snake he'd thought harmless. He muttered some excuse and faded away. Lancaster returned to Cárdenas to see if he could throw any light on this strange piece of interrogation.

"Take no notice of Diego," laughed Ernesto. "He has a thing about *gringos*, even English ones. To him they are all spies, exploiters or manipulators, and even a Marxist journalist from Europe must be motivated by something corrupt, like desire for foreign travel. He believes that no true Marxist–Leninist can live in Europe. As Comrade Fidel has tried to emphasise, the only true focus for revolutionary consciousness these days must be in the Third World. Diego simply takes this proposition further and believes that no one in the advanced West can be a genuine revolutionary."

Cursing the long interruption, Lancaster continued his search for Cristina. She was no longer on the dance floor, nor indeed anywhere in view. He was irritated by the thought that she might have left the party while he had been engaged in the absurd conversation with Calderón – especially since, in a way, the encounter was a result of his own carelessness: the use of different covers in the same town was totally against his service training. For about ten minutes he wandered about listlessly, all thoughts of making the FARC contact suspended. Suddenly he saw Cristina emerge from one of the rooms along the corridor, in animated conversation with the man Cárdenas had introduced to him earlier as a professor of anthropology. He felt an irrational surge of jealousy. Containing himself, he managed to insert himself into the conversation and eventually to edge out the bearded anthropologist.

As they danced, the imp of the perverse rose up in him. Perhaps it was that she seemed not quite as impressed with him as he would have liked. He understood that Colombian girls made a great fuss of *gringos*, often to the irritation of the local males. But Cristina responded to him coolly, almost mockingly. He decided to goad her.

"I was told you could meet some genuine revolutionaries here. The cream of the Colombian left, Ernesto told me. But this seems as bourgeois a gathering as one could hope to meet between here and Boston."

Cristina eyed him sceptically. But if he'd hoped for more of a reaction he was disappointed – there was no sign of a frown on the serene, smooth forehead or of movement in the pencilled black eyebrows.

"I am sorry we disappoint you, Señor. Perhaps Ernesto should have arranged for some grenade-throwing exercises. Maybe that sound is more to your taste than *música caliente*."

Lancaster tried again: "I begin to think that playing at being a revolutionary is a piece of Colombian bourgeois chic. Surely, if you were serious, you'd be in the Sierras with Núñez?"

Cristina stopped dancing and motioned him to an armchair in the corner of the room, the same chair from which he had watched her earlier. She perched herself on the side of it and invited Lancaster to sit in the well of the chair.

"You have said a number of things that require an answer, Señor . . . what is your name again?"

"Frank Pearce," he answered, wishing he could get rid of the unfortunate alias.

"Yes, Señor Pearce, you have seen fit to point the finger at us. Now I in turn will tell you your faults." She considered him calmly, her head on one side. "For a start you are obviously one of those European intellectuals in love with violence. South America to you is a place where you can live out your fantasies of violence. You call *us* bourgeois, we who have seen more of violence than you will ever know. The brutality of the coffee plantation owner or the institutionalised brutality of the state. Take your pick. They are both two ears on the same mule. Yet you come here tonight and because we're not blazing away at each other with sub-machine guns we're just play actors to you."

Lancaster acknowledged the accusation with a slight nod. He did not tell her he had actually served with Núñez. It would be better for her to discover that from some other source.

"The second thing, Señor Pearce, is that you seem to me a vulgar Marxist. For you the only revolutionary is the fighter in the sierras with a bandillera over his shoulders. Yet in any army only fifty per cent are front-line fighters. Even in a guerilla army. For men like Comrade Fabio to succeed they need an urban network. Auxiliaries. People who fight with their mind as well as their guns."

Cristina's spirited defence made Lancaster unsure. He felt himself hovering on the edge of dangerous indiscretion. Suddenly it occurred to him how he could square all the conflicting impulses at play within him. After all, he was operating under cover as a journalist.

"Señorita Cristina, your rebuke is merited. I apologise for my arrogance. But if you really want to explain the Colombian mind to me, perhaps you could help me professionally as well. My editor likes human interest stories – 'How I came to be a revolutionary'. That sort of thing. I'd keep it anonymous, of course. But it would be a great coup if I could get inside the mind of a middle-class revolutionary. The Che Guevara syndrome revealed. Especially if the subject were a woman. What do you say? Then you could show me how utterly wrong I was just now."

Cristina smiled. Lancaster thought it was the only really thawed-out expression he had seen on her so far. "You're very clever, Señor Pearce. I can't really refuse, can I? All right, why not? But when and where?"

"There's no time like the present." Lancaster quickly considered the possible complications of arranging a later meeting at a time and place that would not blow his cover, but decided it was better to ask Cárdenas for the use of a private room then and there. He went back to his host and outlined his scheme. Ernesto smiled obligingly. He could use the guest room, he said.

Cárdenas' apartment was a large residence on the ground floor. The guest room proved to be a small bedroom at the extreme left off the corridor which led from the main living quarters. Its floor was of red brick, uncarpeted, with one or two fleecy rugs thrown across the smoothly polished surface. In one corner was a tall mahogany *bufete*, a combination of chest of drawers, writing desk, filing cabinet and bookcase. In another was a large bed with a crimson damask counterpane and decked with pillows or cushions in covers of delicately embroidered lawn. The decoration of the walls consisted mainly of reproductions of Chibcha artefacts and sunbursts.

Cristina sat down on the bed. "Do you usually interview girls for your journal in a bedroom?" she asked.

"I don't usually interview them at all," replied Lancaster. This, after all, was true. "Do you mind if we have a bit more light?"

The central bulb, as so often in Colombian rooms, provided only a background glow. Lancaster turned on the table lamp which shed a more powerful light over the darkly-curtained room. Rather self-consciously he sat down on the other side of the bed from Cristina.

She watched as he scribbled a few symbols in shorthand. "Then you are serious? You're truly going to interview me?"

"What else did you think?"

"I thought that 'interviewing' was perhaps this month's

euphemism," said Cristina. "You must admit that an interview in a bedroom does sound slightly implausible."

It was Lancaster's turn to smile. "You have quite rightly pointed out my Anglo–Saxon hypocrisy, Señorita Cristina. May I in turn point to a peculiarly Latin neurosis – the idea that a man and a woman can never be alone together in the same room without sexual intercourse taking place?" Lancaster's tone was bantering, but he was also sounding out Cristina's responses. Her reply was matter of fact.

"If I choose to make love with someone I do so. Once I have made up my mind I see no point in beating about the bush. Only I admire a man more if he states his intentions clearly." She looked at Lancaster closely, a half smile on her face.

Again he had the unpleasant sensation of being out of his depth. "I assure you, Cristina, I have brought you here tonight for entirely serious purposes." For the first time he had used her name without prefacing it with "Señorita". At the same time he was aware that what he'd said sounded absurdly prim. Trying to lighten the tone he added: "Between you and me, I always find such interviews an ordeal, even though I make my living this way."

"You didn't seem to find it an ordeal with me on the dance floor. You were very good." Lancaster knew this was untrue but he appreciated the gesture.

"What I meant, Cristina, was that the process of interviewing is an ordeal – not, of course, that anything concerning you could be so described."

"Very gallant, Señor . . ." She had been sitting on the bed about three feet away from him. Now she moved into the centre, arranged the cushions comfortably around her and curled up, her legs tucked under her, only her knees and lower thighs visible below the hem of her dress.

As if in response to the change in mood Lancaster slid off the bed and drew a chair round to the side of the bed, where he sat facing her.

"Would you mind satisfying my curiosity as a journalist, Cristina? How were you first attracted to the revolutionary cause?"

Cristina sighed. "So you are serious after all? A pity. And you *gringos* are so bad at mixing business with pleasure."

Lancaster found it hard to tell how much of the reproach was serious, how much flirtatious banter. A moment later he was forced to conclude it was the former. Once more Cristina displayed that alarming ability to turn on an emotional sixpence, switching mood from one second to another. All of a sudden she was grave, almost sombre.

"Until I was nineteen I was the most ordinary and unexceptional Bogotá girl of the upper middle classes imaginable. No one could have been more bourgeois than I. Then two things happened that changed my life. In the first place, I enrolled for the sociological theory class that Ernesto teaches – and began to see the appalling misery that the wretched and dispossessed in my own country endure. At the same time the answers my parents and the priests gave me when I questioned them seemed more and more unconvincing. Eventually I came to the conclusion that they knew the truth and were consciously colluding with evil."

Cristina paused, as if uncertain whether to go on. She reached inside her handbag and took out and lit a cigarette. She inhaled deeply and continued.

"While all this was going on something else happened. My brother Alfonso, who's four years older than me, was by this time a radical student leader at the National. He organised the strike at the university in sixty-two, when the police occupied the campus. From then on he was a marked man. One evening we were driving back to our home in Chicó from a cinema in Chapinero. Somewhere along the Avenida Tercera a car overtook us and swerved in front of us, forcing us to stop. Four men jumped out, dragged Alfonso from his seat and began to hit him with truncheons. I screamed at them to stop and threw myself at them but I too was clubbed. However, my screams may have unnerved them, for they made off. My head was bleeding from a gash but I managed to help Alfonso into the car. I took the wheel. I remember I staunched the blood from my head with a handkerchief. Steering with the other hand. A slow drive home.

"As you can imagine, my parents were appalled at the

incident. My father is a highly-placed criminal lawyer and he immediately set on foot enquiries to find who was responsible. Using his contacts within governing circles, he was able to form a pretty shrewd estimate that the assault came from somewhere within the DAS, but when he tried to probe further he encountered a wall of silence and eventually a counter-attack.

"The Minister of the Interior, whom he had always regarded as a friend, told him bluntly that he was fishing in troubled waters and would be well advised to put his own house in order first. This oblique reference to Alfonso was made explicit a couple of nights later when an anonymous phone caller threatened that unless my father controlled his 'godless communist spawn' the next attack on his son would be a fatal one. Now my father, though a tough opponent in the court room, has seen the terrible things that can happen to a member of the elite who breaks rank. The upshot was that he advised Alfonso to quit student radicalism. This led to the most dreadful scenes between the two of them. My father called Alfonso a fanatic, he replied by calling my father a coward – it ended with their parting angrily, threatening never to speak to each other again. Alfonso eventually left Colombia, and after a period of political activism in Paris settled in Mexico City."

Cristina paused. Lancaster struggled to find the right words with which to respond. None seemed adequate. He cursed himself for his failure but Cristina appeared not to have noticed. She went on:

"At first I was shocked to think that the secret police could act like that against a family like ours and get away with it. Then I thought about it more deeply. If a man like my father could be pressurised, what about those lower down the social scale? From that moment, with what Ernesto was providing at the university, I came to see a clear pattern in events."

Cristina was talking faster now, trying to get the words out at speed before her agitated breathing prevented her. She was taking deep breaths at frequent intervals. Lancaster fancied he could almost hear the adrenalin pumping.

"Bit by bit I became a Marxist–Leninist. I realised that

we lived in a cesspool in which the *norteamericanos* and our native bourgeoisie collaborated to exploit the working people and came to see that the only possible salvation for Colombia lay in an armed struggle."

Cristina stopped. She seemed drained of energy, and Lancaster sensed that she was near to tears. He did what compassion dictated, moved close to her and squeezed her hand. She in turn moved her hand over his. Then, lifting her off the bed, he drew her to him and hugged her in an uncomplicated bear embrace. For a while she wept, silently and without embarrassment. Lancaster was touched. He had begun by finding her sexually attractive, bright and quickwitted. His verbal fencing with her in the other room had, he knew, been primarily sexual; but then, as she talked, something had happened. Animal sexuality had been replaced by human tenderness. He waited until she was calm again.

"What about dinner tonight?" he said, holding her in a more gentle embrace. "And it's no use saying it's too late. Remember, I know how you Colombians operate. What's that line? To arrive after eight is impolitely late, but to eat before one just isn't done."

Cristina laughed. Already she seemed to be recovering. He went on: "But a good stiff brandy'll do you a power of good. Wait till I get you one."

Re-entering the main room, he noticed how Cárdenas's eyes followed him as he made his way to the drinks cabinet. There he poured two large measures of Courvoisier, reflecting as he did so that he had scarcely touched a drop of alcohol all evening. He retraced his steps quickly, kicking the bedroom door shut behind him.

"Here, get this down."

Cristina was touching up her eyes in the handmirror. He handed her the tumbler of brandy and studied her once again. As before, it was not primarily Cristina's story that affected him. It was the immediacy of her trust and his response to it. Past experience had taught him that he was not a man capable of great closeness. Now, in a moment, his isolation had been pierced.

Suddenly Lancaster started, remembering guiltily that

there was another purpose for which he was supposed to be at Cárdenas' party. For the first time in his professional life he had relaxed his grip on a case: he had spent nearly two hours with Cristina, oblivious to anything else. Only Ernesto and a few of his immediate colleagues were left; the contact with the FARC had not been made. Such was the amateurishness of the whole set-up that Lancaster almost suspected Núñez might have given him the wrong contact, and all he had done was spend the evening at a faculty soirée. Well, if the FARC link had not worked out at least it meant he could concentrate now on Cristina.

They told Cárdenas they were leaving. He looked at Lancaster oddly, then flashed them both an enigmatic smile and said that he hoped they'd come again. Lancaster could not tell what the man's attitude was, only that he seemed genuinely to mean what he said.

He drove to Koster's on Calle 35, off the Décima. Cristina was silent in the car. Lancaster ordered for them both in the restaurant and chose a wine which turned out to have been specially imported by the Belgian proprietor. Cristina, brighter now, joked with him about his choice of eating place.

"Not the most proletarian choice, Frank. You, who chaffed me about Ernesto's apartment!"

Lancaster looked at her unabashed. "I believe in the best in whatever sphere. Food, surroundings, women . . ."

Cristina ignored the heavy compliment. "Comrade Fabio would be amused by you. He says all European revolutionaries are flabby talkers. I remember one French journalist who came here. Fabio said he was the type of man who would cease to believe in revolution once his *café crème* and croissants were threatened . . ."

Another reference to Núñez. How much did Cristina know? Perhaps *she* was the link? In which case had he been deluding himself – imagining that she had come with him solely on the basis of himself?

He was confused by his reactions to her. Respect, liking, admiration, lust – all jostled for pride of place, and although the meal passed pleasantly enough he continued to be plagued by the idea that Cristina's interest in him might be purely professional. Although he was in some senses a man of the world he lacked any instinctive feel for relationships with "real" women. He did not have the effortless knowledge of the sex possessed by the natural womaniser, which permits exactly the right thing to be said at the right moment. Nor was he particularly good at picking up the unspoken signals in which women specialise.

Then as he drew his wallet from his breast pocket to pay for the meal a piece of paper that had been neatly folded within fell on to the table. On it were written the words "ring 364163 for contact". Obviously the paper had been planted on him some time during the evening. For a moment he wondered if Cristina could have inserted it there somehow or was working with a linkman and had distracted his attention at the vital moment, but then he dismissed the idea. She would have had no need to be so devious, he thought, and felt much better about her.

"Cristina, something has come up so that I can't take you home. I'll call for a taxi. But I would very much like to see you again. As soon as possible."

She had seen him retrieve the slip of paper and looked at him with genuine concern.

"I have an inkling of what you may be doing. No, don't explain anything to me. You see, after tonight I trust you, Frank Pearce. Please – come to my apartment tomorrow afternoon." She handed him a printed address card. Like all Colombians of a certain social class she carried around a ready supply. "And remember, if you need my advice or there is any way I can help . . ."

Lancaster paid the bill and rose to help her on with her coat. "Just sit down again, Frank – just for a minute. There's something I want to say to you," she said softly. "I'm so afraid you must be wondering why I broke down and told you all those things. I don't want you to think I'm a shallow creature, one who bares her soul easily . . . The only way I can explain it is that we can sometimes only let ourselves go with people who are outside our problems. Can you understand that?"

Lancaster's answer was cool. "So I'm a sort of psychiatric counsellor, you mean? You probably need one with all that unexpressed anger." It was not the explanation he had wanted Cristina to give.

She sensed his disappointment and touched him on the hand. "I've been very clumsy, I can see that. But I do want you to know how grateful I am. And I hope one day to get the chance to show you *how* grateful."

She leaned across and kissed him on the forehead.

Lancaster came out of Koster's a happy man.

After seeing Cristina into her cab, he steered his car out on to the Avenida Décima. But instead of heading north, to the flat Miller had rented for him, some instinct made him swing south towards the embassy offices. It was now past midnight. The long-distance lorries had already begun their nocturnal runs to Tunja, Chiquinquirá, Bucaramanga and beyond. As he went south they rumbled past northwards, their roofs stacked high with boxes and crates. The lights of the downtown area began to flash past him; in some of the fast-drink *tiendas* he caught flashes of *aguardiente* and *sifones* being dispensed by mini-skirted barmaids. As he neared the city centre he noted the late-night cinemas disgorging their patrons, many with handkerchiefs held tight over their faces, demonstrating the neurotic Colombian fear of catching a cold.

Close to the embassy offices a fine drizzle began to fall and soon he was in the middle of a thoroughgoing downpour. He turned west for the final approach to the subterranean car park of the Edificio Caracal through a maze of one-way streets. The car had so misted up that by the time he arrived he had to wind down the window before being recognised by the gun-toting night porter at the garage entrance. After ascending to the seventh floor in the lift, he made his entry into the offices following the usual speakeasy procedure of presenting passes and documents through the grille of the embassy door. As he walked down to the registry Lancaster called out a greeting.

"Ah, Mr Lancaster. Didn't expect to see you here tonight," said young Peter Holmes, the night duty officer. "You must have a sixth sense. A coded dispatch came in for you not half an hour ago."

Taking the message, Lancaster turned to his office and

unlocked the drawer where he kept his cipher book. As he flicked abstractedly through the pages he gazed out at the night lights of the city. The three guardians of the Andes stood out in a blaze of white light, distinct from the neon of the downtown. On Monserrate the floodlit chapel appeared to link hands with the monastery on the next peak, the two seemingly acting as maids-in-waiting to the massive figure of Christ on the *páramo de Bogotá*. Snapping back to the business on hand, Lancaster smoothed out the message on his desk and reached for a pen.

Fifteen minutes later he knew he had to be at Eldorado airport on Thursday afternoon at three to meet the Braniff flight from Miami. The message was graded "urgentest" and the array of digits at the end of the cipher revealed it as emanating from E. I./J committee. Lancaster was now in an awkward position. If he made the contact with the FARC later that day (Wednesday) he was likely to be committed to leaving Bogotá before the proposed meeting at Eldorado. Yet he could not now deny having received the coded instructions, especially as Holmes could testify that he picked it up almost as soon as it had arrived. He had expected to be recalled, certainly, after Watkins's warning, but not so soon. One way and another his life appeared to be becoming hopelessly snarled up at all levels.

Eleven

But the snarls, if only very briefly, quickly unsnarled themselves.

First, his FARC contact: that very night, before he went to bed, Lancaster called the number he'd been given at Cárdenas's party. The bell rang twice, stopped, he provided Pearce's name, there was the customary *"momentito, por favor"*, a series of clicks, and then a classless male voice with a brisk set of instructions: an appointment at eight in the evening had been arranged for Señor Pearce on the Monday of the following week, in a house on the Tercera near the Quinta Bolivar. The password was to be *Fijo*. The connection was broken before Lancaster could even acknowledge the message.

He sat for a moment, staring at the receiver in his hand. Somehow, he thought, whatever happened the following day when the man from London arrived, he would keep the FARC appointment. Just a few more days in Colombia would see him right.

Second, Cristina: in the afternoon, as she had suggested, he went to her apartment in the university quarter. It was all very uncomplicated. She gave him lunch, and then they made love. She had stood by the window of her living room, looking out at the buildings of the Jesuit University opposite, the Universidad Javeriana, and he had gone to her, put his arms around her, and kissed her. She had responded at once, and with passion, and they had spent the rest of the afternoon in bed: when they weren't making physical love they were exploring with easy tenderness each other's emotional needs, their lives, their beliefs, their hopes and fears.

In this, very unwillingly, Lancaster had been forced to play a part, but he was determined that it would not be for long. Very soon, he swore to himself, she must be told the truth. Also, and for the very first time in his life, that afternoon with Cristina caused him to question his entire direction. For someone as gentle, and spontaneous, and basically generous as she to be a member of the militant left – as her conversation consistently suggested – was already a conundrum. But for her so unreservedly to share her body and her mind with a man like him – and he had always believed he knew himself all too well – sorely tempted him to revise his self-judgments. He had thought he knew what was right for him: remoteness was right for him . . . emotional distance . . . the centreless, impersonal life of an agent was right. Now, seriously, for the first time, he began to wonder.

And third, his Thursday meeting with the man from London: that too, if not simple, at least solved as many problems as it created.

It was immediately clear to Lancaster which of the passengers who had disembarked from the green Braniff 707 at Eldorado airport was the man he had come to meet. A tall, soldierly individual in his early fifties, unmistakably fit and wearing the same sort of military-style camelhair coat as Lancaster had seen on Major Watkins – signally unsuited to the South American climate, even here at nine thousand feet – strode purposefully out of immigration and towards the customs hall.

Lancaster moved across to intercept. "I believe you're here to see me, sir. David Lancaster."

The other man looked him up and down. "Quite. Colonel Durand. E.I./J and all that . . . Pleased to know you, Lancaster." He eyed the airport clock. "I have about two hours – catching the six o'clock out again. Where can we talk?"

The obvious, most secure place was Lancaster's hire car. After whisking the colonel through customs, explaining that his charge was in effect a transit passenger since he would be taking the Aerolineas flight back to Lima that evening, Lancaster led him out into the sun-baked car park.

Durand stared up at the surrounding mountains. "Take me for a drive around the country," he said. "Not Bogotá. I don't want us caught up in heavy traffic. We need time to talk without distractions."

Lancaster decided to head out along the Villeta road towards Facatativá. This was a pleasant tree-lined road, and they could maybe stop for a drink in the improbably-named village of Madrid.

As soon as they cleared the airport complex Durand began: "I don't know how much Rhodes told you in London about this operation and its larger implications."

"Enough. And what he didn't tell me I've been able to piece together for myself. With a bit of help a few days ago from Major Watkins, of course."

"Ah. Then I'll spare my breath on the political implications. Frankly, I don't mind telling you I opposed the idea as a madcap scheme, as did most of the members of E.I./J. But there's many a good tune played on an old fiddle. And now it really does seem that Crombie was on to something after all."

Durand produced from his pocket a box of snuff and proceeded to take a pinch between finger and thumb and inhale it. He sneezed copiously, offered the box to Lancaster. "Want some? It's useful stuff. The only way I could give up smoking after the quack warned me off it."

Lancaster declined in that accommodating way familiar to junior personnel in strictly hierarchical organisations.

"Mind you, Crombie wanted the operation to be so secret that not even MI5 would know of it. But inevitably Five did get to hear of it, I personally believe because of a leak from someone actually on the E.I./J committee. Even worse, someone in Five seems to have leaked it on, as you might say, to the PM. As you might expect, he was livid, and has ordered a complete standstill on all Service operations except those personally vetted by him."

Lancaster nodded.

"What I still don't understand, sir, is why you felt it necessary to come all this way. The Major warned me to

105

expect recall, and I'm prepared for that. But with respect, Colonel, what are you doing here?"

"Hold on, Lancaster, there's more. I was just filling in the background. We're coming to the point and you, old son, are right up there in it."

Lancaster decided not to stop the car until Durand had explained himself, so he drove through Madrid at a steady, inoffensive fifty kilometres an hour.

"One of the points influencing Crombie to pull out all the stops in the first place was his reading of this double in Washington. Now one of the key pieces of circumstantial evidence the chap left behind was an exceedingly cryptic letter to the Hungarian Cardinal Rósza. At first it was simply taken to be a typical bit of metaphysical blathering from the agent, who seems to have been your standard Central European broody intellectual – the kind who can never face a concrete problem but always turn it into an abstract one."

Lancaster stifled the answer that rose to his lips – that the agent's metaphysics was probably just the mirror image of the military who resolutely converted abstract problems into concrete ones. Both sides were lucky in this, of course. They could see black and white where most intelligent men could increasingly see nothing but grey. He listened as Durand continued.

"Well, it turns out that the message to Cardinal Rósza had a more specific content than could have been imagined. Apparently our man in Washington, let us call him Janos, and the Cardinal were old friends who had became estranged after the forty-eight coup. Until suddenly, early last year, Janos appeared in Budapest and sought an audience with the Cardinal. During the interview he expressed serious concern about the Pope's political attitude. He urged the Cardinal to exhort His Holiness to give a clear world lead on the subjects of capitalism and socialism. He also warned Rósza that the Pope would increasingly be used as a focus for pressure groups of the right and left, and that he could be left dangerously isolated if he failed to take a strong line. Janos quoted 'how many divisions has the Pope' to the Cardinal, and gave his opinion that the papacy was worth more than any army to the side that could enlist its support in the ideological battle between West and East. Now this is where the thing gets interesting for us. Janos' closing remarks to the Cardinal were that he feared the Pope's new policy of foreign travel exposed him to serious risk. While he committed himself to neither side, Janos feared there was a real danger that one group might attempt to co-opt the Catholic Church by some stroke that could then be blamed upon the other. Janos did not rule out the possibility that assassination might be used. He was obsessed with the way the Kennedy assassination had been manipulated by the media in the USA so that Oswald appeared as a fanatic motivated by pro-Soviet feeling, whereas Janos knew – so he claimed – that Kennedy had been murdered by forces of the Right."

"I think I see the drift of all this now," Lancaster murmured.

"Well, what our American friends call an 'educated guess' brings us slap-bang down here in Bogotá. When Rósza got the letter he came to the same conclusion. He expressed his fears in a memorandum to the Vatican, a copy of which we have obtained, by means I won't trouble you with. Given what we know of Pope Paul's movements this year, the planned move can only come right here in Bogotá in August."

"But if he knows this, why hasn't the Pope cancelled his trip?"

"Our sources tell us that he has been urged to, but refuses. Apparently he feels he has to give a lead to the Church in Latin America. He has to push his opposition to birth control and to the theology of liberation. To duck out now would be seen as cowardice or weakness. At least that's how the Pope sees it."

"It's funny, you know. When I was in London for the briefing Rhodes mentioned this possibility as a thousand-to-one chance. It seemed absurdly far-fetched, at the time, but I've thrown out the idea as bait a few times to see if anyone would snap at it."

"And has anyone?"

"That's just it. No one has. I was becoming more and

more convinced I was on a wild-goose chase. But now this."

Colonel Durand sneezed again dourly, and mopped his eyes. "What's even worse is that of course Crombie is now under strict orders to recall all agents pending the PM's review. His one chance of saving this department is that you pull his chestnuts out of the fire – unofficially, that is. If you cracked this one that would prove that his instinct has all along been sound. If a plot to assassinate the Pope can be uncovered by the SIS, at one stroke the whole pack of critics, the PM, MI5, the Select Committee – all of them – will be routed."

"And in the meantime I'm on my own to take on who knows what combination, right-wing crackpots, Cuban refugees, 'blow and burn' boys, the KGB or whatever?"

"That's about the size of it, old boy. The only consolation I can give you is that if you succeed in uncovering a plot you'll shoot to the top of the Service like a meteor. It's not beyond the bounds of possibility that you could end by being the youngest Service director ever."

"Come on, Colonel, you don't seriously expect me to believe that, do you?"

"No." Durand smiled grimly. "But I feel embarrassed at leaving you in this mess. The thing is, Crombie can get away with keeping one man in the field – he can lose you in 'overheads' – but no more. You must remember that the Cabinet Secretariat has now given the FO strict orders that no diplomatic postings of any kind, genuine or cover, be made until the PM's review body has sat. There are poor blighters due for leave in god-forsaken holes all over Africa and Asia who'll have to sweat it out, doing damn all until further notice."

"But why can't Sir Ian produce an affidavit from Cardinal Rósza, proving the seriousness of the plot?"

"Lots of reasons. In the first place, the PM is completely fed up with Crombie and would regard any representation from him now as being bogus, cooked up in some back room. Then we're not even supposed to know about Rósza's minute to the Vatican. You know your history, Lancaster, and you know we're the only major Western country not represented in the Vatican at ambassadorial level. Our source is highly placed and one of our true aces in the hole. To convince Number Ten we'd have, in effect, to blow his cover. Remember what a sieve Downing Street is at the best of times."

They talked on, going over the details. Finally Lancaster sighed. "You know the old saw, 'miracles we can do, the impossible takes a little longer'. That's how I feel, sir, faced with this assignment. Where's the threat coming from, for God's sake? Is it the right or the left? Are foreign governments implicated or is it a buccaneering effort? And of course there's another factor – time. When is His Holiness due here? Late August?"

"The twenty-second, according to the best information."

Lancaster turned the car and headed back for Eldorado. "You see these roads, Colonel. There's six miles like this from the airport to Bogotá, open all the way and thronged with crowds. I'd say it was tailor-made for an assassin, wouldn't you? You may rest assured, sir, that I'll do my best. But in the circumstances my best probably won't be good enough."

That evening, during dinner with Cristina, Lancaster sounded her out on the papal visit.

"We see it as primarily an exercise to establish legitimacy," she told him. "The Church in Latin America is increasingly breaking free from the irrelevant dogma of Rome. Look at Camarra, at Romero and at Camilo. This Pope, who is a reactionary to his fingertips, is trying to regain control of a runaway church. He's making a point of supporting the conservative bishops against the radical priests. Some of my comrades were hopeful when he seemed to be backing reform last year, at Easter time, but I knew it would turn out to be empty phrase-making. Now that they see his attitude on celibacy and birth control they no longer look for anything from him."

"So you think a Rome-based Catholic Church is basically a hopeless case?"

"If the Vatican says the Marxist criticism of the Church is unfair, let them prove it. It's no good the Jesuits claiming that if the middle classes show goodwill we can have non-violent reform. This is false consciousness. The middle class can *never* show goodwill in that sense, otherwise they'd no longer be the middle class. No, the Pope has to condemn all *Frente Nacional* posturing and he has to come flat out and state explicitly that only the revolutionary road will work in Latin America. Then and only then will I take notice of him."

Later, over the wine, Lancaster asked what the basic attitude of the Colombian people was to the papal visit, and whether it was such that strong emotions (homicidal, he meant, though he did not say as much) could be kindled by the presence of the Supreme Pontiff. Cristina did not answer the question directly but replied that the attitude of her comrades ranged from indifference to contempt. "For me the visit is at best an irrelevance and at worst an obscenity."

Indifference . . . contempt . . . neither, in Lancaster's experience, was ground for bloody murder.

In the dark days that followed Lancaster often thought that the real turning point in his relationship with Cristina came not when they first made love, but on their later excursion to Guatavitanueva. In the normal course of events perhaps Lancaster might at this stage have expected to be invited to meet her parents, but for obvious reasons relations between Cristina and her family were strained, and the last person she would have wanted to introduce to her apprehensive father would be a European Marxist revolutionary. Their first weekend together, therefore, was spent pretending to be tourists in the model village of Guatavitanueva.

The shadow that hovered over Cristina never completely left her, even during their love-making, but the nearest it came to lifting was on that Saturday at Guatavitanueva, when she clambered among the sandy hills, laughing at Lancaster's fears about the snakes of Colombia, especially the dreaded bushmaster – *el verdugo*, the executioner – which he feared might lurk anywhere off the roads.

Old Guatavita had been submerged when the Muña dam

was built. Guatavitanueva, the new town, is to Colombia what Santa Fe is to the American West. Sparkling new houses had been created in the tradition of colonial New Granada alongside the artificial lake Muña, in the depths of which the old Guatavita lay submerged. It was pleasant to stroll hand in hand among the patios, in the Dominican cloisters, under the overhanging balconies, sustaining the illusion that they were simply an ordinary couple of lovers out on a day's excursion. They sat and drank *anís* and Colombia's special brand of coffee before starting the climb through sandstone hills above the village to another lake, higher up and more sombrely set in the landscape than Muña, and said to be the spot where the Chibcha kings of old bathed each dawn, painted in gold from head to toe, long before the coming of the Conquistadores.

On this particular Saturday, unusually for the towns strung along the spine of the eastern cordillera north of Bogotá, there was a limpid blue sky. The grey clouds that lower over the Andean sierras for most of the year were absent. Lancaster watched as Cristina climbed the rocks and slid on her back down the steep incline between the two lakes like a reckless schoolgirl. He felt great tenderness for her and every now and then stopped to kiss her. And yet basically he found it difficult to react to her spontaneously. When they were talking dialectics all was fine, and in their more intimate moments too; but what happened when, as now, she ceased to be Cristina Amaya the revolutionary and became the girl she had probably been before that fateful night with her brother?

The result was that, delightful as the day was at Guatavitanueva, he was intermittently edgy and morose. He loved her, he was sure of that. What she felt for him he could only surmise, and anyway in one sense what she was feeling was only for a phantom, a man who did not exist. He seemed to be in the absurd situation where he feared he might only be lovable to Cristina if he possessed the political affiliations of someone who did not exist.

His escape from this predicament was provided in an unexpected and spectacular way. The drive back to central Bogotá took about an hour from Guatavitanueva. First there was the unpaved, dirt stretch to Sesquile, then the main Tunja–Bogotá road, asphalted all the way to the Colombian capital. It was while they were driving back along the lakeshore to the turn-off at Sesquile, about half an hour before dusk, that it happened. The bends on this stretch of the dirt road were treacherous, yet it was easy to take them too fast. On the right-hand side sandstone cliffs rose steeply. On the left was the lake, separated from the road by no more than a rim of scrub.

As the giant Mercedes roared around the bend towards him Lancaster saw at once that the driver had misjudged his speed badly. When he tried to apply his brakes the heavy car slewed across the road, its rear door broadside on to Lancaster in his hired Thunderbird. There was just one possible way out of the collision. Sharply Lancaster swung the wheel to the left. The car slid off the road and ploughed sideways through the bushes. By sheer good fortune the lip of scrubland between lake and highway was wider at this point than elsewhere. Lancaster brought the vehicle to a halt in a cloud of dust, its front wheels within inches of the water.

Cristina was first out of the car, running back to see how the Mercedes had fared. It had dented its bumper when it finally came to rest nose-first against the sandstone over-hang, but the passengers – the driver, his wife and two young children – were unhurt, simply shaken. At first the man started to bluster. He was mustachioed and fat, and the macho code would not allow him to admit culpability to Cristina. Only when Lancaster appeared a minute later, having satisfied himself that his own vehicle was road-worthy, did the man have the grace to half concede his error. He saved face amid a feast of back-slapping and hand-shaking, while Cristina did her best to calm his near-hysterical wife. Meanwhile the shock of the accident had reduced both the children to loud sobs. Lancaster picked them both up, hugged them, tousled their hair – and finally calmed them by producing two gleaming fifty-peso gold coins, specially minted for the coming papal visit.

Eventually the Colombian packed his family back into

their car and slowly drove off in the direction of Guatavitanueva. But first Lancaster had taken advantage of the man's weight to help him push the Thunderbird up from the shore on to the road.

They drove on. Cristina was silent until they turned left on to the main Bogotá highway. Then she said: "I can see why Fabio was impressed with you. You needed lightning reflexes back there. But why did you do such a crazy thing? We could easily have gone straight into the lake."

Lancaster sighed. "You probably won't believe this, but as that *chiflado* came towards us I saw the heads of his two little girls in the back, and I knew they were goners if they made contact with us."

"And you did that for two children? Two kids you know nothing about and will never see again? And from the looks of their parents likely to grow up into smug bourgeois too. Why?"

Lancaster did not think that Cristina might be testing him. He replied spontaneously, without pausing to imagine what Frank Pearce might have said.

"I suppose I'd have to say that I value children. Completely and without reservation."

Cristina leaned over and kissed him on the forehead. "That's for being you. For not running true to type. You are not like the others."

"What others?"

"Back there you risked your life to save a couple of kids. Mine too – but that's not the point. Not all our comrades would have acted like that."

"What would they have done?"

"They'd have saved their own skin first and then rationalised the fact that they'd saved it. 'Aren't we more important to the world revolutionary movement than a bourgeois family?'" – Cristina did a fair imitation of some of the people Lancaster had met at Cárdenas' party. "I can almost hear the chorus of self-justification."

This was a side of Cristina Lancaster had not seen before. "If you don't mind my saying so," he said, "you don't seem exactly enamoured of your partners in the struggle."

Cristina smiled grimly. "It's just that I'm not starry-eyed

any more. One of the worst problems about being on the left is some of the appalling people you have to work with. Surely you must have found that?"

Lancaster saw the danger of being drawn into deep waters. He might have to talk about his supposed work in Europe. He tried to get the conversation back on to more general lines.

"Some people are moral lepers, sure. But why should the moral motive for revolution be all-important?"

Cristina looked surprised at the question. "I do what I do because I care. Really care. Perhaps you will understand if I tell you that when I was a girl my favourite saint was Francis of Assisi."

"I doubt whether *he*'d approve of violence." This slipped out before Lancaster could consider whether it was an appropriate remark for his alter ego or not.

"Lenin thought he would have done. For good ends. Did you know he was a great admirer of St Francis?"

Lancaster weighed up for a moment whether this was something he ought to know. He decided to play safe. "No, I didn't. But I have to admit it's a long time since I read my Lenin."

"Never mind," she answered. "You have your uses."

The following Monday, back at his embassy desk, it was put to him that, although his extraordinary FO documentation might give him a roving brief under cover of his Technical Assistance post, his frequent absences were now causing acute official embarrassment. H E had been very put out at a reception at the American Ambassador's house the other night when his opposite number asked: "Who is this new attaché with *carte blanche* to travel the country?" H E's well-known view was that if Service personnel were in his embassy under diplomatic cover he did not want to hear about it. But this deafness would be hard to sustain if one of his staff blatantly exercised privileges not even open to the First Secretaries. After Miller, the Head of Chancery, had put this point to him with surprising vehemence, Lancaster decided not to visit Cristina that lunchtime. He phoned her to say that he would call at her apartment after the contact with the FARC group had been made, possibly around eleven that night.

Lancaster spent the morning catching up on the paper-work expected of a dutiful Technical Assistant. Parker looked in once or twice, then, in the afternoon, disappeared for the twice-weekly embassy conference. Lancaster sat at his desk wrestling with the growing problems of his assignment, his cover at the Embassy and, most of all, Cristina. From his rear window he could enjoy a view almost to the edge of the Bogotá plateau. He watched de-tachedly as a Boeing 737 took off from Eldorado, heading out towards Facatativá before banking and turning round to overfly the city. It seemed that his situation was fast becoming intolerable. As far as Cristina knew and believed he was merely a journalist. He had given her his flat's telephone number only, and excused his many absences by pleading the entertainment of government contacts. Sooner or later, however, he would be revealed in her eyes not only as a tool of Western imperialism but also as a gutless liar. He toyed with the idea of confessing the truth to her that coming night. Yet this would risk exposure, if Cristina were sufficiently angered to pass on his confession to her political associates. And he felt an overriding responsibility to Colonel Durand, and to the Service, and also to His Holiness whose life he was supposed to save, to remain uncompromised and actively employed in the field, at least until after the papal visit in August.

On the other hand, he was now under pressure to remain at his desk in the Embassy. So how important was it that he keep the appointment with the FARC representative? From what he had seen of the ELN guerillas, and from what Cristina had said, it was unlikely that the revolutionary left would go in for schemes of political assassination. If any-thing, the likelihood of such a project being mounted from within the FARC was even less, as they took their cue from Moscow. Lancaster saw every reason to agree with Núñez that after the trauma of the missile crisis the Soviets by the mid-sixties simply wanted an easy life in Latin America. And setting up the Right to take the blame would surely be beyond their resources.

No, all Lancaster's instincts told him to expect the blow to fall – if indeed there was to be a blow, and he was still not entirely convinced – from the right. But how to penetrate the right? Unlike the left, the Colombian right had no need to operate a counter-state. They worked from deep within the government itself and were embedded in the very fabric of the ruling elite. If the coup aimed at the Pope was to come from them he might as well get on the first plane out of Eldorado. To penetrate such a structure would need several years of careful preparation. Besides, the motive for the Right to harm the Pope seemed implausible. Blaming the left was all very well, but the extreme right took its ideology from groups like *Opus Dei*, itself a Catholic pressure group. And Paul VI was not the kind of reforming pope who might have attracted the wrath of the ultra-conservatives.

Monday afternoon passed and merged with the evening. Lancaster ate alone, then wandered up the Calle Diecinueve. Suddenly it came to him that he was engaged in fruitless deliberation. He was like a man who had been dealt two pairs in a hand of five-card stud and was speculating on the killing he could have made with a full house. He had no choice but to follow up the FARC contact. If the attack on the Pope was to come from the Right, so be it. There was nothing that he, a lone agent from a declining second-class power, could do about it. Except, possibly, be there to help when it happened.

His mind made up, Lancaster decided to walk the short distance to his eight o'clock rendezvous. Fifteen minutes later he was at the address – an unforgettable one, 69 *bis*. Pressing the bell at the grille, he gave the codeword *Fijo* (presumably after *Tiro Fijo*) and with a jarring buzz the door clicked open. Ahead of him was a flight of stairs. He started to climb but immediately seemed to fall through the stairs as if they were papier-mâché. He seemed to be falling head over heels, curled up in a ball like a hedgehog. Round and round he turned, now in a whirlpool. When he reached the centre of the pool, total blackness descended.

Twelve

"Good to see you back in the land of the living. Thought for a while there you weren't going to make it. You sure bruise easy."

"Where the hell am I?" began Lancaster, sitting up in the bed. An agonising flash of pain through his head made him sink back on the pillow.

"You might say you've come to the end of your trail, old buddy. You were doing good, fella, too good."

"Do you mind telling me where I am, who you are, and what exactly you're talking about?"

"All in good time, buddy. I'm just the message boy, you might say. Call me Jim."

"All right, Jim. I still don't know what the hell you're talking about."

"Of course, of course. Name, rank and serial number, and remember that you're a signatory to the Geneva Convention. Only the Convention doesn't work here. You know the rules. What do you think this is? Disneyland? You'd better wise up. You'll save us and yourself a lot of trouble if you skip all the horseshit about how you're just some lil' asshole attaché."

Lancaster's interrogator was a smooth-skinned, almost hairless individual in his mid-forties, with the scrubbed appearance and easy smile often associated with East Coast Americans of a certain prosperous type.

"Look, I'll level with you. Then perhaps you might feel like putting your cards on the table. We know that you know a certain amount – exactly how much doesn't matter. The question is, who told you? We need to find out who else is in on this. So you've got two ways to go. Either you tell us or we get it out of you anyway."

"I still don't know what the hell you're talking about."

"Suit yourself." The man turned away and seemed to be breaking the top off some kind of glass phial. Coming over to the bed, he took Lancaster's left arm and looked for the vein.

"Sodium pentothal, old buddy. You'll sing like a bird when you wake up."

When Lancaster came to again he was sitting in a chair. Trying to move, he perceived that he was loosely tied to it. He felt slightly hung over and light-headed. He had no previous first-hand experience of sodium pentothal, but during his basic training a Civil Service pharmacologist had demonstrated its powers as a mild anaesthetic. Smoothskin's claim that it was a "truth drug" was of course ludicrous.

As his head began to clear he became aware of the electrodes taped to his body. The room was dark now, a brilliant lamp was switched on, and two men stood by him. To the left of the glare he recognised the questioner from his last period of consciousness. On the right was a more heavily-built man to whom the other seemed to defer. The heavy man remained in the shadows, so that his features could not be clearly seen. Lancaster thought there was something familiar about his voice.

"I understand you don't want to give a spontaneous account of yourself. Very professional, I'm sure. However, we can infer most of what we want to know from your reactions to the polygraph, even though you're an unwilling subject. After that we can all relax, have a drink and discuss your future."

So that was it, thought Lancaster. The polygraph meant only one thing – CIA. And this was the famous "fluttering" he had heard so much about. Despite his situation Lancaster felt almost like laughing. Through a sheer fluke these men were playing to his strength. Long ago he had worked out with his friend James Ingledew, now a leading experimental psychologist, how all lie detectors could be beaten, even when assisted by narcotic drugs.

The polygraph system was, after all, a fairly crude device

for measuring skin conductivity. Once its basic mechanism was understood the trick was to make nonsense of the traces produced on the electrograph. James had presented a paper at a conference in Edinburgh, arguing that by using the tantric devices of the Eastern yogis breathing and heartbeats could be controlled in the short term, thus producing on the graph traces analogous to the arrhythmic patterns of cardiac patients. The resulting print-out would then be the graphical equivalent of gibberish. And later, in systematic trials with Lancaster as guinea pig, Ingledew had demonstrated that his techniques indeed could in most circumstances beat a lie detector.

"Let us begin," said the heavy man. "You are of course an agent of the SIS or MI6?"

"No."

"Then what are you?"

"A diplomat in the British Foreign Service. Second Secretary, Technical Assistance, Bogotá."

"Have you ever heard of Frank Pearce?"

"No."

"Have you ever heard of Janos?"

"No."

"Who runs you? Durand?"

"Never heard of him "

After half an hour of this, Lancaster's interrogator called a halt. The restraints were taken off and Lancaster sat guarded by Smoothskin until, only fifteen minutes later, the chief of operations returned, coldly angry.

"Very clever. You're good, there's no doubt of that. But I've never yet heard of a man that can survive the *picana*. I'll give you till tomorrow to think it over. Either you talk or I'll burn it out of you. And in your case I'll turn the crank myself." He turned away. "Get him out of here."

Lancaster awoke to darkness and a dankness strongly redolent of the police cells in Montevideo which he had visited as part of his work there. His feet, he quickly discovered, were manacled to the bottom of his bed. Gradually he pieced his thoughts together. He had no idea how long he had been in his present dungeon, nor what time of day or night it was. From this he might have conjectured that his interrogators were trying to break him by isolation and environmental alienation. But then he remembered that the big man had threatened the *picana* – which would render all other methods a waste of time. The running of electric shocks through arms, legs, hands, feet and genitals was by all accounts a form of pain not to be endured. Lancaster shuddered. It seemed that, pursuing the longest of long shots, he had accidentally blundered on a genuine plot. He did not fool himself he could long resist the *picana*. As he lay in the darkness, he thought of Cristina, and wondered how much time had passed since he had last seen her. If he were to hope for rescue, would it be from her friends? Or would Miller get curious about his sudden disappearance? No – neither possibility was realistic. His reputation was one of unpredictability. By the time anybody started worrying seriously he would almost certainly be dead.

"You're an intelligent man, Dave. I don't know why you didn't co-operate from the very beginning. You'd have saved yourself a lot of time and hassle."

The session was over, the ceiling light was on in the bare, white-painted room, and Lancaster immediately recognised the heavy man as the individual he had last seen in the Anglo–American club. The harmless right-wing loudmouth . . . it appeared that he had grossly underestimated Ed Summerby. Sitting in the room with him and the American called Jim, their Cuban "mechanic" Luis Frias and two guards, Lancaster sipped his first coffee since his capture. He had withstood the electric shocks for an even shorter time than he had anticipated. Now, having admitted that he was a British agent and agreed to make a clean breast of everything, his only possible strategy was to try to elicit the maximum information in return. He had no great hopes for his life once his usefulness was over, but was not ready to give up while there was still at least a chance.

He began by pretending that he was enormously impressed by the fact that the Americans were on to him – which was half true anyway.

Summerby was exultant. "You were careless, friend. Where you blew it was in your meeting with Roca. Considering that the contact was made through Danny Green, and he and Pete Heyck are Company men, as anyone other than a bungling amateur might have guessed, you were taking one helluva chance."

That's what an agent's life was, thought Lancaster – for better or worse, one helluva chance. "So Roca is one of your men?"

"He's a local. Unfortunately we've never been able to plant anyone within the ELN itself. Núñez is a cunning bird and he'd spot anyone we could muster for the job, even assuming we could find a man with the guts for such an assignment. But he still trusts Roca, so any contacts made through him we know about."

"So I made a damn fool of myself . . ." Lancaster murmured, praying that he was not overdoing his humiliation.

"That's about how it weighs up, feller. We sent your photograph up to Barranquilla as soon as we heard that Pete and Danny had fed you the idea. So when a British journalist called Frank Pearce called on Roca a few weeks later, Julio simply got out your photo and put two and two together. He probably had it in his desk and was laughing his head off even as he spoke to you. I've always had a certain amount of respect for British intelligence, but they sure sent a greenhorn on this one."

"That's not fair. It looks as if you had me buttoned up whichever way I moved."

"That's as may be. Certainly we have other sources of information. Take Paul Fitch. He's a godsend to us. We don't even need to take the nut on to the payroll. He's so eaten up with imaginary slights to his so-called ability that you've only got to pump him with booze and he'll tell all he knows about Her Majesty's diplomats. I think he hated your guts from the word go. Circumstantial evidence was piling high even before you went to Barranquilla. Then again, Cárdenas's circle has been known to us since sixty-four. It's honeycombed with our people like you wouldn't believe. Need I tell you that the FARC link man is also one of ours? The rest, as they say, is history. What *I* want to know is what you were hoping to gain from these contacts with the reds."

"I'll tell you that when you've answered me one question: Who exactly are your people in Cárdenas's group?"

"I know where you're coming from, old buddy," Jim put in. "It's that little girl of yours. Yeah, of course we know all about her. And you're just gonna have to sweat that one out. Maybe she *is* what she appears to be, and then again maybe not."

Ignoring him, Lancaster repeated his question directly to Summerby: "So you won't tell me who your plants are?"

"Maybe later. Right now I want you to tell me what you were doing playing footsie with Núñez."

Now for it. Lancaster took a deep breath. "You probably know that for some time now the SIS has had wind of a planned assassination attempt here on the Pope. We in London knew that the attempt would be made by a right-wing group. My task was to recruit a counter-force among the guerillas which would assemble in mid-August and strike back at the *derechistas* just before the Pope's visit. British intelligence could then pose as the true bulwark of civilised values and score a propaganda victory – at your expense among others."

To Lancaster it sounded good. He waited anxiously for the Americans' reaction.

Summerby was wary: "How much was known in London of the Company's involvement?"

"They were capable of what you would call an 'educated guess'. It was doubted that such a scheme would have official sanction from the Director in Washington. After all, we are talking about the assassination of a pope. But it could easily be some backroom initiative."

"Then why didn't London contact the Company at the highest level? That way you'd have blown any local station project."

"For the very simplest of reasons. Political in-fighting. With something like this proved against you people we'd have such a lever in future deals with you as you wouldn't believe."

Summerby chewed his lower lip. "So you're in Colombia as what – a high-level representative of E.I./J committee?"

"That's about it." Lancaster relaxed. Clearly his guesses had been good enough.

"They've goofed then. You were about as inconspicuous as a blonde in a football locker room."

"But the point is they know enough of your plans to be able to blow the whistle on them at any moment. I'm supposed to cable in to them every twenty-four hours unless they hear to the contrary, as they did when I was in the mountains with Núñez. Now I don't know how long I've been here, but that probably means that already contingency plans will be on foot to send the heavy squad here."

Summerby still seemed undecided. "You walk a very tight line. You may be bluffing, but . . . well, right now I can't take the chance that you are. For a while you'll be in cold storage." He nodded curtly to Luis and spoke the solitary Spanish word: *selva*. Then he spoke to the other American.

"If we're having a heavy-duty goon squad over from London, Jim, we'd better talk this through."

The two men walked out of the room leaving Lancaster with Luis. The Cuban grinned and spoke to him in *chicano* English.

"Hey, man, you did real good back there. My orders was to waste you."

"So I've got a reprieve?" asked Lancaster.

"You was on death row, man, and the governor's wire came in. If your story's true Summerby'll cry off, for sure. If not, he'll put a bullet in you soon as look at you."

When Lancaster did not appear at her apartment on Friday night Cristina immediately feared that something had gone wrong. After the entire evening had passed without so much as a phone call her fears became certainties. At midnight she rang the *jefatura* of police to enquire whether a blond Englishman had been involved in a car crash that night. Somewhat bemused, the cop at the other end replied: "*Gringos no, colombianos solamente.*"

At 12.45 she telephoned Cárdenas. Ernesto was obviously already in bed, for a sleepy voice mumbled uncertainly, "*Quién es? Ah, Cristina, que hubo.*" But when told of the reason for her call he pulled himself together. He couldn't help her then, but he suggested that Cristina contact him again next morning if the Englishman had not reappeared.

By the time of *that* call, just after eight, Cristina had spent a largely sleepless night. Ernesto, however, was still inclined to play the whole thing down.

"My dear Cristina, there are a hundred and one reasons why a young man like Pearce should go off on his own without warning – even, I dare say, if it meant depriving himself of your delightful company for a while."

"No, I'm serious, Ernesto. This is not some silly schoolgirl talking. I have a very strong feeling that something has gone badly wrong."

Ernesto sighed resignedly. "All right, then. What do you want me to do?"

"Ernesto, you know how I have worked for the movement all these years and never asked anything for myself. But now I do. You must ask cadres one and two for a *trámite de emergencia.*" She could hear the intake of breath at the other end of the line. "You know I can't do that, *pájarita.* Such a procedure can only be invoked in the case of a real and immediate threat to the movement. You know the dangers in the *red urbana.* And you know that Fabio in particular dislikes implementing the *trámite* anyway."

Cristina's next words had a hint of desperation in them. "Please, Ernesto, I'm begging you. Tell Fabio that I will find a means of letting him have a quarter of a million pesos within the year. I will sell the *finca* in Medellin that I inherited from my uncle."

Cárdenas made a curious clucking sound with his tongue. "I'll do what I can. But try to find me a political motive as well as the money. Then I think I could swing it."

"*Está bien, hombre.* But begin the *trámite* now, please." Cristina replaced the receiver, picked it up again and rang the number of her uncle Carlos, chief of protocol at the Ministry of Foreign Affairs.

*

124

The normal procedure was that Jim Everett took turns with Luis Frias as the principal guard. In addition, a local back-up man was always present. Usually little was said, Luis in particular being singularly uncommunicative, but on the second night after Lancaster's confession, when Everett came in to relieve Luis, it was obvious that he was the worse for drink. Immediately he began to bounce conversation off Lancaster in a half-threatening, half-teasing way.

"I hear you're going on a plane trip tomorrow. Ed's taking no chances. And he's got another little goody lined up for you too."

Lancaster looked up from the game of draughts he was playing with the Colombian guard. "What's that, then?"

"You must be joking. Brother Ed would skin me alive. He's saving that particular bundle of joy to tell you himself. Later tonight, when he's through with the arrangements."

Lancaster didn't press that matter. Drunks were much more informative if left to ramble. Instead, he asked: "Where are you taking me?"

"Wait and see on that too, pal. You'll be well out of harm's way, that's all I can tell you."

"Then you're still going ahead with this crackpot scheme? How the hell do you expect to pull it off? And even if by some hundred-to-one shot you did, how do you think you're going to get away with it?"

"The plan's foolproof. You'd better believe it."

"Is this a Company operation, or is some private loony financing it?"

Everett looked at him. Caution warred with drunken boastfulness. The attractions of being in a position to divulge secret information won.

"Yeah, why the hell not. After all, Ed's already told you some of what's going on. Only thing is, he left out the best bits. Like for instance that the whole operation has got Washington approval except that they don't know who the target is. The directorate has sanctioned a hit on Fabio Núñez, and all the paperwork has been approved. But in fact the Latin American co-ordinator in Washington, J. J. Johnson, has his own master plan. He succeeds in getting the okay from the top, then he substitutes his own target –

none other than His Holiness Paul VI. He recruits a handful of men in the Company who think like him – me and Ed, let's say. The only problem then is the station officer in Bogotá. The trick is to recall him for an early leave. With Summerby now running the station, the budget for local back-up already granted by Washington, and a good team like me and Luis in position, the stage is set for the big kill."

"But how did the co-ordinator running Latin America desk know in time that the Pope was going to visit Bogotá?"

"Simple. We had a leak from the Curia as far back as January last that the decision had been taken. So we could work on the set-up before anyone else even knew there *was* a papal visit. That way, it's going to be much harder to pin anything on us when the shit hits the fan."

"But if Washington has approved a hit on Núñez, how are you going to explain when the Pope gets it instead?"

"Easy. Our plan is to frame Núñez. After the job is wrapped up a dead guerilla will turn up with incriminating evidence on him, proving that the ELN wasted the Pope. How does he get to be dead? We terminated him, of course, mistakenly thinking he was Núñez. Unless of course we can get hold of the guy himself – in which case, so much the better."

Lancaster tapped the draughts board thoughtfully. Certainly, if the Pope was killed, the left was going to say it was a CIA job anyway. So what did they have to lose?

"All right, I'll go along with you so far. Let's assume that you've got a plan to knock off the Pope and that you can cover up. But what's the theory behind the whole idea? This man running the show from Washington, what's his motivation?"

"Isn't it obvious? With the Church in Latin America preaching that it may be a Christian duty to take up arms against US-supported governments? I don't have to tell you that ideological struggle's the name of the game. If the clergy here go over to the likes of Núñez we might as well pack our bags and hightail it back to DC. Those feckless mothers on the Potomac can see the danger but they're doing nothing about it. That's where J. J. Johnson – Latin

America desk to you – comes in. He's got a lot of balls. He's damn well determined to fix things. If we can frame the left for the assassination of the Pope we'll drive a wedge between the Church and the Marxists that'll take a hundred years to sort out."

"Now I really *am* convinced you're mad," Lancaster said indignantly.

"You better believe we're not, old buddy. I mean, take yourself. I mean, even before you got here, we were waiting for you . . ."

Lancaster tensed inwardly. "But how could you be? Don't tell me you've got a sleeper in the SIS."

"We didn't need one. Your top man overplayed his hand on this one. And someone in your MI5 was concerned enough to pass on the word to your Prime Minister. But here's a twist in the tail. Your premier's already so leery of the security services that he then gets on to the CIA to ask them to investigate his own guys. How d'ya like them apples? He spoke to our Director General on the hot line and mentioned the possibility that the SIS had started a global enterprise against international terrorism without his approval or knowledge. When the DG passed this on to the area heads in general terms J. J. put two and two together and suspected that you guys might be on to him."

"But why should they be on to him? Even if we suspected the CIA of an imminent masterstroke, why should anyone think of Bogotá?"

"Since Jim here has been stupid enough to let you in on so much I may as well take you completely into our confidence." Summerby was standing just inside the door, having entered unnoticed. "Okay, Jim, I'll take over now. Try to sleep that one off and don't hang any more on till our honoured guest is out of here."

Everett took himself off, mumbling, and Summerby eased his considerable bulk into the chair his assistant had vacated.

"You were wondering, Dave, why J. J. should have expected a visit from someone like you. Well, the story begins in Washington . . . as so much of interest does, wouldn't you agree? Some years ago the Company recruited a high-ranking officer, possibly of KGB status, in the Hungarian secret service. This man's code name was 'Verbunkos'. Let's call him 'V'. Anyway, Washington had good reason to believe in his sincerity – a rabid Hungarian nationalist, he felt he could do more for his country by fighting the Russians from within rather than by going into exile like so many of his brothers."

Lancaster kept his head turned away. This story was becoming dangerously familiar.

Summerby mopped his forehead. "The man V. provided much valuable information but there were always those in DC who mistrusted him. They argued that his intelligence, though very good, was always vague enough to escape positive verification. On this basis, he could simply be another KGB operator, trying to take us for a ride. On the other hand, he could be a genuine double, playing both sides off against the other out of cynical self-interest. In the end J. J. decided to test him out. He pretended to take V. into his confidence and sounded his reactions on political assassination as a tool of intelligence work. V. looked troubled at this. Then J. J. told him that there was a serious CIA plot afoot to assassinate the Pope and blame it on the communists. V. seemed genuinely aghast – which raised the third possibility, that he was in fact a sincere idealist at large in the intelligence community . . . Now, why J. J. decided to reveal the details of his own plot I've never been sure. He told me it was a double bluff. You see, if the KGB reacted he would be able to get the plot denied at the highest possible level, and the Russians would have to question seriously V.'s usefulness to them, past as well as present. While if there was no reaction this would mean that it was safe to proceed. The way J. J. explained it, it was a no-lose situation."

Lancaster waited while Summerby paused for dramatic effect. Whoever J. J. Johnson was, he was obviously as mad as a hatter.

"But then V. did something we hadn't bargained on. Instead of going to the Russians he went to the British. That makes V. his own man, neither ours nor the Russians. Like I said, a genuine idealist, and they're the worst kind. Anyway, he'd been frequently seen in the company of an attaché at the British Embassy. So J. J. decided to take him out before he could be interviewed by senior Britishers. Then, even if he had revealed all to his friend at the Embassy, it would be hard for your people to take the story seriously on the one guy's uncorroborated testimony. But, J. J.'s a cautious man. He alerted us to keep an eye out for someone like you. Just in case."

"What happened to V.?"

"He was terminated, according to plan."

"Prejudicially so, no doubt."

"How else? The only thing we didn't know was how much V. had passed on to the British. Unfortunately it now seems he passed on rather a lot. Which is why, in case you're not bluffing, you're now going to cable in that you will be absent for some weeks in the wilderness pursuing an important lead and that under no circumstances should anyone from the SIS come out to investigate your disappearance, owing to the delicacy of your own investigations. This way I can test the truth of your story. Either London knows all and they'll be here in force in August whatever you say, or they don't and we'll have one less problem to contend with."

"But what gives you any reason to believe I'll co-operate in this phony communication?"

Summerby scratched one fat cheek. "Have you so quickly forgotten the *picana*?" he asked sadly.

Briefly, Lancaster had. He subsided. Then he tried again. "But don't you see there's a contradiction in what you want? You can only test my story if no one from London shows up, but now you're saying that I must *request* that no one does. By your logic, if they accede to my request I'm bluffing and if they don't that means I've doublecrossed you."

Summerby was unimpressed. "Not at all. If the British got real information from agent V. either they will appear in force or the Company itself will when the Brits tip off Washington. But if it's just a case of replacement for you, then after a prolonged absence on your part, a single agent will appear. If that happens we know you've been bluffing and that will make you dispensable."

"I'm dispensable anyway, once I've sent that cable."

"Not at all. If all goes well we may well need another. And obviously there are codes that only you know. It would be great, Dave boy, if between us we could keep everybody happy until . . . after the event. Which is why, by the way, come the morning you're taking a little plane trip."

"Where to?"

"All I'll tell you is you'll need a change of clothing. It's real hot where you're going."

Thirteen

Next morning Lancaster was awoken by a sharp dig in the ribs from Everett. "Rise and shine, pal. Time for your great adventure."

Bleary-eyed, Lancaster called for water and washed the sleep from his eyes but this was wasted labour, for a few minutes after he was completely awake he was blindfolded. Then, hands tied behind his back, he was taken up some stairs and bundled into an automobile. The car spluttered into life. From its sudden lurch forward every time the driver changed gear he conjectured that it was a local man at the wheel. After a long time on a paved road – at least two hours, he reckoned – the vehicle suddenly began scrunching over gravel, bumping and jostling as the driver made none-too-successful attempts to avoid potholes. There was about half an hour of this, then a sensation of travelling on yet a third surface, neither tarmac nor gravel, then a full stop. After a further pause, in which he perceived himself to be alone in the vehicle except for one guard, the main party returned. He was hustled out of the door, grudgingly allowed to urinate at the back of the car, and then frog-marched forward.

The explosion of engine noise provided him with all the explanation he needed. There was a distinctive sibilance in the timbre of the engines that placed the aircraft immediately in his mind as a DC-3. Thrust inside the fuselage, his nose was assailed by a peculiarly noxious mixture of diesel oil and old goat. Then he felt the plane edge forward, slowly gathering speed in the manner of prop aircraft. Its run seemed interminable. Finally it lifted off, banked to the left and curved away sharply.

After about an hour Lancaster heard the undercarriage descend and a few moments later the familiar skidding of wheels on runway. Bundled from this plane, he was then stowed on to another, evidently much smaller, which made what seemed a tortuous take-off, zigzagging and tacking for a full five minutes before settling down to climb gently.

By now Lancaster was tired. After persevering for a while with the monotony of the flight, he lapsed into an uncomfortable semi-sleep, broken by sudden twitches and jumps as he lurched between consciousness and oblivion. When he came to, jolted into wakefulness by a change in engine tone, he perceived clear signs of descent. Once more the familiar friction of wheels on runway, the screaming of engines with reverse thrust, and then complete rest. The door of the plane was flung open and a wave of sticky heat flooded in.

"Okay, *compadre*, you can look now," said a voice, and he felt the blindfold being removed and the handcuffs unlocked.

Now able to see for the first time in many hours, Lancaster was just able to make out that a primitive runway had been cleared in the jungle before darkness obscured all. The sudden tropical night came on within minutes of the little aircraft's touchdown – the flight had obviously been timed with precision. His companions, however, were easy to identify. It seemed that Luis Frias and two of the Colombian guards had been detailed for his surveillance. Neither Summerby nor Everett had made the trip.

The five of them – the pilot was to fly back next morning – spent that night in a makeshift wooden hut by the edge of the runway, evidently where the overseer who had directed the clearing of the airstrip by the Indians had made his base. There was a good supply of tinned food in the hut, and after making a desultory pretence of clearing the interior of insects, Luis' aides prepared a meal of rice and canned stew. Luis offered Lancaster a glass of *aguardiente*. Prompted by the thought that it might be politic to conciliate Luis, Lancaster took the glass and drained it. Luis then informed him that the next day they would be travelling on by canoe to their final destination. Hammocks were produced and

132

strung up. Lancaster was one of those who could usually fall asleep at will and sleep soundly and heavily. So it was that after crawling into his hammock he remembered nothing until next morning.

The sun was streaming into the hut and Luis and the two guards were already up.

"Hey, *gringo*, you like sleep, huh?" Luis said jovially, handing him a cup of *tinto*. "Come and say goodbye to your last link with civilisation."

Lancaster heard the twin-engined *aerotaxi* splutter into life outside. Stepping into the morning haze, he saw the pilot give a wave and begin his run along the strip. His craft seemed more like a model plane than a genuine navigator of tropical skies. It ran slowly along the *pista* as if it were a young bird trying out its wings for the first time. Then a sudden roar and it was airborne, missing the treetops by inches, it seemed, and quickly gone from sight.

"Time for us too," said Luis.

Lancaster was only halfway through his breakfast of coffee and baked beans when Luis' Indian guides arrived by water. He had been completely unaware that a river of considerable width was barely two hundred yards away from the airstrip. There were two Indians in a canoe large enough to take six men with ease. Long and dark, it had been hollowed out of an enormous trunk and was powered by a smart white outboard motor. Evidently the Indians were used to working for Luis, for at a few guttural clicks from him they began loading the supplies he had brought in the *aerotaxi*. Within half an hour the entire party was under way.

On both sides of them dense tropical forest ran down to the very edges of the river. All conceivable shades of greens and yellows seemed to be represented in the palms, myrtles, acacias and pineapples. Red, blue and emerald flashed before them as parakeets and kingfishers flew across the line of the canoe. Occasionally the odd small cayman would be seen in the water. On both sides colonies of ants had built nests by the waterside, high up on tree trunks. As the day wore on and the sun climbed higher Lancaster noticed, as he had in Antioquia when with Núñez, that the colourful sights around him seemed to fade in the sun's brightness, and the nuances of shade that had made such an impact in the early morning became attenuated.

He was aware that he was the only one in the party excited by the Amazonian habitat. The Indians, obviously, had been there before, but Luis and Roberto too were plainly bored, while the other guard, Rodolfo, passed the time by taking potshots at the small caymans and even once at a badly camouflaged sloth on the river bank. Lancaster filed away for possible future use the fact that as a marksman Rodolfo was useless.

The sun was already beginning its steep tropical descent when landfall was made at a bend in the river just beyond a canebrake. Stepping out on to the shore, the Indians unloaded the supplies, hauled the canoe on to land and covered it with loose branches, evidently left there for that purpose. Then they led the way into the jungle along the barest of trails, occasionally stopping to chop away with a machete some new vines that had invaded the path since their journey out. After perhaps three quarters of an hour the jungle opened, revealing a large tribal village. Night was now casting its pall over the Amazon and much the same arrangements were entered into as the night before. Hammocks were slung and a meal served – much better than Rodolfo's stew and beans – consisting of manioc, cassava bread, boiled fish and a joint of bush pig. Lancaster was assigned to a hut by Luis who admonished him: "Don't try no funny stuff, *compa*. I've got this hut staked out by the locals, so just crash out, man, and we'll talk tomorrow."

In the circumstances Lancaster thought this good advice.

Next morning he took stock of what was clearly to be his open prison. The village, which the Indians seemed to be calling a *maloca*, was simply hewn from the forest, separated from the wilderness by a narrow clearing and situated about a mile from the nearest river, partly to avoid the river-bank insects, mosquitos, sandflies and ants, partly to be invisible to anyone passing by river. The only sign of its existence to someone canoeing up or down was a telltale cluster of tethered canoes. Even so, only an expert could find the beginning of the narrow path that led to the village, and only a local could follow the Ariadne's thread of beaten jungle for a mile to the settlement itself.

The village consisted of two kinds of habitation. Where Luis and Lancaster were lodged there was a row of dilapidated, round huts fighting a losing battle with the encroaching jungle, which festooned the doorways. On the other side of the clearing stood the *maloca* proper, the communal dwelling place of the tribe, perhaps eighty feet long and sixty feet wide, the ridge of its roof forming a high peak some thirty feet above the ground. This ridge was supported by a succession of gigantic posts. The cathedral-like appearance of the *maloca* was enhanced when one entered. A central space or aisle running down the centre created the illusion of a nave and the sepulchral gloom inside heightened the effect, since the only light penetrating the *maloca* came from the entrances at either end, separate ones for men and women, and from the occasional rays that broke through the palm fronds in the roof.

Because the conditions in the huts on the other side of the clearing were much inferior to those in the cool and dark *maloca* (for Luis and his party to live inside the *maloca* would have breached tribal taboo) Luis had an arrangement with the headman that the huts would be kept in a livable condition by the Indians.

The natives were not temperamentally a tidy people. Small fires and half-burned logs, the shards of broken clay pots, the remnants of wooden mortars and pestles, competed for attention with rotting palm-leaf baskets and bits of torn matting. The shells of canoes were in frequent evidence, some on their way to completion, others long since abandoned. Beyond the clearing was a rude vegetable patch and beyond that again the manioc plantation. In front of the men's entrance to the *maloca* was a small copse of tobacco plants. There was another surreptitious trail from the manioc to the river, whence the women would return every morning with great loads of manioc, blenched clean by the combined effects of sun and water.

The village community itself contained perhaps sixty persons, apart from Luis and his henchmen and prisoner. They seemed a docile tribe who had evidently been pressed into some form of feudal service long since by Luis and other local CIA operatives. Even the headman and the shaman treated Luis with fear and respect. Lancaster gathered that he was not the first *gringo* to come here. Anthropologically, the Indians fitted the descriptions he had read of the Colombian tribes of the Vaupés, Putumayo and Caquetá, and certainly the ranges of the DC-3 and the *aerotaxi* were not great enough to have taken him much farther south than the equator. It was possible of course that they had crossed into Brazil or Venezuela, but it hardly made sense for Summerby to conduct a Colombian operation outside the national boundaries.

No attempt was made to prevent Lancaster from wandering off from the settlement in the daytime. He could not get far, and anyway the Indians, who seemed to refer to themselves as the "Turami", were obviously expert trackers and could run him to ground with ease if he should be foolish enough to attempt escape. Also in the village only Luis and the two *pistoleros* Rodolfo and Roberto possessed firearms.

Within the obvious limitations of his "village arrest", Lancaster had little to complain of. He was provided with a native manservant to cook his meals, sweep out his hut and keep the insects at bay; apparently fear of Luis had broken down cultural male resistance to this sort of labour. The days were passing, however, and Lancaster chafed bitterly at his inactivity. Soon it would be August. Luis, meanwhile, made friendly overtures. He affected to despise the company of Rodolfo and Roberto and seemed to need to converse daily with Lancaster. To show his distance from his two underlings he insisted that he and Lancaster talk in English. With this barrier self-consciously erected between himself and the *pendejos*, as he referred disparagingly to his men, Luis could settle down for long monologues or harangues. He seemed not to need Lancaster's participation but only his acquiescence or silent approval.

On the very first morning Luis had gone out of his way to engage his prisoner in conversation. "Hey, you know something, man, I like you. Too bad you got in Summerby's way but you got style, you know that, *compa*."

Silently Lancaster acknowledged the sally, so Luis plunged on. "I'm not a bad old guy, you know. I'm a technician, know what I mean, man? Someone else pays and tells me what to shoot at, I'll shoot. That's where it's at."

Luis seemed to need no answer other than a grunt or a nod or a sign that one's attention was not wandering.

"Hey, you know something, man? The honcho in Washington they call J. J., he had a shrink run me over. The guy figured I was perfect material. He alluded it all to my childhood."

Lancaster reflected that if Luis knew that his real interest in the conversation was fixed on the Latin's eccentric use of English he would probably pull out his pistol and dispatch him there and then. So he forced himself not to smile at the "allude" and to many other solecisms.

"My dad, he'd put the right royal business to us if we got out of line. He was one sonofabitch. And my ma, she was a bitch on wheels. All my dad wanted to do was run around with whores, spend money on booze and horses and beat up on us kids. The old lady used to lock the mother out and he'd sleep in a hedge in our yard, drunker 'n a son of a gun. One time my dad, he won five thousand bucks in a lottery – this was before the reds came in, you know."

"Where was this?" Lancaster interjected.

"Ain't I told you before? I'm Cuban, man, born and bred in Havana." Luis looked annoyed at the interruption. "Anyway, my dad collected the money and just did his number, only big this time. All those bucks and he spent the shit out of the sonofabitch in two months. All he ever give me was a kick up the ass. My ma, she used to put out when the ole bastard was whooping it up. Jesus, what a set-up. I don't think the ole bastard cared about it anyway. One time, my sister, she gets herself knocked up and my ma starts all this wailing and crying bullshit. 'What am I going to do? What will the *padrecito* say?' My dad, he says, 'Screw the *padrecito*. Anyway, what you gonna do about the girl? You can't stop the little whore putting out. What you gonna do, put a cork in it?'"

"How did you learn your English?" Lancaster asked, finding it difficult to keep a straight face.

"One time in Havana there used to be these real dude hotels. A lot of times my brother Juan used to clean out the trash in back of the Hotel Miramar. One day he says, 'Hey, Luis, there's a number going here as bellboy.' I goes to the hotel to see the manager. He says, 'Son, can you shoot?' Hell, I been shootin' since I could hardly walk. We had an old car and my dad used to take out two cans of gas. We'd drive the mother till one can was gone, then we'd get out and go hunting – rabbits, squirrels, birds, anything, man. Then he'd fill up the car with the other can and we'd drive home. He couldn't afford no more than that. If we wasted any ammo he'd knock the shit out of us that night. You can bet pretty soon I turned into a helluva shot. Anyway, I says to this *jefe*, sure, I shoot good, boss. He tells me this hotel is owned by someone big in the rackets. A lot of times this guy stays here, but he's got a lot of enemies and some of 'em might take a notion to come in and croak him in his own pad. So all the staff have got to be like bodyguards.

"I was working there, keeping my head down and doing my number, when one day I notice this guy coming up to Mr Dollman's room – Dollman, that's Mister Big, right? Usually they can't no way come up the elevator without two of Dollman's men come with 'em. I calls out, 'Hey, you can't go in there without proper authorisation.' He turns round and fires off a volley from a gun he's got under his jacket. I duck back into the elevator where I keep my Colt and I shoot the mother dead with one bullet. Then the whole hotel is fizzin'. Dollman's chief bodyguard has a conniption fit when he finds out. The two guys who were supposed to be on duty had been suckered away by a pair of broads and the type I blasted was the real thing, on his way to make a hit on Dollman. So Dollman's feeling pretty buggy about the whole mess and there's some real heavy duty ass-kicking goes on in his set-up. When he finds out what I did for him he offers me a job as one of his personal bodyguards. That's how I came over to the States. I worked out of Miami a piece with Dollman, then I went freelance."

"So you've done a lot of jobs in your time. How many contracts did you make in the States?"

"I did about one a year for ten years. In the end I got teed off and became a contract pro for the CIA."

Lancaster reckoned it would be better not to press Luis at this stage on his career with the Company. With luck, the Cuban would feel the need to talk again.

Fourteen

Apart from his conversations with Luis Lancaster was from the very first day taken up with his efforts to learn the local Indian dialect. Here the intuitive grasp of the born linguist helped him. Within a few days he found he had picked up enough to have rudimentary communication with the Indians. He soon learned that they were the Pirano branch of the Tumari and that there had been a schism within the larger tribe. Gradually the Indians' reserve broke down and Lancaster learned that their village was located near the river Curumayo, a tributary of a great expanse of water that the natives called Valeta. After a while Lancaster learned to differentiate between the various male Indians – the women were kept apart and away from his gaze, no doubt in fear of the lust of the white devil.

From the first it was an Indian named Rotilio who had shown the greatest warmth in response to Lancaster's overtures. The ice was broken in a curious way. On his second morning in the village Lancaster walked out to the very edge of the manioc field where there happened to be a fallen tree and in stepping upon it Lancaster disturbed a wasps' nest. Immediately a whirlwind of furiously buzzing insects assailed him. In his panic Lancaster did not head towards the *maloca* but rushed into the forest, only to collide seconds later with a *varasantha* tree from which a new and even more formidable enemy appeared. A cloud of reddish stinging ants descended from the foliage.

As Lancaster, in considerable agony, stumbled half-blindly back towards the clearing, Rotilio emerged from the forest by a parallel track not more than twenty feet away. Immediately solicitous, Rotilio motioned to the *maloca*. On entering it he applied various native salves and ointments to Lancaster's body. Curiously, although Lancaster thought he would have lost face as a result of this incident, the encounter with the ants seemed to break down a barrier between him and the Indian.

As the days passed and his grasp of Amazonian idiom increased, Lancaster also achieved a rapport with Rotilio's son Keshenko. From Keshenko he learned many details of the culture of the Amazon Indians. It appeared that Keshenko had been one of a pair of twins but luckily for him he had been the first-born. The second twin had been instantly drowned, since for the women of many of the Amazon tribes to bear more than one child at any one time is the ultimate disgrace. It is to be no better than the beasts of the forests. Lancaster realised that it was to this and other customs, such as dispatching any infants born with blemishes or handicaps, that the small number of children in the *maloca* could be attributed – there were no more than three in the largest family.

Through Keshenko Lancaster naturally came closer to Rotilio, until one day he was invited to accompany Rotilio and his brother Alirio, with the boy Keshenko, on a hunting expedition. It was not difficult to persuade Luis, who was now well pleased with his captive, to allow him to travel with the Indians on such a trip.

"Sure, have a ball," the Cuban told him. "There ain't no way you can get away."

The next morning the four of them set off into the forest. Alirio and Rotilio carried *macaña* wood bows and a quiver of arrows tipped with curare. Rotilio allowed his guest to examine these shafts. The arrows were made of cane, unfeathered and without notches, coming to a point where the deadly black poison had been smeared. In addition to his bow, Rotilio carried a blowpipe, about ten feet long, made from palm. Slung along his shoulder and crisscrossing the straps of the arrow sheath was a wicker folder, containing thirty or forty darts about a foot in length and no thicker than a pipe-cleaner. The blowpipe was used for birds and squirrels and the smaller monkeys, the bow and arrow for larger game.

As they penetrated the forest Alirio took charge of the machete while Rotilio watched the trees overhead. His favourite quarry was parrots, and Lancaster saw him shoot down four of these brilliantly coloured birds in less than an hour. Later it was Alirio's turn to demonstrate his prowess. As they came to a small stream, probably a tributary of the Curumayo, his sharp eyes detected a flicker of movement on the other bank. The party froze and waited. There was another staccato movement, but not so brief that even Lancaster could fail to recognise a capybara, the giant water rat of South America. Alirio began to stalk it, half crouching. When he got within range he fitted an arrow to the bow and, winding his legs round his quiver to steady himself and provide a primitive purchase on the slippery river bank, waited for the capybara to break cover. Crouching lower, he held the bow at full stretch. Suddenly the animal moved into the open, Alirio loosed the arrow, the capybara was bowled over noiselessly, and triumphantly Alirio brought back his prize.

By the afternoon little Keshenko was staggering under the weight of spoils, so the two adult Indians decided to abandon the hunt and return to the village. In addition to numerous parrots and the capybara, their skill had added several monkeys to the pot. The hunting of monkeys, Lancaster found, was a wasteful business, since only about half of those shot were retrieved. The Amazonian monkeys had a habit of gripping branches as they died, so many of the corpses would be left to rot high up in the trees.

Once back in the settlement, their kill was smoked to preserve it, except for the capybara, which was boiled. Lancaster found that it tasted a lot like pork. Alirio and Rotilio were well pleased with his behaviour during the hunt and it also seemed that among the other Indians he was regarded as good luck – the tally of birds and monkeys that Alirio and Rotilio had amassed had been much better than average.

The next morning was uneventful, and after a time a bored and listless Luis joined him for what the Cuban called a "rap". Lancaster let him run on for a while, then tried to turn the conversation to some more useful advantage.

"When were you recruited for the present job?" he asked.

"Hey, you know there's a funny story wrapped up in that. Right at the start, I wasn't on this case, only Romero, the guy who was going to fill the contract, he got croaked in a shoot-out with the cops."

"Why did they choose Romero for the job instead of you?"

"Seems like there was a lot of folk wanted to know that back in Miami. Some say Romero was mixed up in the Kennedy assassination and the Company wanted him out of the way."

"What do you think?"

"I reckon somebody put the business to him. But I got lucky and picked up his contract."

Lancaster stiffened. He'd been talking about this job in the jungle. A contract was a different matter. "This contract. Who are you supposed to hit?"

"I don't know that myself yet, man. Operation Toro, it's called. Summerby's got some deal cooked up where I don't get to know till just before. But it's something big, I know, 'cause he's got this Colombian heavy-duty type all ready to let fly too."

"Who's he?"

"I heard his name once and I even met him. One mean hombre. He was some kind of bandit chief or something. Then he got mixed up in some of the political bullshit they had down here a few years back."

"So Summerby's setting you up to work under him?"

"Under him? I don't work under nobody. If this mother bugs me, he'll get it. I don't give a shit if he's the biggest goddam bandit chief since Al Capone."

"But you're both working for Summerby? You'll carry out whatever order he gives, no matter who is the target?"

"You pay me enough, man, I'll knock out L. B. J."

As the days passed, Lancaster's acquaintance with Rotilio and Alirio deepened. His knowledge of their language and culture was deepening too. Then, some way into the second week of his abduction, something happened that placed the bond between him and the brothers on a higher plane.

143

One morning Keshenko, who was perhaps eleven years old, went down to the river to bathe. Lancaster accompanied him, for he found the boy a rich source of information about the village and its inhabitants. On reaching the river Keshenko plunged in and swam strongly to the other side. Then, as he scrambled up the bank, he seemed to slip and twist his ankle. He called out for Lancaster to come and help. Just as Lancaster struck out for the farther shore, he heard the note in Keshenko's voice change. Making the fastest crossing he could, he scrambled up the steep bank on the other side and ran to Keshenko. There, coiled and waiting for the boy to move, was a fer-de-lance, its back a line of yellow and black-fringed diamonds. It was a snake with an evil reputation for being prepared to attack without provocation. His hand trembling, he reached cautiously for a large, pointed stone lying on the river bank a few paces away. Praying that the serpent would not come lashing in on Keshenko before he could lay hands on the rock, Lancaster inched forward. Then, in a co-ordinated movement of hand, mind and body he seized the stone and threw it with all his might. It was a lucky shot, and struck the fer-de-lance on the flat part of its head. Like a whiplash the snake seemed to uncoil itself. It sprang backwards and streaked away into the jungle.

Examining Keshenko's foot, Lancaster found it to be badly sprained but no more. After about ten minutes Keshenko seemed to have recovered completely, except for a slight limp. They swam back to the other side, Lancaster keeping close to Keshenko in case he should be seized by a sudden cramp.

When they arrived back in the village and the boy told his tale, Lancaster was embraced by Alirio and Rotilio. But their gratitude went deeper than he realised. That evening Lancaster was approached by Rotilio, who gave him to understand that he, Keshenko's father, stood under a peculiar weight of obligation to him. Clasping both his hands, Rotilio swore that he would do all in his power to repay the white man. Seeing nothing to lose, Lancaster took his chance and asked that Rotilio help him to escape from the camp and almost certain death, as he had helped

144

Keshenko. The tall Indian looked troubled at this, but said he would go away and think how this could be accomplished.

Next morning, Lancaster wandered up to Rotilio's hut outside the *maloca*. Seeing him approach, Rotilio motioned to him to enter. Inside Alirio was seated in a corner; the two brothers had obviously been conversing long and hard. Now Rotilio told Lancaster that they had hit on the following scheme: Alirio was willing to take him downstream to the nearest *maloca* and assist him in finding a guide to the land of the white men. When Alirio returned without him, it would be given out that the two of them had ventured into the territory of a neighbouring tribe in pursuit of a tapir which they had wounded. They had then been surrounded by a war party of Purupuri and Lancaster had been taken prisoner. Alirio himself had made good his escape with great difficulty. In this way, whatever Luis decided to do it would be too late, for by that time Lancaster would be abroad on the great river.

Fifteen

London. July 1968. "But you saw him just a few days before this was written," Crombie exclaimed incredulously, flinging the coded cablegram down on the table. "And that was the occasion when you told him the full scope of the affair."

Durand glanced anxiously round his colleagues. "I have no reason to doubt either David Lancaster's competence or his loyalty. Perhaps he genuinely has stumbled on to something big. That would explain his decision to sign off like this. The real question is, how do we play it?"

Ledbury rubbed the side of his nose and slid his hand into his pocket and then out again – a mannerism which usually denoted the imminent appearance of an opinion he instinctively felt went against the hierarchical grain.

"As I see it, we have two choices. We can saturate the target area with all the agents we originally prepared for this op. – or we can keep out, as Lancaster indicates he wants us to. If we take the former course, quite apart from us catching it in the neck from the PM, the conspirators will certainly be warned off. If the latter, we perhaps say good-bye to an agent who is possibly not quite *comme il faut* anyway."

Durand looked up sharply. "Wait a minute. What exactly is this innuendo about Lancaster's reliability?"

Crombie nodded to Ledbury, who explained. "We decided, seeing that this plot was one of our biggest potential breaks ever, to run an intensive vetting *in absentia* on every aspect of our man in the firing line. What the data banks have produced is slightly disturbing. The recruitment procedures in this case seem to have been absurdly remiss. From close examination of his past and background

Lancaster emerges as more of a political animal than we could have wished."

"How so?" Durand had liked Lancaster at their brief meeting at Eldorado and now regarded him almost as a protégé.

"It seems that when he was an undergraduate he wrote an article for *Isis* arguing that the only viable political ideologies were fascism and communism, and that anyone who deserved the appellation 'thinking man' was forced to choose between these two."

"And this is your evidence?" Durand asked. "How many of you, I wonder," he went on pointedly, "would survive if your undergraduate idiocies were held against you?"

Crombie weighed in on Ledbury's side. "I believe that the question mark raised against Lancaster's reliability seems perfectly valid in the light of his mysterious disappearance – followed by an enigmatic and some would say meaningless cipher – immediately he learns the truth of his mission from Colonel Durand here."

At this juncture Colin Blakely could contain himself no longer. "Surely the critical issue here is not the status of our man in Bogotá – and I incline to Durand's view that we are jumping to conclusions anyway – but the safety of the Pope. Ought we not now to insist to the Vatican that his trip be called off? After all, the security of the Pope is the object of this mission, isn't it?"

"The object of the mission, as I have always tried to make clear, is the vindication of the Service in the eyes of its critics at home and abroad," Crombie remarked icily.

Blakely was stung by the rebuke. "Even if this means the death of a pope? I begin to ask myself whether we are really interested in his safety. We appear to be concerned purely with the rehabilitation of our organisation's reputation. You seem to be saying that if an assassination can secure that kind of payoff, so be it."

Crombie was really angry now. "As far as I am concerned, there need be no conflict between the security of His Holiness and success in our operation – both here at home *and* in Colombia."

"But what if there should be?" persisted Blakely. "Supposing it comes down to a straight choice between scaring off the assassins or allowing them full rein because it suits our book?"

"I really must insist that you cease to waste the Committee's time with these tendentious hypotheses," Crombie muttered furiously. "Let us pass on to the question of what support operation to mount in Bogotá, if any."

So much for the fabled "philosophical" Crombie, Durand reflected bitterly.

Cristina could not come to terms with what she had discovered. Under her bitterness at Lancaster's deception she felt instinctively that this was not the whole story. What they had experienced together was *real*. If Lancaster had made a fool of her there had to be some good reason.

Another problem had arisen. It was Ernesto Cárdenas who had blown David's cover and discovered from the Ministerio de Relaciones Exteriores that he was not a journalist but an accredited diplomat with the British Embassy. This information had been relayed through the *enlace* to Núñez, who had already dispatched a man to Bogotá in response to Cristina's plea for help. A second man was then detached from the guerilla force with instructions to countermand the orders given the first. The men sent down to Bogotá were two of Núñez' most trusted lieutenants. The first was Andrés Valencia who had been with Lancaster in the attack on the train. The second, dispatched with explicit orders to shoot Lancaster on sight, was Antonio Penata, the best marksman in Núñez' army. Both were now holed up in Cárdenas' apartment, awaiting developments.

Cristina felt an acute tug between love and duty. It was true that Lancaster had behaved unforgivably and that as a result she had put the movement at risk. But Penata and Valencia proposed to shoot him down like a dog, without giving him a chance to speak in his own defence. Nobody, it seemed, in the passion roused by the discovery that Lancaster was not a comrade but a spy, had asked why he should suddenly have vanished from Bogotá, leaving not a word behind him. This action was clearly incompatible with his role as an agent if only because such a disappearance must inevitably result in his cover being blown.

Most important of all to Cristina, however, was the fact that he had pierced through her emotional defences as she had never imagined possible. For her, until David, men had been creatures she took for her pleasure; the cause of revolution was all. With Lancaster, on the assumption that he was committed to the same cause as she, both sex, and revolution, and indeed love, had seemed to flow into one. Now that this had been shown not to be the case, the wholeness of her life had disintegrated, leaving her torn between her emotions as a woman and her duties as a revolutionary. If only she could make sense of his betrayal! It was essential that Lancaster make contact with her first if and when he returned to Bogotá. She needed this so desperately that she almost returned to the religion of her childhood and prayed for it to happen.

Summerby relit his cigar. "This way we've got three possibilities: first, the helicopter, second, on the run in from Eldorado, and third, in the Plaza Bolivar."

"And you've definitely ruled out anything at Mosquera?"

"Yes, for the very good reason that the diversion wouldn't work up there. Acosta will rise to the bait in the centre of town, where he figures he could trap Hernández, but not in the open country."

"And what if either of the first two hits scores a home run? What happens to Hernández then?"

Summerby exhaled histrionically. "One way or another he has to be liquidated. He knows too much already, and is a cunning enough bird to figure out the other angles once holy hell breaks out, as it will. But don't worry about that. Acosta and the DAS will pick up the tab for us on that one."

But Everett still did look worried. "Have you told Luis yet that he's to make the hit?"

"He won't know till the day before. The less time he has to think out all the fine points the better."

149

"And you're sure he won't chicken out once you reveal the target?"

"Listen, I know Frias from way back." Summerby spoke with an exaggerated confidence to reassure his aide. "If I made the price right he'd bump off his own mother. He's had presidents and prime ministers in his sights before now, and he wasn't joking when he pulled the trigger."

"Which jobs has he been responsible for? Some real lulus, by the sound of things."

"Listen, Jim, not even I know the all of it. Only J. J. could draw you the whole picture. But the less you know in this game the less chance there is of anyone getting any fancy ideas about how you're a security risk and therefore dispensable. Believe me, there's money to be made out of *not* knowing what I know."

"So when do you call him back from Amazonas?"

"Just as soon as I hear from J. J. what I'm to do about Operation Toro. The latest is that J. J.'s got to figure out some angle involving the British before he can give me the green light. I got to hand it to that Britisher, though. He's played one real cool hand. Even now I don't know what to make of him. All I know is no limeys have shown up since we snatched him."

"But apart from this, everything's A-okay, right?" There was still unease in Everett's voice.

"Everything's in position. The operatives are bought and sold. Now just pray that nothing prevents that plane getting here on the twenty-second." Summerby swivelled firmly round in his chair to indicate that the subject was now closed.

Sixteen

It was three days after the affair with the fer-de-lance that Lancaster and Alirio made their break. Alirio had taken a canoe a few miles downstream and hidden it in the undergrowth by the bank, since they could not use one of the canoes tethered at the village landing point if they wanted the fabricated story about an encounter with the Purupuri to stand up. He and Rotilio had laden it with the necessary water and provisions. On the appointed morning Lancaster casually mentioned to Luis that he and Alirio were going to bag a pig. Luis had made no objection, and even ventured a weak joke. "Pig, eh? I've bagged a pig or two before now, only those pigs had two legs."

Alirio then led Lancaster through some three miles of dense and matted foliage which they had to scythe through with a machete, until they emerged at the point on the river where the canoe was stowed. But having to hack a path through the greeny gloom cost them a good three hours and by the time Lancaster dragged his weary body into the canoe the sun stood high in the sky.

For the first ten miles along both sides of the river the forest presented a solid, forbidding wall, but towards evening the dense screen suddenly fell back from the water's edge, leaving rocky outcrops where landfall was possible. Now the problem was to find a camp site at least relatively free from forest insects, from the seething masses of ants, mosquitoes, termites and sweat bees. A passable spot was eventually found and Lancaster spent an uncomfortable night, observing bitterly how unaware Alirio seemed to be of all but the very worst of the discomforts. Alirio told him they were approaching rapids through which his dugout

151

could not possibly come safely. They would have to abandon the river and take the canoe across country to the next river system. Such portages to the next stretch of serene water could often be as much as five miles long. But even though the first one on which Lancaster and Alirio pushed their canoe could not have been longer than half a mile and the pathway was largely flat and the canoe's hull slid on rollers cut by Alirio, it still took the two men two hours' hard struggle to cross it.

During the seven days that followed their escape, Lancaster lost count of the rapids they skirted, the long sections of portage they pushed the canoe over, the number of river systems they entered. While he felt a genuine affection for Alirio, their conversation was necessarily limited, and he mainly passed the time learning what he could of the marvels of the forest, which were in fact less exotic than he had expected. Despite the reputation of the Amazon as an area teeming with wildlife, and although he and Alirio sometimes heard the coughing and grunting of jaguars at night, actual sightings of animals were rare. The only creatures they saw on a regular basis were monkeys and the ubiquitous insects. The most common species of monkey in these parts was the marimba, which created an impression of gigantic size as it used its long limbs to swing from branch to branch high above them, rattling twigs, pointing at the canoe and squawking defiance.

The shaggy brown spider monkeys, too, were frequent companions along the banks of smaller streams. Their pinched, miserable faces seemed to contradict the careless ease of their existence in the forest. Their movements were amazing: now a slow swing like a pendulum, now a scuttling motion like the spiders they were named for and, best of all, a sustained and rapid bird-like flight, when their prehensile tails flailed wildly, giving the monkeys a gyration of five limbs, almost propeller-like. But whereas the monkeys might excite Lancaster the insects only depressed him. Alirio's lighting of the fire each night to cook their meagre meal was the signal for a horrific onrush of all shapes and sizes: mosquitoes, spiders, termites, the gen-gen fly, and always ants – red, tiger, sauba and especially the leaf-cutter variety.

At last Alirio brought them to a sizeable settlement, one he had visited before and where he claimed there were white men and great civilisation. He was partly right, but although the village had a single ruler, a large class of Indian workers and a middle class of *mestizo* underlings attached to the court of the ruler, his "white man" proved to be a Syrian merchant, Antiochus Arnese, who had strayed out of his Mediterranean orbit decades before. As Lancaster had no money and no means of identification it was difficult to persuade this man to help, but at last he agreed – for an exorbitant fee – to take Lancaster as far as Leticia on the Brazilian border. There he could obtain funds and pay off his courier. Even at this stage Lancaster had misgivings about the man, but he had no choice. Having decided to trust himself to the Syrian, Lancaster bade an emotional farewell to Alirio, with much hugging and embracing. The last sight Lancaster had of him was that of a gently paddling figure disappearing round a bend of the river.

After twenty-four hours, during which he was provided with brackish bath water, meagre food and – the only real blessing – a sixteen-hour stretch of uninterrupted sleep, it was time for his own journey. The Syrian had told him that his man Umberto would take him by canoe to the next set of rapids, then across country by portage to the Putumayo, where they would change boats. At last Lancaster had some idea where he was. After consulting his host's maps he realised he must have been held by Luis on one of the tributaries of the Caquetá. The Syrian's proposed route would take him by back creeks on to the Amazon itself.

Lancaster's instinctive misgivings were to be borne out. The journey to the portage and across to the Putumayo went without incident, but once on the broad artery of a major tributary of the Amazon things started to go badly wrong. Umberto insisted that the rest of the journey could only be made by pirogue and that Lancaster himself would have to travel in the *pamakari*. The *pamakari* was in theory a delightful deck awning, designed to protect the traveller from the sun, but in practice a hideous assembly of stifling leaves so arranged that its occupant had to lie down, facing straight ahead, with a forward view only, and in a hot and dusty atmosphere far worse than that outside. But Lancaster protested in vain: Umberto insisted that no European could survive the heat of the tropical sun in the middle of the Putumayo.

Sweating and uncomfortable, surrounded by old rice sacks and peering sourly out at the daylight, Lancaster was forced to spend the rest of the day walled up in his stifling tunnel, until finally the combined effects of physical deprivation, poor diet, rough living and sheer stress caught up with him and he slept.

When Umberto prodded him awake it was dark. Gradually he made out the situation. It appeared that Umberto, with the mindlessness that Lancaster had already suspected, had not attempted to look for a place to spend the night until, far out in the middle of the Putumayo, he and the pilot had been overtaken by the twilight gloom and had taken a quick decision to tie up for the night alongside a *playa*, one of the tiny sandy islands in midstream. Now he explained to Lancaster the perils of a night spent on a *playa*.

"Two things you got to look out for, Señor. The current hereabouts is fast. This boat can get knocked away from its moorings. If we're cast adrift, the current will smash us against the dead trees in the dark. The other thing is the snakes. At night the boas rise up out of the water. They like to worm their way down inside the *pamakari* and fetch out whatever's in there. Keep your wits about you. Otherwise the last sound you hear in this world will be the splash as you disappear underwater in the coils of a *culebra*."

The night that followed was the worst since Lancaster had left Alirio's village. Next morning he cornered Umberto and made his feelings plain.

"Listen to me, *doble hijo de puta*, I'm not spending another minute in that black hole. You'd better make up your mind, because the only way you're going to get me back there is as a corpse."

Umberto, taken aback, fingered his automatic pistol.

True, he could shoot the *gringo*, but then his boss would never get his money. So he bowed to the inevitable and agreed to let Lancaster travel on the open rear end of the craft. And so it was that a few hours later, when a chance presented itself, Lancaster was able to escape, just before the Putumayo serenely joined the Amazon inside Brazilian territory.

Since Umberto baulked at taking the pirogue through, they hauled the craft ashore and began to prepare for a gruelling five-mile trek around the obstruction. But just as they started to move into the labyrinth of twisted roots and swampy terrain through which the path led they saw a party of Indians emerging from the jungle. They were about three hundred yards away, and coming towards them. Seizing the chance presented by this distraction, Lancaster rounded furiously on Umberto. "This is it, you bastard. I'm going back upstream and take my chance with these Indians."

"Not so fast, *gringo*," Umberto shouted. "You're coming with us whether you like it or not. You made a promise to Señor Arnese and you're going to keep it. When I've got payment of the money, then I let you go. But not before."

"Don't give me that stuff about promises. Your boss promised to get me to Leticia – he didn't warn me I was going to be stuck with an idiot like you."

"Listen, *gringo*," Umberto cut in." Do you think I'm going back to him empty-handed? We're going on together, I tell you." He drew his pistol. "And no more arguments."

All this time the Indians, perhaps twenty in all, had been watching this altercation between the *blancos salvajes*. Now they began to shuffle past, pulling their canoes down to the water's edge. The first group of about half a dozen had just come up to the spot where Umberto was standing when, panicking, he wildly let off a shot into the air, perhaps hoping to convince Lancaster that he really did possess the ultimate deterrent. Unfortunately the effect of this deafening sound in the silence of the wilderness was to create pandemonium. The Indians were terrified and fled from the scene, one of them cannoning into Umberto and sending him sprawling, knocking the automatic out of his hand. Immediately Lancaster seized his opportunity. Springing over to the grass where the pistol had landed, he retrieved it and trained the weapon on Umberto and the pilot.

"Now *you* listen," he said. "You take that contraption and get out of here. And you can tell Arnese from me that he's a crook. For the price he was charging me I could have travelled first class on the *Queen Elizabeth*."

Umberto began to whine: it was not his fault that things had turned out the way they had, it was the racketeering of *el jefe*. He had warned Arnese that no good would come from trying to cheat such a *buen caballero* . . . "At least, Señor, let me see if any of the Indians will help us upstream."

But the tribesmen, interpreting the pistol shot as a hostile act, regarded Umberto with suspicion and wanted nothing to do with him. Lancaster, on the other hand, they saw as their defender. Trusting to his newly-acquired skill with Amazonian tongues, he tried his luck talking to them. Some words were not the same as the dialect he'd learned, but many were similar and others common. Lancaster managed to explain the help he wanted, using signs when words failed. The Indians explained that they were going back upriver past the rapids and were then cutting across a network of river systems back to their village. Three days' journey away was the military fort at La Pedrera.

Lancaster was delighted. Things had taken a miraculous turn for the better. Eagerly he prepared to accompany the Indians, leaving Umberto and his pilot to follow them on the laborious upstream paddle as best they could. The two of them were soon lost to sight on the winding river, their curses fading quickly in the still jungle air.

By comparison with the ordeal of his journey since leaving Luis at the *maloca*, the days that followed were idyllic. One event only disturbed the trip to the Indians' village. One morning he awoke from a sound sleep in the rude hut where they had made their overnight stop to find blood dripping on him from the hammock above. It transpired that a vampire bat had bitten the toe of the man in the upper hammock and drawn out a great deal of blood. The foot of the unfortunate victim was bandaged, he was wrapped up tightly in blankets and forbidden to stir. Apart from the loss of blood there was some disease the Indians feared, and from his guides' mime of its symptoms Lancaster deduced that the bats often carried rabies. On enquiring how it was that such a wound could be made by the vampire without instantly awaking its victim, he learned that the bats drained out the blood with a kind of anaesthetic effect so that the prey felt nothing.

Two of the company were left behind to nurse the wounded man while the party pressed on to the village. Pausing only overnight to thank the headman and acknowledge his hospitality, Lancaster had his guide take him on to La Pedrera, a journey which took a further four days. To the casual traveller there would have been little remarkable about this encampment on the very border with Brazil, simply a drab slope of grass running back to the edge of a clearing with half a dozen military buildings neatly arranged to face across the Caquetá river to a steep wooded knoll on the other side, curiously at odds with the flat jungle around. But to Lancaster La Pedrera was a glad sight, for it represented the possibility at last of making contact with the outside world.

He said farewell to his guides, trying to convey the extent of his debt through his limited command of the native dialect. Then he introduced himself to an amazed commandant. Yet what most impressed him at La Pedrera was neither the commandant's ready welcome nor the hill rising out of the jungle like a tidal wave. It was something altogether simpler. Inside the major's office he noticed the calendar. The date was 14 August.

Seventeen

Lancaster's luck held. The army supply flying boat was due at La Pedrera in two days and Major Gómez, the genial commandant, guaranteed that it would take him down to Leticia. Lancaster debated whether to use military channels to re-establish contact with the British Embassy, but decided against it. Lengthy explanations would be called for if he reported back, which the unofficial nature of his operation could ill afford. And in the meantime one of Summerby's killers would be preparing to line up the Supreme Pontiff in his sights. Lancaster's urgent need now was to be reunited with Cristina, and to see if by some remote chance he could still deal with Summerby.

Waiting for the flying boat was an agony. Despite the efforts of Major Gómez, who was delighted to have an articulate and knowledgeable guest, to make his stay in the fort a pleasure, Lancaster was restless and distracted. His anxiety was only finally laid to rest when the big Catalina came flopping down on to the river soon after daylight on the Friday morning. The pilot had been warned of the extra freight, and Lancaster was expected for the short hop to Leticia.

Up to this point Lancaster had no fear of counter-measures from Summerby. Even if Luis had been able to radio news of Lancaster's escape – and there had been no obvious sign of a radio in the village – the area Summerby would have to cover was too vast. No, it wouldn't be until Bogotá that serious trouble could be expected. And on the journey there Leticia was no more than a necessary staging post.

Although there were a hotel and a cinema in the town, the work of a buccaneering American wildlife entrepreneur,

Leticia was still a somewhat dispiriting place. But at least the lines were open to the outside world and Lancaster was able to telex his bank in Bogotá for funds.

After booking into the hotel, Lancaster made enquiries about planes due out for Bogotá. His misgivings concerning Leticia were confirmed with the news that the weekly Avianca DC-4 called on Thursdays and the S A M service on Wednesdays. Were there any other planes leaving Leticia? he asked the hotel clerk.

"There is the Peruvian flying boat that goes to Iquitos on Tuesdays and comes back on Wednesdays, but to Bogotá, no, Señor, I am afraid not. No one in Leticia ever needs to go up to the city that urgently. There is nothing else, Señor. Unless . . ."

"Unless what?"

"Señor, I give you this information *sin compromiso*. I do not know how reliable they are but there are two partners, Jesús Jiménez and Antonio Gutiérrez, who have an old aeroplane. Sometimes it is chartered, I know. It is said that the plane is now *cogido* – no good. Some say its owners can't get the parts, others that they are too lazy to maintain it. I cannot recommend them to such an important *caballero* as the Señor, but if the Señor was prepared to take risks – and Jesús and Antonio are definitely men who have their price – then they might be able to help. Tell them Elias sent you and if it should be they can assist you, Señor, I hope you will not forget your humble *servidor*."

Leticia was a small place. Just ten minutes later Lancaster was knocking at a shabby door directly off what passed for one of the main streets in the town. A padlock hung from the door, useless. Getting no answer, he turned the loosely rattling handle and pushed open the door. Entering, he found himself in a muddy patio, in the middle of which were the communal bathing facilities of the individual rooms. Each room was slatted with clinker-built planking which served as a wall but did not reach right to the floor. From one of these rooms emerged an old man, followed by a motley collection of chickens, dogs and cats.

"*Los señores Jiménez y Gutiérrez?*" Lancaster demanded.

"*Por allá,*" the old man grunted, pointing to a set of

rooms in the corner, obviously the elite apartments of the house.

Lancaster went up to the first door and knocked loudly. A sleepy and belligerent voice answered, "*Quién es, por dios. Que vayase, sin verguenza.*" Ignoring the fighting talk, Lancaster called out, moderating his perfect Spanish to that of the usual Englishman in these parts: "*Señores Jiménez y Gutiérrez?* How would you like to make five hundred US dollars apiece by flying me up to Bogotá?"

There was a brief silence, then the same voice called out "*Momentito!*" There were vague scurrying sounds and a scraping noise as of furniture being rearranged. Then, after a few more moments' silence, the door opened and a pretty young Indian girl in a short fawn dress scuttled past him. Behind her a large, bearded man emerged blinkingly into the daylight.

"What is this about five hundred dollars? You have them here? You can show me?"

"Señor Jiménez?" Lancaster queried.

"No. Gutiérrez. Antonio. *A sus ordenes.* You want a plane, no?"

"Yes, right away. As soon as you can manage it."

Gutiérrez turned lazily and bawled over his shoulder. "Jesús, we got business."

"How soon could you be ready to leave for Bogotá?"

"Not so fast, Señor. I said nothing about Bogotá. It is true we have an old kite and maybe if we coax her she flies and maybe not, but not even Jesúsito and myself would take her up into the cordilleras."

"How far can you get, then?"

"Tres Esquinas or Florencia, maybe."

"No good." Lancaster thought quickly. "How about Villavicencio?" From there he knew there would be a taxi service through the mountains to Bogotá.

"Villavo? That's a long haul. I don't know whether the old girl's up to it."

"At least that way you wouldn't have to fly over mountains. Couldn't you run up to the Meta, keeping the Sierra de la Macarena on your left, then follow the Meta into Villavicencio?"

At this juncture the next door along opened and a much smaller, clean-shaven individual emerged. With him too was the inevitable local girl, who made for the street after looking at Lancaster and giggling. Gutiérrez yelled at the newcomer affably. "Hey, Jesús, what you say to Villavo? Five hundred US dollars each?"

Jesús, after muttering a formal *"buen dia"* at Lancaster, took his partner aside. Lancaster left them to whisper and gesticulate in the corner. From the *"hombres"* and *"carajos"* that broke through the curtain of muttering, he gathered that the partners were by no means unanimous. Finally Antonio came back.

"We'll do it, Señor, *si dios quiere*, but it'll cost you seven hundred and fifty dollars each. And we want the money in cash, up front. Apart from the gas and the risks with this particular *avioncito*, we're – how shall I say? – not exactly welcome in Villavo. A slight misunderstanding with the *alcalde*'s men. You are a man of the world, Señor, you know how it is."

"US dollars on the Amazon are not easy to come by," Lancaster replied. "But get me to Villavicencio tomorrow and I'll pay forty thousand pesos each." Which, even for a five- or six-hour flight, was daylight robbery.

"Cash in advance, Señor," added the taciturn Jesús.

"Agreed. But just in case the two of you get any funny ideas once we're airborne, understand this. Here, throw this in the air."

The bank in Leticia had had some silver pesos on display, commemorating the visit of Paul VI to Colombia. On a whim Lancaster had bought a couple. He handed one of them over to Antonio with instructions to hurl it high. Then drawing from his briefcase the Colt that he had purchased a few hours ago in the gunshop near the airport, he put a neat hole through the silver peso as it reached the top of its trajectory. Even Jesus whistled his appreciation. At the sound of the shot there was an instant cacophony of squawks, yelps and barks, and a moment later the old man reappeared.

"Por favor, Señor," he began to protest, but a neatly placed fifty-peso note in his palm cut him off in mid-sentence.

Mumbling "*Muchissimas gracias, caballero,*" he hobbled away. Surprisingly it was then Jesús, not Antonio, who broke the silence.

"Perhaps we ought to feel insulted that you could so doubt us, Señor, but I do not blame you for your caution. I for one applaud a man who approaches life with a rational calculation of the consequences of his actions. I think we can do business *sin apuros, Señor.* You have the sacred word of Jesús Jiménez that, God willing, we will get you to Villavo. Now we have the problem of our temperamental mistress. Eh, Antonio?"

Antonio nodded. "Señor, if ever you fail in your own business, be assured that there is a bright future in Colombia for a man with your talents. Come, we will try out the *avioncito.*"

At the very corner of Leticia's airstrip, on a feeder lane from the main runways, stood a battered dirty aeroplane. To his amazement Lancaster saw that this was no little *aerotaxi* but a genuine DC-3, similar to the plane in which Summerby had shipped him out of Bogotá, but almost certainly in far worse condition.

They jumped out of the old jeep Jesús and Antonio used for conveying freight to the plane. After climbing into the Douglas Jesús revved up the starboard engine. Even to Lancaster's inexpert ear the motor seemed to produce a familiar, healthy tone. The port engine, however, produced a kind of clucking noise, and whenever Jesus gave it full throttle it nearly died.

"Like I thought," said Antonio. "We got a whole afternoon's work on this baby at least."

He and Jesús set about stripping off the cowling to identify the fault. Lancaster wandered out of the airport compound, which was only manned in midweek when the weekly planes were due in, and on into town. It was 5.30 p.m. and almost dark when he returned. Jesus and Antonio were still clambering over the fuselage in their grimy blue overalls.

Antonio greeted him gaily. "Hey, man, I think we fixed it."

He put both engines through their paces, and there was

no trace of the earlier spluttering and coughing. Satisfied, both Antonio and Jesús climbed down and began to shed their overalls.

"Okay, we go tomorrow at dawn," Antonio said. "*Si dios quiere*, we should be in Villavo by noon. At any rate, Señor, be assured that you'll either be there or all three of us will have breathed our last, for if the old lady lets us down over the country between here and the *llanos*, forget it. No one could survive in there."

Jesús cut in. "Perhaps the señor would care to join us later on for a drink."

Lancaster didn't like the idea of their having a night on the town before such a flight, but suspected that they would down their fill of *aguardiente* whether he joined them or not. So he went down to meet them in the bar of his hotel at eight.

Both men seemed already well on their way to oblivion. Lancaster watched appalled as the two of them consumed their *aguardiente* in typically Colombian fashion, holding their throat muscles open and seeming to pour the neat spirit straight from glass to stomach. Inhibitions were soon released on both sides, however, so that by the time Lancaster staggered back to his bed, well after midnight, he felt strongly that an ineffable bond of friendship had been forged between him and his pilots.

At six the next morning Jesús and Antonio emerged from their *rincón* as composed as if they had spent the previous day in monastic contemplation. Lancaster by contrast was still addled as he counted out the 80,000 pesos he had withdrawn the afternoon before under the gaze of an astonished bank manager. This was big money even for Bogotá, but in Leticia it almost counted as the treasure of Eldorado, and things might have gone hard for an un-escorted Lancaster in a town where the withdrawal of such sums was likely to draw in *bandidos*. But he had experienced no problems. Perhaps his shooting reputation, spread by the old man, had gone before him.

The limpid brilliance of the early morning helped to compensate for Lancaster's hangover. It was one of those god-given dawns that Colombia is so rich in, with the golden god of the Chibchas in strong relief against the profound cerulean.

The swamps around Leticia glittered in the morning sunlight as Antonio swung the Douglas effortlessly on to the main runway, exerted full thrust, then moved forward rapidly, bouncing over the few ruts and depressions on the *pista* before taking off smoothly on a northern track. From his position inside the empty vault of the plane Lancaster gazed down on the dark green of the forest, broken only by the glistening water of swamps and the infrequent chocolate-coloured rivers. Occasionally he lent an anxious ear to the engines, dreading to hear the spluttering sound again, but the steady drone continued without a break.

About three hours out from Leticia, when approaching the headwaters of the Vaupés, they ran into thick cloud and a sudden squall. The plane bumped and shuddered and the rainwater trickled down from leaking joints in the ill-maintained fuselage. Suddenly the DC-3 hit a severe airpocket and the door to the pilots' cabin swung open violently. But Antonio and Jesús, so far from being alarmed at the turbulence, had their feet up on the control panel, their pointed cowboy boots obscuring the dials and Antonio was unconcernedly humming *"Todo tiene música!"* a popular Colombian ditty of the moment.

Such aplomb was vindicated only minutes later when the plane emerged from the clouds into a serene sky. Again the same brown streams wove their twisted way through the green carpet below. Once or twice Jesús came back into the passenger area for a brief chat or to point out a landmark. Antonio, by contrast, did not appear to come out of his reverie until they were nearly at their journey's end, over the Rio Guaviare, where the dark green of the jungle abruptly ceased and the lighter, more parched green of the *llanos* took over. Then Antonio came back to point out the distant sandstone peaks of the Macarena.

He was called back into the cockpit by Jesus who suggested that they begin their descent into Villavicencio. Twenty-five minutes later, shortly before noon, the upper waters of the Meta were in sight from the starboard window, and the great bulk of the eastern cordillera on the left.

Executing a textbook approach and landing, Antonio brought the plane in along the Villavicencio runway, raising just one small cloud of dust as he pulled the Douglas to a standstill.

Neither of the men wished to stay long in Villavicencio: the memories of the *jefatura de policia* were too long for them to risk more than the briefest stopover. So Lancaster took his leave of two men he would have liked to know longer. His fears for their honesty had been groundless, and Jesús and Antonio seemed genuinely sorry to part from him.

It was now 17 August. Walking on into Villavicencio from the airstrip, Lancaster learned that *colectivos* ran up to the capital every hour, taxis hired on a collective basis. He needed time to eat, and to buy himself some presentable clothes, so he hired a *colectivo* for his exclusive use, which he arranged to pick him up at the Hotel Meta at 3.30. Next he checked into the hotel, taking a room on the half-day basis common to Colombian provincial towns – *una alcóba no para dormir*, as the local euphemism went. Best to relax for a while, to reflect and take stock.

Villavicencio had still not been completely integrated into the twentieth century. With its cinemas and banks it stood as an outpost of the urban civilisation of Bogotá, but in the curious mixture of tethered horses and ancient motor cars that littered the main square it resembled nothing so much as the photographs of towns in the American West taken in the first decade of this century. Here the cattle barons of the *llanos* came in for their monthly tryst with *aguardiente* bars and the ladies of the night. The raw flavour of the town was richly conveyed as Lancaster walked through the streets. The savoury smells of chicken, *arroz con pollo*, mingled with the cheap perfume of the girls and the dung of the plains horses.

The taxi arrived on time – surprisingly for Colombia, but then exclusive use of a *colectivo* usually entailed a large tip over and above the fare. The road into the Andes climbed steeply out of Villavicencio, twisting and curving as the car climbed from sea level to 12,000 feet. By now Lancaster was no longer surprised that Colombian drivers took blind corners so fast, as if the mere existence of a paved road in itself guaranteed security. The mountains presented a spectacle even more ravishing than the forests. Thickets of rhododendrons and acres of daisies massed in white and pink, red and purple. The slopes of the green mountains were awash with pale lemons and rich golds.

It was with a wrench that Lancaster tore himself away from the view to concentrate his mind on the job awaiting him in Bogotá. One little incident, however, brought him sharply back to earth. Searching in his pockets to check that he had transferred the documents he would need in the capital to his new clothes, he came upon the coin that he had hit with the Colt for his demonstration to Antonio and Jesús. He noticed that the bullet hole had gone straight through the head of the impression of the Supreme Pontiff.

Eighteen

Afterwards, she could not decide whether it had been good or bad fortune that the phone rang in her apartment while Ernesto was visiting. In the mixed astonishment, relief, excitement and latent resentment with which she heard his voice she conveyed to him nothing of the perils that lay in wait. But her snatched delivery, the staccato "Yes, darling, at once, of course," would have alerted a far less shrewd observer than Cárdenas to the identity of the caller. Shaken, Cristina replaced the receiver. "He will be here in half an hour," she said resignedly.

"You understand, Cristina, this is not something I *want* to do, but something I must do," Cárdenas explained carefully as he dialled the six digits of his own phone number. "Professor," he said into the mouthpiece, "the manuscript will be delivered here in half an hour. It would be advisable if you could be here in person when it arrives in order to sign for it."

Cárdenas then quietly left the flat.

Fifteen minutes later there was a screech of brakes as a green Volkswagen Beetle drew up outside. Valencia and Penata, the men Núñez had deputed to execute Lancaster, burst in.

"When he comes to the door, be cordial and invite him in. Don't arouse his suspicions in any way." Penata rapped out his instructions in the peremptory manner he used with his *guerilleros*. Unused to having his orders queried in any way, he was surprised to find that Cristina demurred.

"If I do, you must give me your word as a comrade that there will be no instant execution. You must allow him to speak his piece and explain himself."

"For such a beautiful comrade, how could I refuse,"

167

replied Penata. He was more than a little taken with Cristina himself, and the political hatred he felt for Lancaster was beginning to be overlaid by a growing sexual jealousy. "Andrés, come into the kitchen. It is better he see no one but Cristina when he arrives. That way he will be off guard. But remember, Señorita Amaya, the order from comrade Fabio still stands as regards this *gringuito*, and not even for you will I fail to carry it out."

Cristina said later that she lived through several lifetimes in the minutes before Lancaster finally arrived. Should she break with her comrades for the sake of this man who had so deceived her? On the other hand, could she stand by and see him gunned down? Seconds before Lancaster arrived she decided what she must do.

She heard the car draw up, heard him enter the ground floor, mentally counted the seconds while he called the elevator, got into it and ascended to her floor. Then the noise of footsteps in the hallway, and finally the sound of the bell.

She opened the door.

"Cristina," he cried and threw his arms around her.

Only when he already held her in a close embrace did he notice her tension. He was about to ask her what was the matter when Valencia and Penata emerged from the kitchen, their automatics trained on him. He cursed his carelessness in having come to her apartment unarmed. He had left the Colt in the glove compartment of the car, thinking that with her, at least, he could relax his guard.

Penata indicated with a leftward flick of his gun that he should move away from Cristina. Lancaster disengaged himself and slowly edged away.

"Now, Señor *espión*, before we carry out revolutionary justice Comrade Cristina has requested that you be given the opportunity to plead in your own defence." Penata's tone became sarcastic. "You will please to keep your remarks brief. Our esteemed comrade has doubtless compelling reasons of her own for wishing to believe your lies, but we ourselves are not interested in them. You have made a laughing-stock of us. Still, let it not be said of the ELN that we ever condemned a man unheard."

"Does it make any difference what I say?" replied Lancaster. "You've obviously decided that I'm guilty, according to your lights. Am I on trial for political crimes or simply for having dented your sense of honour?"

Penata drew himself up. "You are guilty of every possible counter-revolutionary treachery. Can you produce one single argument why we should preserve your miserable skin a minute longer?"

"I can," came a voice from the kitchen door.

Unnoticed, Cristina had slipped away. Now she returned, a Smith and Wesson revolver trained on Penata in an expert two-handed grip.

"Lay down your guns – you as well, Andrés – or I swear I'll blast Comrade Antonio to kingdom come right where he stands."

There was a raw edge to Cristina's voice that gave even a tough campaigner like Penata pause. He dropped his gun.

"Both of you, throw them down. You – " she indicated Lancaster "– quick, get them."

He dropped to the floor and retrieved the automatics.

"You little fool," Penata hissed at her. "Do you really think you can get away with this? Even if we fail, don't you know that Comrade Fabio will never rest till he has destroyed you for this? From this moment on you're dead to the movement, you're finished, you've nowhere to go. Who would have thought that you of all people could be brought so low by a well-hung *gringo*?"

Cristina stepped back a pace, but kept her gun steady. "Maybe this man has ruined himself and me," she said softly, "and maybe there's no way out for us, but at least he's going to have a head start. David, tell him the truth. No matter what it may be I want us all to hear it, now, here in this room, so that there may be no misunderstandings later."

"Listen, Antonio, and listen well," Lancaster began. "It is true that I deceived you about my identity, but that is my only crime against you and your men. Do you think you would still be secure in those mountains if I was really what you think I am? I collected enough information while I was with you to be able to bring down several battalions of the

Colombian army and an American helicopter gunship on you long before now if I was really a hostile agent."

"But why then did you lie to us?" Cristina pleaded, clinging to the straw of hope he seemed to be offering.

"I'm waiting, *gringo*. Your story had better be good," added Penata.

With passionate intensity Lancaster explained his mission. ". . . and that was why I visited you and was planning to pay a call on the FARC in Tolima – to see if assassination figured in your scheme of things. I learned enough when I was with you to know that it didn't. But what I did not know then was that your movement has been infiltrated by the CIA – or rather a subsection within it, working to its own rules – and that it is these men who are behind the papal assassination plot. And by the time I had discovered that, it was almost too late. I had already got too close for comfort, and when I went to fix the contact with Fuentes and the FARC – Cristina can bear me out on this – I was abducted. I've spent the last six weeks festering in Amazonas."

"But if you were kidnapped, how did you escape?" It was Cristina, wishing to believe, who asked.

Lancaster then gave her a shortened account of his adventures. "I'll try to bring things up to date. This splinter group within the CIA has a well-prepared campaign. The two ringleaders are American and they've got a Cuban hit man in on the act, presumably to carry out the contract on the Pope. There's also some Colombian bigshot involved – someone from the *violencia* days. What I'm asking you both, Antonio and Andrés, is that you should help me prevent this plot."

"Me? Help you?" Penata laughed. "The killing of a pope may be a world-shaking event to you people, but hardly to us. As Comrade Fidel said of the Kennedy assassination, it would simply be a case of an intelligent bandit being slain by unintelligent bandits. Even if I believed you, why should I care one way or the other?"

"Because, my friend, the fanatics who are planning this have it set up so that the revolutionary left in Colombia takes the rap when the Pope is gunned down. The idea is to discredit the Latin American left by pinning a papal murder on them."

Penata stared contemptuously at Lancaster and was about to begin another tirade when Valencia spoke for the first time: "You remember last Sunday, Antonio, when I took that ride downtown and you warned me not to? Something happened then that I found hard to believe. Later I thought I had imagined it, but after the *gringo*'s story I'm not so sure. You remember José Alejandro?"

"The comrade who joined DAS and fed us information? You can't have seen him. The DAS found him out over a year ago and tortured him before stringing him up in the *jefatura* with piano wire."

"No, no, not José. But you remember the photographs of the most wanted men he got out to us? You were one of them. We were mainly interested in which comrades they were after and how they graded them. There was another man they were keen to get. You don't forget a face like that. Efraim Hernández was his name. Well, on Sunday I went into a little *tienda* on Tercera to buy some *pielrojas*. As I went in, I practically collided with this big *mozo* coming out. He looked as though he wanted to knife me on the spot. But I was closer to him than I am to you now, and I'd swear it was Hernández."

"Well?" said Penata impatiently.

"Well, don't you see? If the *gringo* is telling the truth, the man the *yanquis* are using might be Efraim Hernández. This kind of thing is exactly what he'd be hired for."

Penata remained thoughtful for a few seconds. Then he addressed Lancaster again.

"If the Pope is in danger, why doesn't your secret service alert him? Why don't you tell the police, the DAS, the Vatican security services? Or if you know of a plot, why not publicise it in the newspapers? If what you say is true there are many effective ways of proceeding, yet you ask for the help of a couple of revolutionaries who must be much more your enemy than the CIA could ever be. How is this?"

"In the first place, Antonio," Lancaster replied quietly, "I am not your enemy and have never been. The enemy for my country is still identified as the Soviet Union. Now you yourself have little cause to favour the Soviets or their allies. Look what the Bolivian CP did to Che. The Soviets don't want another Cuba here or anywhere else. They don't want the political trouble it brings from the Americans, and they don't like the bill for a million dollars a day."

"But you are still the *yanquis'* cousins, no?"

"So it is said. But when even cousins come up with a crazy plot like this they must be stopped. And besides, there are many in my organisation who would like to steal a march on the Americans. They would give a lot to expose a case like this and leave the Americans with egg on their faces."

"Okay. So what about my other questions?"

"Publicising a case like this in the newspapers won't work. In the first place, the big guns like *El Tiempo* would think twice before offending the Americans, especially with Lleras breathing down their necks. Then, even if they *did* take the idea seriously, the CIA would deny it, and their denial would have the ring of truth. Don't forget, this is not an official Company venture – just a couple of crazies operating within the Company. Over and above that, rumours of assassinations on popes, presidents and kings are ten a penny. Visits like this always bring out the cranks, the anonymous callers and letter-writers. So you need hard evidence. And what *do* you have? Very little in any detail. The same goes for the DAS and the Vatican police angle. To tell them there will be an attempt on the Pope's life, but you don't know how or where, wouldn't exactly encourage them to take you seriously. As for persuading the Pope not to come here because of the security risk, that's been tried and Paul won't hear of it."

Penata seemed grudgingly impressed by Lancaster's logic. "All right, let's say I believe all this – what can *we* do that the Colombian authorities won't be doing anyway?"

"There are several cards we can play. In the first place, we can put pressure on the Americans. If they're using the man you call Efraim Hernández as a key part of the operation we can cut down his scope for action by giving the DAS a strong tip that Colonel Acosta's old rival is in town. If we give Acosta a list of US-rented and leased properties not covered by diplomatic immunity, and he raids them as possible hiding places for Hernández, then the opposition will know someone's on to them. That *could* scare them off. Another move will be for me to tip off the Director-General of the CIA through British channels that his Latin America desk is running an independent operation. Lastly, I've got a pretty good idea of the general whereabouts of the village where I was held, and I know that the CIA man there is Cuban, a Batista man. So if reliable information could reach the Colombian authorities that a Castroist guerilla leader is arming and training Indians in a village on one of the tributaries of the upper Putumayo, with an airfield nearby, the Colombian military would probably have to go and take a look."

Penata glanced at Valencia, who shrugged non-committally. "How do we know we can trust you?"

"You don't. I can only point to the last six weeks. If I'm lying, why didn't I betray you long ago?"

There was a long silence. Finally Penata spoke. "All right. We'll go along with you for a while. But remember, till the Pope departs and no longer. So what do you want of us?"

Lancaster hesitated. His problem now was to find a way of appealing to the two men's *machismo*. They needed action – a background role would never satisfy them. He seized on the idea of asking them if they would be willing openly to challenge Hernández and the Cuban to armed combat. He hardly believed that such a theatrical battle would take place, but the very act of issuing the challenge itself might well stir things up.

Penata immediately accepted. Valencia seemed less sure of himself, but had been put on the spot and could hardly refuse. Then Lancaster told them that, after making himself conspicuous about the city for the Americans' benefit, he would issue the challenge by telephone to Summerby at the US Embassy. Inevitably his high profile would be taken as a deliberate provocation by the two assassins, to which they were very likely to respond.

The embassy man who took the call would deny knowledge of Frias and Hernández, but the message would undoubtedly get through to Summerby – and to prevent him from concealing the challenge from his hired gunmen Cristina would mobilise all her contacts to place the story in the popular newspapers: after all, what could be more newsworthy than a report about a challenge to the old *violencia* from the new?

And meanwhile Lancaster would carry out his other suggested steps, alerting the Colombian military, contacting London, and warning Colonel Acosta of Hernández's presence in the city. Always assuming that the DAS didn't know of it from their own sources, the Colonel would be very grateful.

"So now," he concluded, "you must get word to Comrade Núñez of all that we have agreed today. Tell him also, as a token of my good faith, that his contact the journalist Julio Roca is in Summerby's pay. There are traitors everywhere. Tell him to be careful."

Penata and Valencia received back their revolvers. Their radio, Penata said, was in Cárdenas's home, which they were using as a hideout. Warily they left the apartment and minutes later Lancaster heard them start up the Volkswagen and drive away.

For a few moments Cristina looked at him, saying nothing. Then she rushed at him and pummelled his chest with her fists. "You bastard, *loco inglés*, why didn't you tell me? Did you think you meant so little to me that I would not respect your confidence?"

Lancaster felt curiously clumsy, caught between guilt and desire. There was so much he needed to explain, so much he did not even fully understand himself. Trying to find the right words, he took her hands and drew her down beside him on the sofa.

"Darling Cristina, I wanted to tell you . . . I just couldn't find the way. I went through agonies. I even thought of resigning my job. But life isn't that easy – I couldn't just walk away. If I'd pulled out London would have sent professionals after me. At the very least there'd have been debriefings in England, security checks, vetting procedures, follow-ups . . . And there was still the assassination plot – did I not have a duty to prevent it if I could? . . . But believe me, my dear, however the next few days work out, this is definitely my last mission. When it's safe to do so I swear that I'll resign."

He paused. "Can't you see that my recent experiences with the CIA have increased my sympathy for your cause? I may not be a convert yet to revolutionary guerilla warfare or to Marxist–Leninism, but at least I understand your reasons."

Slowly but surely their former intimacy returned. "Have you any idea," Cristina asked him, "how close you came to being shot by Antonio? I've seen him in action and I know. It's just luck that we're both alive."

Lancaster leaned forward and kissed her lightly. "Why do we take so much for granted, most of all from those we love? You saved my life. What more can I say – except that without you my life would be worth little anyway. Many times when I lay awake in that village near the Putumayo I thought of you and how I might never see you again. That was far more important to me than the Pope, this mission, or anything."

Cristina smiled sadly. "There are worse jungles than the Putumayo," she said. "When I thought you had betrayed me I – "

He kissed her again. "That's all over now."

She stiffened. "The danger is not over. The American, Summerby, will not give in easily." She drew back, suddenly thoughtful. "What exactly do you hope to achieve with Antonio and Andrés?"

"Frankly, much less than I pretended. I had to stall, try to convince them that they had to work with us. But I'm afraid in the end the whole thing won't add up to much." He shook his head dejectedly. "How the hell am I supposed to find the four musketeers with only four days to go?"

"Musketeers?"

Lancaster laughed grimly, "I mean Summerby, Everett, Luis and Hernández. They've got the whole of Bogotá to range free in. But we can't just sit here and do nothing. There are plans to be made. Sooner or later they're going to have to show their hand, and when they move in for the assassination itself, I aim to be there."

Nineteen

All cables from Colombia were to be sent to Sir Ian immediately on decoding. The cipher clerk had been amazed at the order when it was first issued, and even more surprised when it was repeated on his notifying his section head. Such a directive was unprecedented. Even in the case of defector debriefing operations or in high-level exchanges of agents it had always been the head of the relevant area desk who would handle the ciphers. Sir Ian had even paid a personal visit to the registry clerks handling incoming cables from Latin America, to emphasise the absolute necessity for all material bearing a Bogotá coding to be brought to him without any intermediate stops. The Head of Latin America desk was moved by these unorthodox proceedings to request clarification from the directorate. Crombie's secretary replied with an A notice – Service slang denoting material so secret that only A-grade personnel (in effect the members of E.I./J committee) were authorised to read it.

When the long-awaited cipher did arrive, therefore, the decoded message was whisked up to the twenty-first floor by special courier.

The Colombian military, at first sceptical, had become detectably interested when Lancaster provided a wealth of circumstantial detail. Anticipating their response, he had made the call from a public phone box in the Centro Colombo–Americano. Inevitably the military would have time to trace the call, since he needed a good ten minutes to give comprehensive instructions on how to reach the *maloca*, but this would nevertheless avail them little once they learned that it had been made from an American stronghold. The army chiefs' natural reaction would be to construe this as an important but unofficial and unattributable piece of intelligence which for reasons of their own the *norteamericanos* preferred not to transmit through normal channels. Finally, when Lancaster produced his trump card, the mention of Cuban involvement, the colonel in charge of military counter-espionage was put on the line. His eagerness to get at the declared enemy of all Latin–American military elites was unmistakable.

After speaking to the colonel, Lancaster hung up and wandered ostentatiously through the Centro, making sure that he was recognised and that the library staff and others were forced to ask whether he needed any assistance. Then he drove out to the US ambassadorial residence in El Chicó and asked the guard at the gate whether Señor Summerby was available, insisting that the guard make enquiries of the residency staff through the field telephone in the porter's lodge. Then, when Summerby was not to be found, back through the clogged traffic of Chapinero and the Avenida Décima to the US embassy offices, where he again asked for Summerby, again ostentatiously, to be told that the latter was temporarily "out of Bogotá". Lancaster was not surprised – indeed he would have been surprised only if Summerby had appeared. So now the news of the Frias and Hernández challenge would have to rely on Cristina's press contacts.

The final stage in the operation was the call to the DAS. As expected, one mention of Hernández did the trick. Once again the case officer tried to keep Lancaster on the line while the call was traced, but this time he did not make the call a long one. Acosta's desire to catch up with Hernández was such an obsession that anyone who bore news of him would be subjected to the full resources of the Colonel's interrogation cells.

"Take a pew," said Evelyn Oldham.

The British Ambassador was one of the old school in the FO. In a more professional foreign service it would have been difficult to imagine him rising past Third Secretary, yet in the British system this quintessential

177

amateur was not far off his "K", as the in-service argot had it. Oldham's policy had always been that he wished to know nothing about the activities of such SIS personnel as came under his aegis via diplomatic cover. David Lancaster's activities, however, had been so blatant as to elicit comment from his fellow ambassadors, egged on by the political officers and secret-service personnel under their command. Thus it was the particular form his protest to London should take that now exercised Oldham and had led to the present conclave with his Head of Chancery, Miller.

"I understand our mystery man's popped up again. Our sources report a renewal of cable traffic with London, and the chappy's even been seen around Bogotá ." HE frowned portentously. "I don't want us to get our wires crossed on this one, Dick. I appreciate we can often get valuable spin-offs from these clandestine activities, but this fellow Lancaster has made us into a laughing-stock. I'm proposing that unless we get an apology from someone appropriate we should make it a point of principle not to co-operate in future. What d'you think?"

Miller steepled his fingers. "Two weeks ago, sir, I would have advised you to tread carefully. When Lancaster arrived here I got a distinct impression of someone already groomed for a high position among the Provisionals" – this was how Oldham and Miller habitually referred to SIS agents. "To have objected to his activities, however unorthodox and tiresome, might have meant treading on some powerful corns."

"Let's get to the point, Dick," said Oldham irritably.

"Excuse me, sir, I was going to say that all previous experience would tend to counsel caution, but this morning I received this." He handed the Ambassador a hastily scribbled note. "This latest message takes him over the edge and into impertinence. So I agree with your suggestion about a formal complaint."

"What on earth does the bloody man mean? 'Circumstances compel me to relinquish my position in the Embassy prior to returning to London. Explanation impossible through these channels'."

178

"He appears to be laying claims to a status which, if genuine, is inconsistent with the sending of such a message."

"To say nothing of being damned high-handed. Things have gone to the dogs in MI6 since Crombie took over. I've said it before and I'll say it again, MI6 should be firmly under the thumb of the FO, or at the very least a good, solid, down-to-earth policeman like Manchester."

"Just as you say, sir. Would you mind giving this Adlon your approval? This is what I've said: REQUEST IMMEDIATE RECALL LANCASTER PENDING FULL-SCALE ENQUIRY INTO ORIGINAL POSTING."

"Good chap, Dick. Bang it off straight away."

From the wall behind Acosta's desk came the sound of low moaning, and a thumping noise as of blows being struck: Acosta clearly did not believe in concealing from visitors what went on in the DAS interrogation centres.

Summerby was mildly disappointed. Acosta had been on the Company-sponsored Public Safety Programme in Miami and had been considered a star trainee. One of the objectives of the Miami course had been to get across the idea that these crude forms of interrogation should only be used as a last resort.

Summerby's own dealings with Acosta had not always been successful. Under Colonel Jiménez there had been a fruitful interchange of information between the DAS and the CIA, yet on the few occasions Summerby had dealt directly with this new *jefe* he had found him disturbingly opaque, mistrustful, hostile, even at times insolent. For this reason he had taken a more than usual delight in recruiting for the Company Jaramillo, the No. 2, and Vásquez, the No. 4-ranking DAS officials. Both had been approached independently, so that neither man could suspect he was working for the same organisation, and had been entered on the Company payroll at a retainer of 10,000 pesos monthly each.

It was from Jaramillo that Summerby had learned of the current flap within the DAS on the subject of Efraim Hernández. Apparently Acosta had been tipped off that

Hernández was at large in the city and he was now moving heaven and earth to uncover him.

"Señor Summerby, this is a surprise and a great pleasure," Acosta began, unconvincingly. "We are always glad to see our respected North American friends here. If there is any way in which I can help you, please tell me. We are *a sus ordenes*."

"What I have to say is a matter of some delicacy," replied Summerby. "I understand you have an interest in a certain notorious individual currently believed to be in Bogotá."

"You are, as always, well informed," Acosta replied, his heavy eyebrows raised questioningly.

"I imagine the same person who gave you the information also passed it on to us," Summerby bluffed. "The point is – and here I'm going to be very frank with you – we already knew this, as we commissioned the said individual to carry out for us a contract which bears closely upon the well-being of our two nations. It had been my intention to let you know of our arrangement once our mutual friend's task had been completed. I have of course no authority to prevent you from picking him up before he can finish his work. But, as you can imagine, that would be unfortunate, since he is probably the only man who can help us in this particular case."

"And you are here for what, exactly?"

"Frankly, I have come to ask you a favour, *mi coronel*. It would go ill with our plans if your men were to be seen too openly pursuing their quarry. Just give me a few days, with the heat off, and I will personally deliver to you this man you need so badly."

"Your offer is most generous," mused Acosta. "But in order to avail myself of it and to satisfy my political superiors I would have to be convinced that my self-denial was genuinely in a good cause. What guarantee do I have that the well-being of Colombia is served? Do you have any convincing proofs that your project is vital to the security of the hemisphere, as you suggest?"

"You will appreciate, Colonel, that just as you owe obligations to President Lleras and his Cabinet, I too must satisfy my political superiors in Washington. We are both

180

men of the world, and if I tell you that our current operation is to be conducted at the highest security ranking you will doubtless understand the impossibility of my divulging more. But, at a more personal level, I think you can be assured that my superiors will be suitably grateful. It is within my gift to nominate a Colombian representative as our official guest at the coming OAS conference on hemisphere security in Washington. The invitation comprises first-class travel, first-class hotel and entertainment, *et cetera* – and I mean '*et cetera*' in the sense so dear to your national liberator – plus a reasonable stipend of, say, two thousand dollars to cover out-of-pocket expenses on the trip. The Embassy will get round any problems that may be raised by your superiors by insisting that it is you and only you they wish to see at the Washington meeting."

"And in return I have your assurance that you will deliver this man to me before the end of the month?"

"You have my word on it. One thing, though. I would like your guarantee that you will take no prisoners; that you will shoot down this man who insulted you and all his men, without quarter."

"That is not a favour for yourself you are requesting, but one that you are giving to me," replied Acosta. "*Con muchissimo gusto, a la orden*, Señor Summerby."

Tuesday morning brought Lancaster two shocks. The first was a report in *El Tiempo*, not about the Hernández challenge but rather that the army had uncovered a Cuban sabotage and infiltration unit in the Amazon. This too he had expected. According to the communiqué, however, the Cubans had occupied an Indian village, had lined up the adult males, and had summarily executed them by firing squad. The motive both for the original occupation and for the shooting of the Indians remained obscure in the report, which simply stated that according to army intelligence the Cubans had intended to establish a *foco* for guerilla warfare in the jungle.

Piecing together what was the more likely explanation, and allowing for journalistic exaggerations, Lancaster surmised that when Alirio returned from guiding him Luis, already enraged at the disappearance of his prisoner, must have refused to believe the Indian's story. Fearing therefore that Lancaster might have made good his escape with the active help of Alirio and the connivance of others, and anticipating that the Englishman would alert the military authorities, Luis Frias had cut his losses and returned to Bogotá. But not, it seemed, before he had shot Alirio and Rotilio and possibly Keshenko too in reprisal. So now the contest between Frias and Lancaster was no longer that of two professionals but a darker, more primeval vendetta. Lancaster took an oath that when the papal visit was over, whatever the outcome, he would make it his business to seek out and destroy the Cuban.

Then the second blow fell. The reply from London to his cable stated: IMPERATIVE YOU RETURN LONDON SOONEST ANSWER OLDHAM CHARGES. CROMBIE.

This made no sense. Whatever charges the idiotic Oldham might make could relate only to Lancaster's status as an SIS agent, which obviously Crombie knew about already. So why this excuse to get him back to London? Not for the first time he wondered whether anyone in England was really interested in the purpose of his presence in Bogotá. After a few moments' reflection he sent out another coded message. REQUEST CLARIFICATION YOUR EXLON 2345. PRESENCE HERE TILL END OF MONTH ESSENTIAL IF OBJECTIVE TO BE FULFILLED. CONFIRM OBJECTIVE STILL SAME URGENTEST.

It was, at best, a holding operation. But, with the Pope's visit now only two days away, that was all that was needed.

"Operation Toro has three possible stages."

Summerby placed one elbow on his desk and raised the first of three fat fingers. "First, there is the helicopter sabotage attempt. If this works, there is no more for us to do. But the official decision has not yet been taken about whether to fly the subject direct from the airport to the cathedral or whether to proceed with the motorcade. We must assume that the second stage will have to be implemented."

Another finger was raised. "This is where I expect our

best chance will come. Now, the early part of the subject's drive from Eldorado is too risky. There are no buildings near enough to the highway, and no cover, so that escape afterwards would be almost impossible. Obviously the best bet on paper is to wait until the Plaza Bolivar itself, but this is dangerous since all the buildings in the main square will be under tight surveillance. No, our best opportunity will come before that, as the subject comes off the Avenida de las Americas and starts passing through the city centre on the way to the plaza. Officially no one knows the route for tomorrow's motorcade but in fact the DAS has already decided on it, so I know the exact itinerary."

Summerby paused. Neither Frias nor Everett spoke, so he continued.

"If you look at the plan I have drawn up you will see the upper-storey window I have designated for the targeting. At this point the papal convoy will have been forced to slow because of the crowds. It will still not be stationary, of course. Do you think you can do it, Luis?"

"With this little goody I've got, no doubt about it," Luis replied, patting his Armalite-type rifle.

"Well, we've got to tread carefully," said Summerby. "Lancaster's play of the Hernández card nearly scuttled the diversion plan. Luckily I was able to fix Acosta, so the bulk of the police will be drawn away at the vital moment. Luis, you'll have every chance. Using the elevator to the cellar, you should be able to make your getaway without too much hassle."

"Just don't screw this up the way you did the Amazon job," said Everett bitterly.

Luis's eyes flashed. "You got no call to be talking like that. You don't like the way I handled it, maybe you like to get in the firing line yourself. Perhaps you like to take this baby and go do the job. If not, shut up and just don't shit me."

Summerby intervened. "We know you'll do a good, clean, professional job, Luis. What's bothering Jim is that in the heat of the battle you might go over the top tomorrow and try to take out others. You never did tell us why you felt it necessary to execute half that village."

"They let that lousy limey sonofabitch walk away from me, that's why. I tell you, Señor Summerby, right now I want nothing better than to go after this Englishman's ass. But I'll see the contract through, just like I said I would."

Summerby nodded. "And after this is all over, Luis, you'll have not only our blessing but all the back-up we can give you to settle with Mr Lancaster."

The cable from London had provided Lancaster with final proof of what he had come increasingly to suspect – that it had never been London's intention to do anything actually to save the victim of Janos' coup, not even when it had been demonstrated that the victim was to be the Pope. Clearly Sir Ian Crombie's principal intention all along had simply been to secure a political advantage over the CIA and KGB.

About Colonel Durand's part in things Lancaster wasn't so certain. He seemed an honest man. Perhaps Crombie had fooled him. Perhaps Crombie had fooled the entire E.I./J committee. But Lancaster found it no consolation to remind himself that Sir Ian himself was now in trouble. The system that had allowed one Crombie to climb to the top would allow another.

No, whatever the exact truth of this particular business, the Service was now utterly discredited in Lancaster's eyes and he told Cristina as much that night when they were sitting, quietly talking, after dinner.

"Cristina, I'm disillusioned with my way of life. I think you ought to know that, whatever happens in the next few days, I'm going to resign my post in the British Service. It won't be easy, of course – in their terms I know too much, and so I'm dangerous to them."

She reached for his hand and held it tightly between her breasts. "If you fear for your life, why not go to ground? I'll stay with you."

"You don't know these people. There's nowhere to hide that's far enough away. No, I've got to return to London. There's a chance I can persuade them that I'm harmless. If I can, then I'll be allowed to retire peacefully without dishonour."

Cristina drew him to her and kissed him. "You've been very honest with me, David. But I think that even you are not free of a certain *machismo*."

"Perhaps I'm not." He met her eyes. "But would you really respect a man with none at all?"

She thought about it. Slowly she shook her head.

Before they went to bed that night Lancaster and Cristina rehearsed all the preparations they had made with Penata and Valencia for the coming day, and attempted to draw up a balance sheet of what they had achieved so far. As they had expected, Summerby and Everett had gone to ground. They were unavailable at any of the US Embassy's listed numbers, and at their private numbers an answerphone monotonously repeated in English the formula that Mr Summerby and Mr Everett were unavoidably absent on US government business.

There was clearly even less chance of locating Luis or Hernández. The challenge, finally printed in the newspapers, had turned out a damp squib. Detailed enquiries conducted by Penata and Valencia of all guerilla contacts in the city had revealed not a whisper of any unusual preparations. Even the DAS, it seemed, were relaxing, inclined to the opinion that the leftist guerillas would not put in an appearance, nor would there be demonstrations by the radical clergy asking for the Pope to endorse revolutionary violence and the "politics of liberation". According to everything Penata was able to learn of the mood inside the DAS, the main worry was that the enthusiasm of the peasantry might overflow its bounds and the Holy Father get pelted with flowers.

As to the other obstacles they had attempted to place in Summerby's path, Lancaster and Cristina knew only that the army must have taken their bait and launched a massive airborne sweep along the Caquetá to have found the *maloca* within so short a time after their tip-off. A follow-up story in the Wednesday *El Tiempo* spoke of tens of thousands of soldiers being deployed along the Caquetá and its tributaries in a spectacular search. The newspaper played down the fact that this operation seemed to have yielded them no real benefits, since Luis had in fact already flown the coop. As to whether the leak about Hernández would inspire the security forces to any special action, they could not be sure. Probably Acosta would be forced to weigh the importance of the possible capture of Hernández against his other more pressing commitments.

Everything pointed, therefore, to the fact that when Penata and Valencia arrived at the apartment at dawn on the morning of the twenty-second, the four of them would be as much in the dark as ever. They had no detailed strategy whatsoever. The three men would simply patrol the possible motorcade routes from Eldorado airport to the city, while Cristina kept in touch with them from the airport itself by radio. Lancaster had decided that the airport was the least likely place for the attempted assassination: security would be easiest to enforce there and almost certainly excellent.

For Cristina the whole adventure had become a nightmare. She was at this eleventh hour ready to clutch at straws, and such a straw presented itself from an unexpected source. Turning on Lancaster's short-wave radio, which was tuned to the BBC World Service, she heard the first news of the Soviet invasion of Czechoslovakia. The final item in the report stated that in view of the gravity of the international situation there was now a strong possibility that the Holy Father would not after all fly to Bogotá.

Relieved and delighted, Cristina rushed into the bathroom where Lancaster lay soaking to tell him the news. If the papal trip was off, then their worries were over . . .

From what he already knew of the Pope's determination, Lancaster did not share her optimism. But he kept silent. For the first time since his return to Bogotá he saw something like real contentment on her face, and he had not the heart to spoil it.

Twenty

Rome. Wednesday, 21 August. The Pope spoke, for the last time before his flight, to an audience at Castelgandolfo. Some observers thought him ill. His face had a strained, ashen look belied, however, by the forceful and optimistic sentiments he expressed. "Terror, violence and revolution are not the answer to the exceedingly sad situation that exists in Latin America. For us the solution is, as always, love – not weak and rhetorical love, but that of Christ and the Eucharist, love that multiplies."

All cheered; but by no means everyone was convinced.

Bogotá heliport. 10 p.m. Wednesday, 21 August. Joe Martin finished the game thirty dollars down. Disgusted, he prepared for the night shift. Guard duty was part of air force life, but there seemed to him nothing more futile than guarding the helicopter: who'd ever want to steal a helicopter, for Christ's sake? Joe's mind was slow and was still concentrating on the heavy losses he had suffered in just half an hour with his buddies in the locker room. Joe had never realised that poker was not his game, nor had he been told by USAF recruitment that he had been taken in on the lowest possible IQ band consistent with military service.

After basic training Joe had been assigned to routine duties in Panama and had been sent down to Bogotá with a company of US Air Force men to present the Pope with the giant twenty-five-seater helicopter for use during his visit. Neither Avianca nor the Colombian Air Force had been able to come up with a helicopter suitable for the Friday flight between Bogotá and the Eucharistic field at Mosquera, so the Americans had stepped in. Hence the presence of a none-too-bright farm boy from Colorado Springs in the Athens of the Andes.

However, on this occasion Joe's simple-mindedness stood him in good stead. When he approached the helicopter shed and found that instead of the six regular local night staff only one was to be seen, and that one a man not wearing the official security flash given to all local employees, Joe pulled out his revolver and fired. His shot was poor but it hit the man in the leg. Wheeling round, the intruder fired rapidly three times and Joe fell to the ground. His assailant hobbled out of the hangar and disappeared into the night.

The shots broke up the poker school in the locker room and brought men running from all directions. Joe was badly wounded but not fatally. Two shots had entered his right shoulder and another his left. There were badly shattered bones but no vital artery had been pierced. Joe was lucid enough while a stretcher was being brought to relate what had happened. The duty officer immediately ordered an enquiry, with a view to finding out in particular why the six local employees had not been at their station. Their story was that a man had arrived with an official-looking letter of commission from the DAS, requiring them to undergo further security screening. Obediently they had gone into the general office to wait, leaving the "señor doctor" by the craft.

Suspecting a possible attempt at sabotage, the duty officer, Major Mayotte, then ordered a meticulous inspection of the helicopter by his engineers. They gave it a clean bill of health and Mayotte concluded that Joe had disturbed the intruder before any damage had been done.

Next morning, however, when the chief USAF pilot on the mission test-flew the helicopter at Major Mayotte's suggestion, one of the engines failed and the pilot had to exert maximum thrust on the remainder to keep the empty craft airborne. The vibrations from the engines as a result of this emergency manoeuvre were so powerful that entire houses near the heliport were badly damaged. Ceilings were brought down, windows blown in, and four garden walls collapsed. The helicopter was grounded while USAF personnel began to work against the clock to have it ready for the Pope's use the following day, only too relieved that the craft would after all not be needed for His Holiness' journey to Bogotá from the airport that morning.

Bogotá. Calle 23. 7 a.m. Thursday, 22 August. Efraim Hernández surveyed his arsenal. Unlike most of the jobs he had been involved in, he would go into this one with unlimited ammunition and a wealth of weaponry – Belgian FALs, Russian AKs, Armalite M Carbines with sights, and for close fighting the much-feared Makarov revolver. With a dozen hand-picked comrades he could stand off Acosta for hours unless the Colombian brought up tanks or artillery – unlikely, for he would have lost face by calling in the army. And the beauty of it was that Hernández and his band had a guaranteed getaway route through the improvised tunnel and into the sewers. How much more promising this engagement was than his last, legendary joust with Acosta – then a mere lieutenant – when, despite his bravado afterwards, Hernández had been convinced he was a dead man and would never break out.

According to Summerby, he could expect the shooting to start any time after ten. To win his golden hoard of dollars, he had only to keep Acosta at bay for an hour! No problem. His sole regret was that there had been no opportunity to meet the challenge of those two crazy guerillas, but Summerby had forbidden it, promising him and Frias that there would be plenty of time afterwards.

Hernández ran over his defensive plans once again with Elias Palencia, his second-in-command. It was just like old times; the morale of his veteran followers, newly arrived from Huila, had never been higher. A thousand dollars a head for an hour's work picking off the despised *policieros*! It was like taking *caramelos* from a baby.

The Presidential Palace. Bogotá 8 a.m. Thursday, 22 August. The Minister of the Interior winced as he surveyed last-minute security reports from civilian and military sources. Soon he would have to leave with President Lleras for

Eldorado to meet the cause of his headache. Although he now had 15,000 troops and police under his command he was still worried by the risks to the Pope's safety, especially on the six-mile drive from the airport to the Plaza Bolivar. The problem of policing the Eucharistic field next day was also a nightmare. Out of 750,000 pilgrims it only needed one to be an assassin. Stray lunatics or discontented nationals the Minister could not provide an adequate defence against, especially in a city reckoned the second most violent in the world. But he felt proud of the way he had pre-empted any threat from foreign agents. Their most obvious way of getting to the Pope was through the international press corps – foreign correspondents being in the Minister's book synonymous with members of the intelligence community – so he had dealt with the problem simply and effectively. Having issued *cédulas* for journalists in May, first making them produce photographs in quadruplicate and applications in quintuplicate, he had announced on Tuesday, two days before the Pope's arrival, that these credentials were no longer valid and that new documents would have to be issued. It had amused him the previous day to look out into the corridor and see these eyes and ears of London, Paris and Washington vainly queuing up like anxious peasants before his surly and unpunctilious aides.

For the Minister's future career, much depended on this papal visit. A Conservative in Lleras' administration, he was being tipped as the possible presidential candidate for the National Front in 1970 when, in accordance with the Pact of Sitges, it was the turn of the Conservatives to provide the chief executive. Moreover, the President, in a Cabinet meeting at the beginning of the month, had made it clear that he intended to turn Paul VI's trip to his own advantage and to that of the National Front. He would meet the Pope as head of state to head of state, but would hold himself carefully aloof until he had heard the Pontiff's speech at Mosquera. The aim of the ruling elite was to play down anything to their own discredit coming from the Pope's lips, and to play up every positive statement. It was constantly to be stressed that the visit was in itself a sign of the Vatican's belief in Lleras as a desirable innovating force.

This was all the more important as a new threat to the Liberal–Conservative coalition had manifested itself in the 1966 elections – the growing power of the ANAPO party of General Rojas Pinilla. Some alarmists in the Cabinet had argued that by 1970 Pinilla might be unstoppable, in which case the elite would be forced to have recourse to electoral fraud, which would be hard to conceal from the world. Therefore the President preferred that his successor be elected genuinely, and the papal seal of approval on the "radical" measures of Lleras, even if given only implicitly, would be a priceless asset.

In fact the President's policies were no more radical than those of any leader since Bolivar – he knew that and so did all his colleagues. Indeed they had often laughed at L. B. J. and the *norteamericanos* for their naive belief in Latin American "free" elections and "constitutional" government. The *gringos* were so desperate not to have to confront an authentic military regime that they absurdly overrated any civilian administration and lauded its contribution to the "free" world. All these advantages, however, would be jeopardised by any incident that tarnished Colombia's image of stability in the world. Hence the responsibility on the Minister; and hence his pained expression.

London. Sickle House. 2 p.m. 22 August. Sir Ian Crombie returned from his lunch at Prunier's disconsolate and irritable. God defend me from all amateurs, he thought. Richard Burton, Charles Doughty, Sidney Reilly, T. E. Lawrence – all of you – you should *not* be living at this hour. It seemed clear that for reasons of his own Lancaster had not heeded the instructions sent him to pull out of Colombia. No doubt the imbecile saw the whole thing as a moral crusade and was in danger of destroying an edifice that Crombie personally had wrought to compass the downfall of his enemies. He made a note for the future that the Service must find some way of winnowing out all potential recruits possessing the smallest spark of abstract idealism.

As for the present, drastic action was clearly called for. He would discuss the measures to be taken with Pug

Hammond alone. E.I./J committee was no longer reliable, and certainly not Colonel Durand, who seemed to have taken it upon himself to pose as Lancaster's guardian angel. Pug would know the precedents; there were ways and means of squaring these things. In the meantime he could only hope that not a whiff of London's involvement would find its way from Bogotá on to the international airwaves. If this were to happen, it would happen soon, he reflected, noting that by local time in Bogotá the Pope would just about be arriving now.

Bogotá 6 a.m., 22 August. Summerby felt himself to be within a hair's breadth of the objective he had pledged himself to fulfil in his last meeting with Johnson. Within forty-eight hours he hoped to be able to report to J. J. that the left in Latin America was smitten hip and thigh. He idolised the man and always had. For a long time it had been his hope that somewhere in the Company there would be a man like himself who would make no bones about his contempt for the hypocritical nonsense called democracy to which his country was so impossibly shackled. He could thus still recall the thrill when J. J. had told him, at a Langley training course: "Democracy is cowardice and liberalism the pet dog that trots along at its heel. How can we defeat our enemies if we have always to fight them with one hand tied behind our back, worried about what the *Washington Post* will say, or Senator Fulbright, or the intellectual community?" Summerby had treasured those words as a disciple the utterances of a prophet.

He had had misgivings, certainly, especially when Luis had made such a mess of looking after the Britisher. And Lancaster was still at large . . . But what could he do now? He was a minor irritant, and could be left to be dealt with by Frias later.

Twenty-One

"So there it is, Cristina. I'm afraid your last hope has gone. In some ways it's just as well. How do you think we could have proved my story to Antonio if the Pope hadn't come?" It was before dawn and the BBC had announced the take-off of the Avianca 707 from Da Vinci airport.

Neither Lancaster nor Cristina had slept much that night. Both were glad to be up and doing despite the lack of sleep. Lancaster kept feeding bullets into the chamber of his Smith and Wesson, squinting down the barrel, then unloading and starting again. Normally Cristina would have been irritated by this, but this morning she was gloomy and preoccupied.

"Antonio's got problems enough with Fabio on his back." She went into the kitchen to brew some *tinto*, and continued to talk to Lancaster through the door of the bedroom where he lay sprawled across the bed, still nervously counting and re-counting the bullets. "Fabio was never the coolest of men, but your visit to the camp seems to have unhinged him. I could almost pity Antonio. The only way he can play fair with you is to risk Fabio's fury."

Lancaster put down the Smith and Wesson and searched in his jacket pocket for the crude sketch-map he had drawn. "I've changed my mind. I don't think it's very important *which* route the Pope takes. I've decided to station myself near where the highway from Eldorado funnels into the centre. I know how Luis thinks, and I'm sure that's where he'll strike."

"What about the other links in the chain, David?" she replied. "The phony guerillas Summerby wants to take the

193

blame? How is Summerby going to set that up, and where? And what about this diversion from Hernández?"

Lancaster walked through to join her in the kitchen. "Don't worry, that'll come. About the substitutes, who knows? That was the one thing they didn't fill me in on. But bodies are never hard to come by, for a man like Summerby."

Cristina tried for a last-minute reprieve from the coming ordeal. "Are you still absolutely sure it's worth proceeding, *querido*? Your chances of doing anything are zilch." She spoke the last word in English. Lancaster thought it had an odd sound, then realised with a jolt that they had always spoken together in Spanish and he didn't know how good her English was, or even if she spoke it.

"And isn't there a danger that the DAS will stumble on our frequency by accident?" she continued.

"Highly unlikely. Antonio and Núñez used these walkie-talkies in a bank raid in Bucaramanga in sixty-four, just before they went into the jungle, and no one got on to them."

"This is Bogotá, not Bucaramanga."

"Okay, I take your point. But all British studies of Colombian intelligence suggest that their radio monitoring is perfunctory. If they had the CIA working closely with them on a big operation then yes, I would be afraid. But in the nature of the case we know that can't happen . . . Of course we could get unlucky. Some ham operator could tune in on us and tip off the DAS; but if we keep our messages coded there's no reason why anyone should suspect anything."

It was after ten on Thursday morning. While Penata and Valencia were on roving patrol along the now officially announced route into the centre of Bogotá, Lancaster took up his position at the intersection of Carretera Eldorado and the Avenida de las Americas. Cristina remained at Eldorado, discreetly in the background, in radio contact with the other three. Because of the thousands who thronged the airport, the observation platforms and the exits, she was not able to see the details of the papal arrival;

but over the loudspeaker system, rigged up to relay the Pope's message of greeting on landing, she could follow most of the sequence of events.

The airport had been closed for all flights scheduled to arrive that Thursday morning. There were, however, still a few stragglers from a delayed Braniff flight which had arrived several hours behind schedule at 8.30 a.m., and the inevitable Colombian businessmen elite for whom security requirements had been waived.

The Avianca flight bearing the Pontiff was itself a little late. A cheer arose from the crowd as the Boeing 707 suddenly appeared. All planes appear suddenly on the approach to Eldorado, on account of the need for a sudden descent once the *altiplano* is reached; a gradual descent would take planes straight into the opposite cordillera of the Andes.

The white and silver Boeing touched down at approximately 10.20, local time. The staircase was brought forward and the doors of the 707 thrown open. The familiar aquiline profile of Paul VI, keeper of the keys of Peter and much-criticised head of the Holy Roman and Apostolic Church, stepped into the harsh light of intermontane Colombia. A gust of wind tugged at his robes as he began to descend the gangway. Slowly and deliberately, looking all of his seventy years, the Pope descended to the ground. As Carlos Lleras moved forward to greet him, from thousands of devout Colombian throats there arose the cry *"Viva el papa!"* A twenty-one gun salute was counterpointed by bell-peals from over a hundred city churches.

Cristina tried to concentrate on the loudspeakers. To her disgust, she heard the acclamations of the crowd give way to a stereotyped speech of greeting from the Pope, who, with Lleras at his shoulder, called for "peaceful and orderly progress" in Latin America. He spoke in Spanish, very well, marred by the very occasional lapse as a light Italian intonation crept in, but the content of the message sounded to Cristina as vacuous as reformist commentaries on Colombia had always seemed.

At last the speech ended, and it was time for the motorcade to begin. Cristina communicated this to her comrades.

The Pope got into an open black limousine especially equipped with a high seat at the back so that he could gesture with outstretched arms in the familiar papal way to the crowds lining the route. The enthusiastic and deep-packed multitudes were held back by the police as the papal convoy made a right turn out of Eldorado and began to drive slowly into the city. It was now 10.50, and the drive would take about twenty-five minutes.

From his window on the fourth floor of the Edificio Libertador Luis surveyed the scene below him. The crowd was more heterogeneous than he was used to. Men in dark double-breasted suits carrying umbrellas, more as a sign of Anglo-Saxon gentility than because rain was likely in Bogotá in August, rubbed shoulders with *campesinos* and Indians in floppy hats and *ruanas*. Elderly women in black shawls crossed themselves and threaded their rosaries while they muttered their *"Virgen Marias"*. Dark-skinned children, both *mulato* and *mestizo*, were there in swarms, and Luis noted with concern that his escape would not be easy. So dense were the throngs on the side streets leading to the Plaza Bolivar and back to his position that any form of hasty get-away was ruled out.

Summerby's original plan had been that after the hit he should descend by elevator to the basement and thence through the coal chute in the block's boiler room at the back of the building. Now, however, the crowds were such that the spill-over had encircled the block. He would simply have to mingle with them and take his chance. At least he could still be at the back of the building before the people there could have discovered what had happened at the front.

Although this was the biggest job he had ever carried out single-handed – his attempts on Cuban and US presidents had been as part of a large and well-rehearsed team – Luis felt no nervousness. Everett had half-expected he might demur when he heard who the target was, but in this he misread his man. Summerby's reading had been truer. Luis simply remarked that he had no time for *curas malditos* anyway, and would get some satisfaction from taking out the "biggest bastard of them all".

As a boy Luis had profoundly despised his village priests: not just their casual cruelty to the boys in their school, but much more their cupidity and the way the women would fawn over them, offering them the choicest cuts of meat amid the aching poverty of their families. The Pope, eh? Well, if that guy reckoned he could change bread and wine into the body and blood of Christ, he sure as hell ought to be able to protect himself against one man's bullets.

Luis sensed that his moment was drawing near. There seemed to be a new stillness in the crowd below him, an electric expectancy. The police were now trying to push the spectators back from the roadway long enough for the Pope's car to pass. Looking down towards Eldorado airport, Luis glimpsed the outstretched arms of a white figure in an open car, seemingly a miniature version of the figure of Christ on Monserrate. He made last-minute adjustments to his Armalite, then squinted down the sight, adjusting it to achieve the exact range and focus he needed. He figured he would be able to get off three volleys before giving away his position to the security forces.

But then, as he zeroed in on the section of the crowd immediately beside the road where the car would pass, he checked in astonishment. There, down among all the people, was the *gringo*, Lancaster. Luis shook himself and blinked. There he was, distinctly – the man he had last seen in a jungle clearing in Amazonas, the man he had actually liked, in whom he had confided, the man who had made a fool of him and humiliated him in Hernández's eyes. He had kept out of Efraim's way since his return to Bogotá, but the shame was with him always.

This was an opportunity too good to miss. One simple adjustment of the sights, one careful aim, a squeeze on the trigger, and he was a man among men again.

And if he killed the Englishman now, this minute, who down there in the noisy crowd would notice? One sound among so many, one body falling . . .? Luis checked his breathing, steadied his hand on the window sill. Lancaster was still in his sights. Honour demanded that he should die. And as well as honour, common sense, for Summerby had placed a price of twenty thousand dollars on the Englishman's head.

Lancaster moved. Momentarily a lamp post masked him. Luis had time for second thoughts: the papal car was approaching – why risk the possibility of creating a diversion, halting the police outriders, diverting the column? There would be time enough, as the Pope passed, for both killings: two shots each would be plenty.

Luis relaxed and wiped away the sweat gathering in his eyebrows. He dried his hands. Memories of another motorcade came to him, another car, another crowd, a day very like this, hot and bright, but under a *norteamericano* sky . . . Lancaster was out from behind the lamp post, turning, seeming to look straight up at him. Behind Lancaster the papal car was still some hundred and fifty metres away, the distance laid out below Luis as if on a map. He waited. There was a striped canvas blind above his window, casting a deep shadow. Lancaster would see nothing.

Luis had decided to take out the Pope first, just in case there were problems. For the *gringo* there would always be other days, but for the contract there was just this one chance.

Lancaster, however, was something else. Lancaster was a question of honour.

Now the papal car was close, no more than sixty metres. Lancaster's head disappeared behind a mass of flags being waved in the crowd. It would reappear: there was still plenty of time. Luis raised his Armalite, looking for the head above the white robe and spread arms. And at that moment someone in the crowd beside the car swung a noisy football rattle.

It was a small thing. Luis himself hardly heard the sound. Certainly no one in his right mind would have mistaken it for gunfire. But nerves in the papal motorcade were taut, and just for a second His Holiness' driver panicked. His foot twitched down on the accelerator, the car jerked forward, and on his seat high in the back the Pope lurched momentarily backwards, then forwards again. It was not a significant movement and, as the driver immediately checked himself, it went generally unnoticed. But to Luis it made the difference between success and failure.

He had fired and missed. Lancaster seemed to have heard the shots and was pointing upwards. Luis took a snap decision, fired at him, lost sight of him in the melee. Suddenly there was no time at all. He swung the Armalite round to his right, to the now-receding figure of the Pope. But he was distracted, his aim was poor, and again he scored a complete miss. A woman in the crowd just behind the limousine pitched forward on to the road. By now the escort was alerted and the convoy speeded up. Luis saw grim military faces scanning the windows of the adjacent buildings. There was no time to waste.

When Lancaster heard from Cristina that the Pope had left Eldorado airport he had checked on the whereabouts of Penata and Valencia. On the plane's arrival they had abandoned their fruitless patrol and were now stationed in the Plaza Bolivar. Their impossible brief was to prevent any attempt that might be made on the Pope's life while he made his speech from the cathedral balcony. Then Lancaster had signed off. He himself had a strong intuition that Summerby's assassins would make their bid Dallas-fashion, on a moving motorcade rather than on a static target in the main square. For one thing, the confusion caused would be greater, and hence the cover better for an escape. Drawing on his own experience, he reckoned this block on the Avenida Libertador as a prime location, since it was the point he himself would have chosen. For fifteen minutes after signing off from his comrades he moved up and down, slowly and with difficulty, through the deep crowd. Finally, when his watch showed that the Pope would pass in about three minutes, he managed to push his way to the front. He then turned to examine the windows of the building behind him. They were dark and still, many of them shaded with awnings, and he could see nothing.

The cheering around him intensified. Looking to the right he saw the first of the cars approaching, perhaps five blocks away. The convoy came nearer, the police outriders helping to part the mob as their colleagues on foot linked arms against the weight of eager humanity. Lancaster, staring upwards again, shaded his eyes against the sun. Nearby a man waved a rattle above his head. The clacking sound triggered alarm in the jittery escort: the convoy gathered speed. Just as the papal car swept by Lancaster felt an agonising blow against his shoulder. He staggered and would have collapsed at the roadside but for the press of people holding him up. Fighting the nausea caused by the sudden pain, he looked towards the receding figure of the Pope – all seemed to be well. Pandemonium had broken out in the crowd around him. Excited voices gabbled incoherently. He was on his knees now. From the babble he made out that a woman had been seen to fall as the papal limousine swept by. Already word was spreading that there was a sharpshooter at one of the windows opposite. By now the Pope's escort was alerted. A police cordon formed, and after a while a squad of heavily-armed riot cops ran up. Fingers were pointed skywards and eyes trained to the higher floors of the surrounding office blocks.

By this time the press around him had parted and Lancaster slumped full out. He vomited and several people shouted for a doctor. Eventually a squat, profusely sweating man arrived and deposited his briefcase on the pavement. After a few minutes' examination he pronounced Lancaster's situation not serious: he had been shot once, in the shoulder. It was simply a case of removing a bullet and treating a minor gunshot wound.

"You are American, yes?" he asked. Lancaster groaned, unwilling to argue. "So sorry, Señor. A foreign visitor gunned down. That's bad image. But it's everyday life in our Athens of the Andes."

Cristina had followed the motorcade into the city as far as the intersection of Carrera 20 and Calle 20. When the crowds made further progress by car impossible she tried to reach the Plaza Bolivar on foot. The ancient heart of the city was where the Pope was due to give his address after the ceremony in the cathedral. But when progress by foot itself became impossible because of the throng, Cristina contented herself with watching proceedings on a television set in a *tienda*. After a two-minute speech from the balcony of the cathedral, the Pope disappeared from sight.

As the disappointed crowds began to disperse Cristina found her attention caught by the commentator's words. He remarked that all had gone as planned on the first stage of the Pope's visit. There had been no disturbances except a police gunfight with bandits in the south of the city. They had tried to take advantage of the Pope's arrival to hold up a store. Also, there were reports of two people in the crowd having been mysteriously shot, one of them an English diplomat. Both had been taken to the Mercedes de Pérez hospital.

Guessing something of the truth, Cristina hurried to the hospital. It was not difficult to discover where Lancaster was being treated, since the shooting had created something of a sensation among the nursing staff, less from the nature of the case as from the flotilla of police who had arrived with the patient, klaxons sounding and lights flashing. Despite the police presence, Cristina's distinguished family name got her to the bedside of the "English diplomat" with little difficulty. The surgeon in charge told her that he would have no objection to the patient's discharging himself that evening, provided he signed a form absolving the hospital authorities from any further responsibility.

Lancaster, still drowsy after his anaesthetic, seemed in good shape. He smiled and clasped Cristina's hand tightly before lapsing into sleep.

The police were unsuspicious. It was true the Englishman had been found to be carrying a gun, but he also possessed an official permit, so that was that. The inspector simply asked Cristina routine questions about how she knew Lancaster (from the Press Club, *como no*), and whether she had witnessed the incident. No, the inspector said, they were not able to suggest any motive for the shooting, but the proximity of the Pope's car at the time suggested that some amateur killer had tried to get a shot off at His Holiness. It had to be an amateur to have missed by such a margin. But she was please not to mention his off-the-record remarks to anyone, as the Colombian authorities were anxious that no unfavourable publicity attach itself to the papal visit, and the foreign press would certainly try to build the incident up into a sensational story. Cristina acquiesced with the customary bland Colombian *"está bien"* and made arrangements to return that evening for Lancaster.

Twenty-Two

At 10.50 a.m., just as the Pope was leaving Eldorado airport, Hernández heard from Summerby that he was about to tip off Acosta anonymously that his old enemy was in conference with *violencia* veterans in the house on Calle 23. No more than ten minutes could then be expected to elapse before Acosta's men arrived. Hernández listened with silent satisfaction, replaced the receiver, and for a full half-minute continued whittling away at a block of wood with the long slashing blade he used in street fights. Then he rose slowly and barked out crisp orders to his men.

Hernández had made his preparations with professional thoroughness. He and his men were provided with masks against tear gas. Heavy wooden barricades, about ten feet high, had been erected behind the windows in the house, formed partly from the more solid items of furniture, and partly from a variety of lumber Hernández' men had brought for the purpose. In the barricades they had constructed embrasures commanding wide fields of fire. Hernández would direct operations against all frontal assaults, while his lieutenant Palencia's job was to watch out for attacks from the rear or the sides. Palencia would use three of the *guerrilleros*; the other seven would remain with Hernández.

Like many of the undevout and even blasphemous, Hernández was deeply superstitious. He liked the idea of just twelve men defying the DAS. Twelve was a number with mythic overtones – there had been twelve apostles, and juries too were composed of twelve members . . . All in all, the omens were more propitious for combat than on any occasion he could remember.

It was two minutes past eleven by his watch when Acosta's vanguard made its appearance. Three police cars arrived at the end of the road, where they could be seen by Hernández' lookout from the upstairs window. Cautiously but purposefully a dozen men, four from each car, began to creep along the pavement towards the house, until they reached the entrance to the driveway. Hernandez' strict orders were that his men should hold their fire until the main body of the police began to approach the front of the house. When firing commenced Palencia's group were to use a heavy machine gun in an emplacement at the upstairs window to destroy the police vehicles at the end of the road.

Since the anonymous caller had not informed Acosta of the degree of Hernández' preparedness, the precautions exercised by the police were of the simplest kind. As a result they came boldly into the open on the approach to the front door and were totally unprepared for the devastating fire they then received from the defenders. At least half a dozen were killed immediately. The wounded survivors scurried back towards the end of the road to get the heavier-calibre weapons they had brought – only to see their cars enveloped by flames as Palencia's gunners set about their work.

A runner was sent immediately for reinforcements. Torn between this major conflict and the shooting of some foreigner in the wake of the papal motorcade, Acosta had no hesitation in diverting the majority of his force to Calle 23. And so it was that Luis Frias, delayed by the crowds and facing an impenetrable cordon of policemen, was suddenly reprieved. The policemen broke up, doubled smartly away, and so the way was open for Luis to make good his escape.

It was 11.30 before the full weight of Acosta's fury descended on the Hernández group. No less than four dozen heavily-armed special police took up their stations at the corner of Calle 23 and Carrera 3. Colonel Acosta directed the assault in person. He soon found the range of Hernández' gunners, their blind spots, the killing ground, and the limits of the upper-storey machine gun. Deploying his men behind various stone walls, hedges and trees, he proceeded to soften up the defenders by a devastating barrage of sub-machine gun fire.

Hernández had anticipated these tactics. Although his men occasionally had to duck – for some of the shooting brought down plaster from the ceilings – for the most part the barrage spent itself on the barricades. Throughout the bombardment Hernández watched for the moment when Acosta would order his men closer. He expected that assault troops would have to be sent in with grenades and, sure enough, at about 12.10 Acosta gave the order for half a dozen men to emerge from cover and enter the garden. The luckless handful got no further than the first yard on to the lawn before a withering volley rang out and all six were dropped in their tracks.

The groans of the dying had a potent effect on Acosta's team. To prevent any drop in morale and to take advantage of the spontaneous blood lust of his men, now thirsting for revenge, Acosta immediately ordered a frontal charge en masse. For Hernández and his men it was like picking off ducks in a shooting gallery. The upper-floor machine gun scythed through the charging ranks, while those who survived were exposed to fire from the barricaded lower windows. One or two penetrated to within grenade-throwing range, but the handful of missiles they managed to lob caused little damage. Two contained tear gas, which drifted harmlessly among the masked defenders.

At 12.30, smarting under his humiliation, the DAS commandant called up his reserves and requested reinforcements from the city riot police, the veterans of countless campus clashes at the National University. This time his trump card was to be the use of water cannon. His colleague, Colonel Vicente Gómez, commander of the riot control squad, had long been keen to try out his new equipment, imported at the beginning of the year from the USA. It was claimed that these cannons had a range of up to one hundred metres, though generally used at about a third of that range, and had been perfected after the 1965 Watts riots in Los Angeles. One hundred metres was about the distance from the street to the barricaded front windows held by

Hernández' men, and Acosta reckoned that even if the jet of water would be largely spent by the time it hit the wooden defences it would impair visibility and create confusion, so that his men could at last advance into the garden without coming under the raking salvos from the house.

Shortly after one o'clock the water cannon arrived. Gómez had come too, eager to see how his expensive equipment performed. After a quick conference the two commanders agreed to launch an immediate assault, and the massive hoses, already linked to the water mains on Calle 23, were trained on the front of the house.

When the deluge began Hernández's visibility was reduced almost to nil. This was a counter-stroke he had not foreseen and he had no contingency plans for dealing with it.

Summerby had provided him with a flame thrower against the possibility that regular troops of the Colombian army would be called in at an early stage. This, Hernández saw, was the key. Quickly he motioned to one of his men to help him with the unwieldy cylinder. After explaining his plan to Palencia, he took another two men to cover him during the sortie. Leaving by the back door, the three men edged round the side of the house. When they got to the front, Hernández paused for a moment. Acosta's men, overconfident, had not yet begun to infiltrate the garden. Clearly Acosta had not imagined that Hernández would be able to improvise any realistic counter-attack. The massive water-cannon tank was parked just out of sight of the house, to the left, but closer in to the defenders than the intersection of Calle 23 and Carrera 3, so that it was out of sight of the upper-storey machine gun. Hernández and his men dodged round the arc of the cannon's trajectory. Reaching the street, they saturated the waggon bearing the deadly water with flame.

The first inkling Acosta and Gómez got of Hernández' presence was when they saw the water tank going up in flames. Now the extreme difficulty of manoeuvring the unwieldy machine was manifested, for it toppled over as soon as it caught alight. Again and again the baleful cylinder belched out fire, and the all-conquering jet could no more

206

be trained back on itself than the guns of a tank could be turned against its own armour. So sudden and devastating was Hernández's attack that his little party was able to make good its retreat back to the house before Acosta thought of ordering a pursuit.

The destruction of the cannon produced profound depression in Acosta. It seemed that he had no option now but to call in the army and let them pound the house to pieces with heavy armour. Gómez was no help, but rather sat dejectedly on a low wall at one end of the street, murmuring over and over to himself incredulously: "*Hijo de puta, hijo de puta*". An hour ago the potential scourge of all Colombian students who dared to follow the example of their Parisian or North American confrères had stood gleaming in the garage of the *jefatura*. Now it was a burnt-out shell, whose cannon mouth still dribbled water while the machine itself smouldered with ebbing flames.

By 1.45 p.m. Acosta had finally steeled himself to bear the humiliation of calling in the army. So it seemed that the legend of Efraim Hernández would live on. The ballads and folksongs would tell how Colonel Acosta was twice worsted by the hero, who only finally went down fighting against the entire might of the Colombian military machine. Still, there was nothing for it. If this defiance went on much longer he, Acosta, was in danger of dismissal for incompetence, never mind public humiliation. The ruling coalition would brook no major scandal on the very day of the Pope's arrival, when they were attempting to burnish the country's image in the eyes of the world.

Almost as Acosta lifted the telephone in his car to compose the necessary number, he heard his name requested from HQ: "Mr Summerby for Mr Acosta."

"Yes. Of course. You're sure?" Acosta listened and made notes, interrupting the caller only to request an exact detail or two. When the caller had finished there was a new light in Acosta's eye.

"Señor Summerby, I will never forget this. You have helped me more than you will ever know. *Mil gracias y hasta luego!*"

*

By now, however, Hernández had more than made good his side of the bargain with Summerby. Of his men, four had been wounded, but only slightly, while outside on the lawn lay the bodies of possibly two dozen of Acosta's crack paramilitaries. By any standard, it was a great achievement, and he gladly gave the order to withdraw.

The trap door in the cellar was opened and the men began to descend into the tunnel beyond that would carry them out on to the Avenida Gaitán, to freedom, and to a place in the legends of Colombian folk heroes. Palencia was the last one down. As the stutter of his AK gave way to silence behind them, his comrades made their way by torchlight along the passage to the connecting door opening on to the main tunnel of the Bogotá sewers. Leading the way, Hernández found the rusty circular screw-action connecting door difficult to move. Main force was needed by half a dozen of his men to turn it. At last the circular hatch gaped open. Eagerly Hernández' men crawled through it, then lowered themselves on to the ledge above the sewage channels beyond. The door was left open for Palencia, who had been told to follow the main column, closing the cellar trap door behind him. When Acosta's men broke into the house they would be bound to find the trap door, but only after a thorough search of the building, and by then the guerillas would have escaped.

They formed an Indian file behind Hernández on the narrow ledge and crept forward. The air was foul and rats scuttled in front of them, fleeing the glare of the flashlights. Down, down they went, descending steeply at times, towards the main sewer into which all the tributaries fed.

At this junction Hernández stopped to read Summerby's map, playing his flashlight over the simple diagram. On the blueprint a right turn along the next channel was indicated. He stopped for a minute and listened. There was only the sound of falling water and the occasional lapping noise of the shallow river against the iron causeways. Hernández bellowed and listened to the heavy resonance of the echo. Satisfied, he ordered his troop out on to the main watercourse.

Just as he was about to turn into the next canal and begin

the steady climb upwards he stopped. Something was wrong. All of a sudden he was sure the jammed circular doorway had been an omen. The gambler's intuition that had kept him alive for twenty years made him pause at the intersection. Powerfully and insistently his sixth sense told him to turn back. In the next second a glaring searchlight was trained full on the guerilla party and a voice, which even in these depths he recognised as that of Acosta, called through a megaphone for them to surrender. "*Que rindense en seguida si quieren sobrevivir. Manos arriba.*"

Hernández's answer was a burst from his machine gun, a refrain taken up by his party. But this time it was the last stand of doomed men. Acosta, with the detailed information Summerby had given him, had baited his trap too well. An inferno of heavy-arms fire brought to its end for ever the legend of Efraim Hernández. Some of the men fell dead where they stood, Hernández among the first of them. Others tried to escape back the way they had come, but Acosta had corked this escape route too. A party of his men had been hidden in the next tributary downstream from where Hernández's guerillas had emerged. This rivulet was about halfway between the Gaitán exit and Hernández's point of entry on to the river. These now emerged to deal the *coup de grâce* and to bring the life of a folk-hero to an inglorious end in a Bogotá sewer. No balladeer would sing this last chant of Efraim Hernández.

Twenty-Three

The high-point in the drama of the papal visit had been reached, but there were still several acts left. Lancaster could not afford to discount the possibility that Summerby might try something at Mosquera. Released from the Mercedes hospital into Cristina's care, in the car home he scanned the evening papers for any clues to Summerby's future actions. *El Tiempo* and *El Espectador* carried lengthy front-page stories of the Pope's mass ordination of priests in the special Eucharistic arena on Thursday afternoon, when the Pontiff addressed a giant gathering from an open-air circular temple. Antonio and Andrés had been there too and reported nothing untoward. Evidently Summerby had gambled everything on the motorcade attack and had had nothing ready for the afternoon.

To Lancaster a curiosity of the day's news was that the shooting in which he had been involved was not even mentioned. The whole presentation of the Pope's progress from Eldorado to Plaza Bolivar was upbeat, a triumphant example of Paul VI's charisma and confirmation of the devoutness of the Colombian man in the street. On an inside page there was a brief paragraph which stated that Efraim Hernández, the notorious bandit, had been killed by police while resisting arrest. Hernández, it was reported, had been reduced to petty theft in the *tiendas* of Bogotá, and it was an aggrieved shop-owner, who had previously been robbed by the bandit, who had recognised him in south Bogotá and had called the police. Reading between the lines, Lancaster wondered if the coincidence with the papal visit was too great. Possibly Hernández had been causing a diversion for Frias's benefit. Either way, it seemed likely that Luis was still at liberty.

Penata and Valencia were waiting for him on his and Cristina's return to her apartment. The issue of his *bona fides* was still unresolved: Antonio had promised a truce only until the Pope's departure, and remained sceptical that there had ever been a plot to assassinate the Pope.

"I accept that you were shot, *inglés*. Someone wants you dead. You are clearly mixed up in deadly affairs. But so far you have not provided me with any evidence that your many plots have anything to do with the Pope, still less with a scheme to discredit the left."

"Talk sense, Antonio," said Cristina sharply. "How do you think David came to be wounded at that very time on that very day? Surely even you must think it a pretty far-fetched coincidence that David should be shot at when he was standing within yards of the Pope?"

"Then why has your assassin not struck again?" asked Penata. "If he is after the Pope, not the *inglés*, why was he not in the Plaza Bolivar? I was there and saw no sign of any threat."

"What did you see exactly?" asked Cristina, hoping to defuse a tense situation. The ploy worked. Antonio lapsed into his Marxist-Leninist mode.

"I saw the fallacy of liberalism and reformism. The world will never change just because some old priest exhorts it to. How do you get the multinationals to disgorge what they have stolen from South America? By an appeal for kindness? By a warning that God sees all and will judge all? No; as Chairman Mao says, these things can only come from the barrel of a gun. Does the Holy Father tell us how we can achieve justice peacefully? He does not, nor can he, because there is no way it can be done."

"You seem to have been so engrossed with the Pope and his words that you would not have noticed the enemy even if he had made a move," Cristina said.

"Enemy? What enemy? Señor Lancaster's enemy perhaps, but that is all. "And now what, Señor Lancaster? The Pope departs for Rome tomorrow, and yet you are no nearer proving to us the truth of your statements. Meanwhile I have to take some action and report to Comrade Fabio. For all I know, you could even have had yourself

211

wounded by an accomplice – " he said this sarcastically, looking at Cristina " – to make your story about the Pope stand up."

Afterwards it seemed to Lancaster little short of miraculous that the phone rang at that moment. In his anger Penata strode forward to answer it.

"*Si, si.* I am authorised to take all messages on his behalf." Then a long pause until "Indeed." After a few more moments of listening, he said, "I am Señor Lancaster's aide in all this, so you can talk to me as if to him. Yes, I know everything about the case." Again a pause, one lasting perhaps three minutes. The anger seemed to drain out of him and he glanced half-quizzically, half-perplexedly at Lancaster as he took notes on a piece of paper. "Of course. *Lago de Tota, como no.* Tomorrow at eleven? I see no objection." He hung up.

"It seems I owe you an apology, Señor Lancaster." Penata sat down slowly. "That was the American Summerby on the phone, and in his raging at you he confirmed in detail the story you have given us. His fury was better than any truth drug."

"So now you're convinced you've not been on a fool's errand?"

"More than convinced. Summerby wants us to meet him at a spot near Lake Tota tomorrow morning. He says the matter is a personal one between you and him, but as he will be bringing friends you are quite welcome to do the same. Your Señor Summerby must have some Latin blood in him, no? I did not think *gringos* were affected by *venganza.*"

"It's more than that," said Lancaster. "Summerby's finished with the Company. He's made a mess of the job and his famous J. J. will have to ditch him to save his own skin. In fact, he may well feel that Summerby is too dangerous to be left walking round alive. Summerby knows this. The only card he has left is the possibility of wiping us out. He could then present this either as a libation to his master in Washington or – who knows? – he may hope to dump the blame for the whole affair on us and the British when the Company investigates it. Whichever way you look at it, this meeting has to be the last throw of a desperate man. And that's what makes him more dangerous than ever."

Lake Tota was a dismal and curiously dispiriting place. At certain times of the year this bleak stretch of water, perched nine thousand feet above sea level, was frequented by the trout-fishing fraternity in the Bogotá oligarchy, but in August it was deserted, its two almost empty hotels nestling in rival bays of the nearer shore. The farther shore, beyond the unprepossessing village of Tota, was cold and uninviting. From Tota an unpaved road wound down the ribs of the eastern cordillera and into the *llanos*, but few ever went down from the plateau to the great plains by this route; the favoured itinerary for those with ranching business in the vast *llanos* was east from Bogotá to Villavicencio. The far shore was thus an ideal location for both Lancaster and Summerby. The hills and bluffs encircling it were even used on occasion for shooting practice by *bogotanos* determined either to increase their marksmanship for the hunt or to exercise themselves in noisy *machismo*, so that the sound of gunfire would be greeted with no surprise by the locals.

Lancaster and his party took up their position in a cold and dreary copse a mile inland, at a point almost directly on the other side of the lake from the Hotel Tisquesusa. The three-hour trip from Bogotá had been effortless – an excellent paved road ran all the way from the capital, through dreary Tunja, up by Paipa, tucked in at the waterside of a small lake, and thence through the Sogamoso valley to the big lake itself. The hospital had insisted that Lancaster keep his injured left arm in a sling, so Cristina drove.

Lancaster saw the meeting as a final settling of accounts, after which he would quit the Service, disappear to Mexico with Cristina, and arrange his rehabilitation with London from there. To this end he had written a somewhat incoherent personal note, uncoded, to Colonel Durand. Cristina was worried about his state of mind. He was no longer the seemingly effortless master of a given situation she had come so to rely upon, and she sympathised with

213

him deeply. The strain of the last few weeks had been enormous, and for this reason alone she looked forward to nightfall with a longing unlike any she had experienced before. By dusk on this day the business with Summerby would be settled one way or another: either she and David would be making final preparations for Mexico, or . . . she did not allow herself to dwell on the alternative possibility.

If she was fearing for Lancaster's sanity then he, in the car that morning, was having similar thoughts about Summerby. What was the American's purpose in this meeting? He could conceivably be planning to eliminate Lancaster and his comrades, but this seemed unlikely. The terrain around Lake Tota, though ideal for crude gun-fighting, was not suitable for an ambush – there was too much cover, for one thing – and in any case it was common sense that a planned wet job was never carried out at a pre-announced locale. There was always the possibility that the opposition could have taken pre-emptive action, or even enlisted the support of local security forces. No, the more Lancaster thought about Summerby's request, the more bizarre it seemed.

Expecting Summerby to arrive by car along the dirt road that wound round the edge of Lake Tota, Lancaster had placed Valencia as lookout on a point of rock at the roadside. The place Summerby had chosen for the confrontation was a two-hundred-yard stretch of baked mud between the rocks and the lakeshore. But the American proved to have another trick up his sleeve.

It was just eleven when a chattering noise in the sky roused Lancaster's party from their somnolent wait. A slate-grey helicopter flew low over them, circled, then moved in close. At first Lancaster thought it intended to attack them, and shouted to Penata and Valencia to take cover. The two guerillas flung themselves to the ground beneath the car with rifles ready – but the helicopter pilot was simply reconnoitring before landing.

Great whorls of dust were churned up as he settled on the shore of the lake, across the open space from Lancaster's Thunderbird. Three men got out. Lancaster recognised them at once as Summerby, Luis, and Everett. Luis and

Everett took cover behind the helicopter; Antonio and Andrés released the safety catches on their weapons. Cristina stayed with them, armed with her favourite Star.

When the clattering rotors had slowed to a halt, Lancaster hailed Summerby: "Okay. Let's talk, if you want to talk."

He motioned towards some humps of rock that looked out over the lake. Summerby followed him down to the shore, walking easily, giving every impression of a man relaxed. Lancaster, by contrast, was nervous and edgy. He began the conversation, eager to get it over.

"I didn't know the Company ran to gunships for their station directors."

"Company, nuts. This is on loan from Acosta. The bastard owes me a favour."

"Lucky you. Well – suppose you tell me why you've asked for this meeting. It's not every day that a man sits down in conference with his erstwhile torturer."

Summerby spread his hands. There was an aura of Pennsylvania Avenue about him even as he perched on a rock at Tota. "You've every right to be mad, Dave. I don't deny it." Lancaster noticed the ingratiating use of his shortened first name. "I know I've no right in the world to expect a sympathetic hearing from you, Dave, but I'd like you to give it a try. Hell, you're probably in as much of a fix as I am."

"How d'you figure that? You're the one who's bungled the job. You may remember, I told you you'd never be able to pull it off."

"You may be right. Then again, you may not. Maybe there's more to Luis' foul-up yesterday than you know. Anyway, you've been in this game long enough to know that when the chips are down both sides play against the middle. And the time's come now when you and me are just those two guys in the middle."

"What exactly are you talking about?" said Lancaster sharply.

"Hell, I see no reason not to tell you. The way I figure it, you and me could still end up partners. You know the good Colonel Acosta, of course? Well, me and the Colonel are

215

thick as thieves, and it seems that J. J. sent in a squad a couple of days ago to silence me after I'd done my work here. Acosta monitored their arrival. They were surprisingly frank with him. The story is that I'm a traitor to the good old US of A, a danger to hemisphere security, Public Enemy Number One in spades."

"Why should your J. J. want to dispose of you? After all, if Luis had been successful you'd have been his blue-eyed boy."

"That's what I thought. But it seems J. J. intended to eliminate me whatever the results of Operation Toro. The document authorising my termination which Acosta saw was dated twentieth August – that's before the Pope even got here. Luckily for me, Acosta is so pleased at having nailed Hernández with my help that he tipped me off last night. And maybe your position's not so hot either. He mentioned that there's a gang in town from London too."

"Okay. So you're in a hell of a mess. Perhaps I am too. But why should I of all people want to help you?"

Summerby stared out over the lake with a glazed expression, as if his thoughts were far to the north, in Washington.

"Because, feller, according to J. J. you already have helped me. You can figure his play. If London have a man on hand who can testify that he and he alone ordered the strike against the Pope, then J. J.'s in deep trouble. The only way to counter that is to insinuate that we're in it together. He's obviously fed the line to London and they've swallowed it. Who else is an MI6 squad looking for in godforsaken Colombia but their own man? They're sure as hell not looking for me. Besides, Acosta confirmed my hunch. He told me that the story from the Arlington heavy brigade was that I was in league with a Britisher called Lancaster. How else could Acosta have got that name? He doesn't even know you. So now the only problem you've got to face is which set of bombers hits you first, the RAF or the USAF."

Lancaster reflected that by disobeying Crombie's cable he had indeed played into the hands of the mysterious J. J.; that part of Summerby's story made sense. He hesitated, then decided to see what other cards Summerby might hold.

"All right, let's say I go along with your crazy theory. What do you propose next?"

"Let's start from basic propositions. We've both got gorillas on our tails, right? Now, shooting it out's far too risky. Let's assume instead that you were willing to sacrifice your two men, and me to give up Frias. That way we've got the bodies of proven guerillas and gunmen to verify our story about the Pope, and puts us in the clear, right? But that won't work either. You see, like I told you, J. J. wants to off me whatever . . . The point I'm making is I don't exactly have a whole bunch of options. Our best hope lies in getting our information right to the top in Washington. I've got to get to the Director-General himself and bypass J. J., and if you support me by presenting your credentials as a British field agent working to uncover a plot against the Pope we can lay a charge that stretches back to the good ole boy himself. J. J.'s then stymied. What do you say?"

"I say you're crazy. Just tell me this: What's the percentage for me? I can clear myself without getting into this far-fetched lunacy of yours. All I need is a confession from you or your aides over there."

"I thought you'd say something like that. Obviously you need to be persuaded. I think you underrate the danger you're in. I hope you're not a Catholic, Dave?"

"No."

"Then you won't mind if I say that nobody really gives a shit about the Pope. Okay, J. J. had a great scheme and it snafu'd, but as the great Sam Goldwyn would say, that's all water under the duck's back now. What makes you dangerous is not that you've stumbled on a plot to liquidate Paul VI, but that by accident you've blundered into something much bigger."

"Keep it up. You're bluffing a treat."

"Look, I don't know the half of it, only the crumbs J. J.'s let fall from his table, but even what I *have* heard would scare the shit out of me if I was a Britisher. Why do you think Frias there, who's a crack shot and has been in on some of the biggest deals of the decade, fired at you and not the Pope and so blew the whole operation?"

"I think I know why. It's a personal matter between us."

"Because you made a monkey of him in the Amazon? Yeah, I heard about it all. Don't you believe it; Frias is a pro. It's because when I radioed J. J. to inform him of your meddling in our little affair we got back something we didn't expect. We were instructed to find you and eliminate you at all costs. J. J. was afraid you were getting close to the big one. Operation Churchill."

Lancaster could not contain himself. He burst out laughing. "Operation Churchill? Not even the CIA could devise something that ludicrous."

Summerby looked almost hurt. "You think so, huh? Well, how about this for starters? We all know that the *Soviets* have penetrated the SIS. But it would never occur to anyone that the SIS might be penetrated at the highest level by its so-called *ally*. Suppose that in the innnermost circles of British intelligence there was a sleeper, convinced of the necessity for his own country of the US winning the Cold War – and any hot ones, for that matter. Let's imagine a man in the Churchill mould, profoundly dedicated to the ideal of Anglo-American friendship and deeply suspicious of the British Labour Party. A man who hated it and thought it a Trojan horse for international communism."

"Such a man would be as mad as a hatter and as such a fitting comrade for your own J. J."

"Maybe. I'm not going to debate with you on that. But J. J. told me there *is* such a man, and that his cover is in danger of being blown by your activities here in Colombia. Also, suspecting that I would be as sceptical as you are, he provided some back-up evidence."

"I would be most interested to hear it."

"Well, you remember J. J. told me long ago that the Prime Minister in Britain had requested that the CIA investigate the British secret service on his own behalf, because he suspected it of treachery and disloyalty to the Labour government?"

"I remember distinctly the uncomfortable circumstances in which you first told me the story."

218

Summerby shifted his weight uneasily. "The request went to the Oval Office and was passed to the directorate at Arlington for immediate action. An investigation was conducted in Britain and it was discovered that there was indeed a plan for a coup against the Labour government. It was to be led by the armed forces and there was to be a provisional government of the patriotic right, with a figurehead leader close to the royal family to ensure continuity. The report was processed and passed to the Director's office. He in turn was prepared to hand it to the President who, as you know, has a soft spot for your PM. Then, suddenly, the report was suppressed. The word around the Company was that if the British learned the details of the coup they would soon trace the leading member of the SIS who had colluded all these years with Washington. This individual was too deeply involved with the preparations for the coup to be able to escape detection. In the interests of the continuing deep penetration of the SIS by the agent, the top-secret memorandum being prepared for the President was suppressed and a harmless routine bulletin prepared instead.

"Now what worries me is this: J. J. was powerful enough to extend his tentacles into the directorate itself to extract all this information. And this is just the bit I know, probably the tip of an iceberg. That raises three questions. How much more is there to this Operation Churchill? Was the highly-placed plant in London in on our operation here? And, for us, the sixty-four thousand dollar question: can we get to the directorate before J. J. gets to us?"

"Let me understand you. You're saying that I'm now a prime target because as a result of uncovering your own plot against the Pope I came dangerously close to revealing this other business, this Operation Churchill? Which, incidentally, I still don't believe in."

"Think about it, Dave. It adds up, you know. If you informed London of a plot by the CIA to assassinate the Pope, a plot the directorate in Washington knows nothing of, heads would roll. So the new broom comes in, starts sweeping out the files, and a lot of compromising stuff surfaces. And neither side wants that. The sides against the middle, Dave. It's the way things go."

"There's only one thing wrong with all this. The whole ingenious story rests on your say-so. There's no independent evidence. How do I know you're not just a brilliant spinner of yarns?"

There was a look of something like desperation on Summerby's face now. He twisted uncomfortably on his rocky seat, then got up and began to pace along the shore. Lancaster followed him.

"Talk sense, man. Where would I be able to make all this up? Think back to the time we had you staked out. Think back to the things I told you then. There was stuff I couldn't have known any other way than through a leak from London. Besides, what about this posse from London? Now they haven't exactly flown all the way from England just to say happy birthday. For God's sake, Dave, let's put all our cards on the table and level with each other. It's the only way we're going to get out of this mess alive."

Lancaster stopped walking and faced him. "You're crazy. And I don't do deals with torturers. Frankly, I prefer to take my chances with my own people. I'm quitting, Summerby. And if I do it right, maybe I'll live to a peaceful old age."

Summerby flailed his arms wildly. "You're passing up the best deal you'll ever get, Dave. For Christ's sake – I've got money . . . I'll cut you in on the stake Hernández was to have got. You'll be – "

"Save your breath. I came to Lake Tota because I wanted to hear what you had to say. Now I've heard enough." He drew his revolver and backed away. "We're on neutral ground here, Summerby. I suggest you remember that. You're outnumbered, and if there's shooting you wouldn't stand a chance."

Summerby hesitated. Behind him, from the shelter of the helicopter, Luis shouted: "Hey, *jefe* – we're wasting time here. Why don't we finish these sons of bitches now, eh?"

Lancaster continued to retreat, his concentration razor sharp. Summerby, alone now and vulnerable in the middle of the open space between the helicopter and the car, called back: "Can it, Frias. I'm the ham in this particular sandwich.

220

And like it or not, feller, you need me alive. No Señor Summerby, no pay-off. So calm down, will you?"

Turning his back on Lancaster, Summerby lumbered towards the helicopter. He paused. "You'll regret this, Dave. No guy's ever turned down Ed Summerby and got away with it."

Lancaster glanced round. His group was reasonably well placed: if there was a shoot-out the Thunderbird might not give as good cover as the helicopter, but there were rocks behind it, and dead ground away to the left.

By now the American had reached the helicopter. Lancaster ran back the last few strides to the car, dropped behind it and braced himself. But Summerby had reckoned the odds: he called to Everett to cover them while he and Luis climbed into the helicopter. Luis went first, then heaved up the fat man. Everett warily followed them.

Summerby pointed upwards with one thumb, the rotors began to turn, and in a moment the machine had lifted off, leaving behind it a thick red haze of dust. As it heeled and sped away across the lake, Antonio and Andrés broke from cover and ran down to the shore to watch it. Lancaster joined Cristina. But the moment of their relief was very short.

The helicopter turned and headed back towards them, losing altitude as it came and travelling flat out. Antonio and Andrés saw the manoeuvre just too late. As they sprinted for the protection of the car the helicopter swooped down on them, strafing them with machine-gun fire. The two guerillas fell to the ground, raked with bullets. Lancaster and Cristina were luckier. By the time the helicopter reached them they were crouched in the shadow of the Ford. And as the aircraft turned to make its next pass over them Lancaster had time to jump from his cover, retrieve the sub-machine gun Antonio had dropped, and race back to the car. Wincing with the pain from his injured arm, he checked the weapon. When the helicopter whirred in close above them again, he let fly with a burst from the heavy gun.

His shots went wide, but the pilot sheered off, and once more Lancaster and Cristina survived.

The helicopter continued on its course as far as the edge

of the lake, then banked before coming in on them yet again. Suddenly there was a mighty explosion. An immense red and yellow fireball hung in the air for a second, then plunged down into the lake. Instantly the fireball was snuffed out as the shattered fuselage and assorted debris sank from view. Only the big rotor blades remained. Thrown clear of the wreck, they spun crazily for a few seconds, then came to rest in the no-man's land between the rocks and the lake shore. Finally, after the ear-shattering noises, silence returned to the waters of Lake Tota, broken only by the gentle sound of ripples, as if from a stone thrown into a pond, lapping on the beach.

Twenty-Four

Lancaster spoke first. "Let's get out of here. The *jefe* at Tota may have been alerted. And after him will come the DAS."

Cristina stared down at the dead bodies of her former comrades.

"Aren't you going to bury them?" Her voice broke. For a moment she was close to tears. Then she controlled herself, looked almost accusingly at Lancaster. "Antonio and Andrés were good men, David, and they died for *your* cause, not theirs."

"We're all comrades now," Lancaster told her. "Nuñez can be content that they met a hero's end, befitting freedom fighters. But this is no time for brave speeches. Do you want to be here when Colonel Acosta and his men arrive?"

"He too has run true to form, David," Cristina said thoughtfully.

"What d'you mean?"

"It takes a Colombian to know how another Colombian's mind works. That helicopter didn't blow up simply to oblige us. Acosta set up his *yanqui* friend. No wonder he was ready to lend him his favourite toy."

So that was it, thought Lancaster. *The colonel owes me a favour*, Summerby had said. The favour was really to Summerby's boss, J. J. "So he booby-trapped the helicopter . . . But how did he get his timing right?"

"There's an old trick we know about from the Cubans," said Cristina. "You don't use clock devices or altitude fuses or anything like that. Fidel's people learned it from the Cuban exiles in Miami, who no doubt got it from the CIA."

"What is it?"

"A sound trigger – sound of a distinctive pitch and

timbre. You can programme it any way you like. Gunfire, for instance. That way Acosta could be sure the bomb didn't explode too soon. He set the device to go off two minutes or so after the first shots."

"He must have been pretty sure there'd be some shooting."

"Knowing Summerby, wouldn't you have been?"

Lancaster shrugged. That the monstrous Colonel Acosta should triumph over anyone, even Summerby, disgusted him. But it could not be denied that the deaths of the men in the helicopter were highly convenient to people other than himself. For one thing. The CIA's detailed knowledge of the guerillas and their network of contacts had presumably died with them. And for another, the Pope was now safe from them for the rest of his stay in Colombia.

Lancaster's own situation, he realised, was less ideal. If the heavies from London ran true to form, they would shoot first and ask questions never. Not to mention the rest of the opposition . . .

He returned to the Thunderbird. After a moment beside the two dead bodies on the shore, Cristina joined him. She was pale and shocked, so he drove the car, resting his left arm on the open window.

For a while she was silent, then she turned to him. "Where are we going, David?"

He frowned. "Bucaramanga. Bogotá is too hot for me now on every count. My own people will be looking for me. And the Americans. And probably Acosta. When those bodies are found there'll be road blocks south of Tunja, so the trick is to fly crooked."

"And after Bucaramanga?"

"Eventually, London. Colonel Durand's my only hope. If only half of what Summerby told me back there is true then the Service is in dangerous shape. Corrupt men, Cristina, and in high places . . But direct flights to London are sure to be monitored. So I suggest Mexico City – but not direct from Bucaramanga. It's the most likely airport from Lake Tota, and if Acosta acted fast he might be able to put a check on all international flights out of there. So I'll go via . . . Bogotá."

She glanced sideways at him, horrified. "That's crazy."

"I don't think so. It's the last place anybody'd expect. And transit passengers don't even have to show their passports. Even if Acosta traces me to Bucaramanga, by the time he gets word to Eldorado airport the chances are I'll be up and away. And even then not to London, as he'd expect, but to Mexico City."

Cristina nodded slowly. "And what will you do in Mexico City?"

"I haven't thought it all through yet, but I have contacts among the British community. They'll help us to get the resources we need. Somehow I'll be able to negotiate a safe conduct from there to London."

"And will I go with you to London?"

Briefly he removed his right hand from the wheel. He put his arm round Cristina's shoulders and held her tight. "I'd never go without you," he said quietly.

In Bucaramanga Lancaster immediately made his way to the Avianca office, where he learned that the afternoon flight to the capital would connect there with a non-stop Varig flight by Boeing 727, originating in Rio, to Mexico City. Lancaster warily queried the information, anxious that he and Cristina should not be caught by some idiotic clerical misunderstanding.

A 727, could that be right, *all* the way to Mexico City?

Well, perhaps not *always*, conceded the Avianca official. With a full quota of passengers and a heavy payload, it was not unknown for the Brazilians to lighten their fuel load before leaving Eldorado airport. Although it boasted the second-longest runway in the world, owing to the altitude a full carrier like the Varig 727 often needed every inch of the *pista* to get airborne, and taking off without full tanks was an excellent way of reducing the plane's dead weight.

Where did it put down again in such circumstances? Lancaster wanted to know.

"Usually in Managua," the clerk told him, "but occasionally in Panama City."

"Never in Colombia itself?"

"It has never been known, Señor."

Reassured that he would be clear of Colombian territory by that night, and further encouraged by a provisional passenger manifest that showed the plane to be almost half empty, Lancaster purchased two one-way tickets to Mexico City.

The hour-long flight by Boeing 737 to Bogotá left on time. It was a perfect evening for flying: dusty blue skies, golden sunshine, no wind. From 27,000 feet the peaceful greens, greys and browns of the eastern cordillera were hard to reconcile with the sudden and violent death that still awaited him if he were to make just one mistake. Already his morning's bloody encounter with Summerby was becoming blurred and dreamlike. Once on the journey he even asked Cristina: "Did it really happen? Is Summerby dead? And Andrés?"

"Yes," said Cristina quietly. "These things have happened. But they are part of a life that's gone for ever. Put it all behind you *querido*. Just think of Mexico and the future."

This counsel of perfection Lancaster had found difficult to follow, but the glories of the lush Colombian landscape gradually began to calm him. He was in good spirits as the plane began its descent into Eldorado.

There was now a two-hour wait before they could board the plane to Mexico. The transit passengers' lounge gave them an excellent view of all incoming aircraft so that Lancaster and Cristina could see the arrival of their plane from Manaus, en route from Rio to Mexico City. For a while they watched a few craft make the rapid descent into Eldorado, but the procession of 720s, 737s, 707s, DC-4s, Aviancas, Braniffs, Sams and Aerocondors soon bored them and they moved back into the bar.

Both were very nervous. The transit lounge seemed safe enough, not overlooked, part of the special secret world that airports create, but only when their Varig craft was airborne would they feel totally secure. Cristina looked round at their fellow-travellers. Most were clearly Colombians, but she could distinguish the odd sprinkling of Mexicans. Lancaster was always amused by this ability of hers to differentiate the particular *mestizo* type of Mexico from other South Americans. This evening Cristina's mental count gave her two Brazilians, six Mexicans and a solid phalanx of fellow-countrymen. There were also two *gringos*: one a tall, greying, distinguished man of about fifty; another, smaller, thirtyish, angular and intense. Visiting academics: she recognised the type at once and gave them no further thought.

At 7.30 the loudspeaker announced that the Varig flight from Manaus proceeding non-stop to Mexico City would be the next to arrive. At 7.45 its passengers were called forward for customs formalities, including the payment of airport tax for use of transit facilities. This might be the danger time. There was the remote possibility that their passports, although ready stamped and endorsed in Bucaramanga, would be examined again. But even if that happened there was no certainty that the emigration officials here in Bogotá would have been alerted.

The crowd jostled forward towards the passageway to the departure gate. Here the men of emigration control waited. Cristina and Lancaster had arranged to have the exact money in peso notes to pay the airport and exit taxes. Any delay to query the amount of tax or to give and receive change might lead to an innocuous question. And then perhaps another, less harmless, and so on . . .

As the crowd edged forward, eager to pass the tollgate and emerge into the open space of the departure area, Cristina heard a loud thud – possibly a heavy suitcase being man-handled from a trolley on to the floor behind her. She paused, was urged on. Looking over her shoulder she saw that a large Mexican woman was immediately behind her where David had been a moment before. She was puzzled.

Suddenly from several places behind her in the queue there came a piercing scream. One of the Colombian women was pointing down at the ground and gabbling hysterically. Cristina knew at once. Her sleepwalking of the past few minutes, her inattention to her place in the crowd, her failure to notice that David was not with her in the queue, these lapses of concentration had been fatal. She struggled through the shoving throng and fought her way backwards.

As she bent over David's body the truth suddenly came upon her. The crowd, the confined space, the press of people, the thud of the suitcase. Frantically she eased one hand inside David's jacket, already certain of what she would find: the hot, sticky, crimson patch that she seemed to have seen already in her dreams. It was there, above his heart, spreading across his shirt. She looked at his jacket. In its breast were three telltale punctures, powder-singed grouped there by an expert.

"David, David, David!" she screamed.

The emigration officials ceased their rubber stamping and fumbling with their peso notes, drew their pistols and came forward. Somewhere a whistle blew. There was shouting and the sound of the running boots of the airport police. The two *gringos*, where were the two *gringos*? Wildly she jumped up from Lancaster's body and ran up and down the amazed ranks of passengers looking for the two men. Was it the *viejo elegante* who had the gun with the silencer? Or was it the smaller weasel-faced one? The two were nowhere to be seen. Then for Cristina everything whirled into a nightmarish vortex of sights and sounds and smells, the barking of commands, the babel of excited voices, the heavily-perfumed jowls of the anxious police commandant, the jagged cross-cut rhythms of whistles, alarms, sirens . . .

As she lost consciousness, Cristina's last thought was that she had never told David really how much she loved him.

Epilogue

In May 1981 Geoffrey Staines, a young, newly-recruited graduate to the Intelligence Evaluation Section of MI6, was assigned the task of working back through the Service files to see what background material he could produce on previous assassination attempts on popes or rumours thereof. This was of course in the aftermath of the unsuccessful attempt on the life of Pope John Paul II in Rome.

Among the reports which had circulated down the years Staines lit on a résumé of a case in which the SIS had been involved in 1968. The dossier stated that there had been a strong tip from usually reliable sources that an attempt was to be made on the life of Paul VI during his visit to the Eucharistic Congress in Bogotá in August 1968. The memorandum was not particularly informative: it remained silent on the issue of whether there really had been a plot, but simply recorded the historical fact that Pope Paul's sojourn in the Colombian capital had been uneventful. There was a throw-away comment, however, that there had been an SIS operative in Bogotá under embassy cover who had been shot dead by "assailants unknown" during the Eucharistic Congress. There was a cross-reference to a file in Personnel which contained the career details of the agent.

Out of no more than idle curiosity Staines put in a routine request slip for the file in question. It was at this point that his interest was really awakened, for the slip was returned from Registry marked "File not available. Please cancel or upgrade request." Upgrading the request needed the counter-signature of his controller, James Franklin. Franklin, liking the thoroughness Staines brought to his work, took the unusual step of telephoning the office of the Head of the Service. The secretary was cagey, but promised to raise the matter with Sir John. Next day she rang back to say that Sir John had confirmed that the file had been removed from Personnel during Sir Ian Crombie's incumbency for reasons concerned with "the good of the Service." At this point Franklin wisely lost interest. He knew the ways of the organisation well enough to realise when he was being politely warned off. But for the enthusiastic Staines the case of Operative X (File reference 1936/7/8/LA/C/8) became an ever-tantalising mystery.

The problem was that there was no obvious focus for Staines' quest. In Service terms thirteen years is a long time. Most of those who would have been principals in any drama played out in 1968 were either in retirement or had moved on elsewhere. Still, Staines persisted, and finally he was able to establish the important fact that Agent X's controller at the time must have been a Colonel Eric Durand, who had retired from the Service in 1975. Colonel Durand, it seemed, now lived in Reigate in Surrey. Fortunately for Staines, Durand's telephone number was included on the information sheet, otherwise the quest might have ended right there. It was strict policy that all retired Service personnel went on to an ex-directory listing.

It was still a long shot. Durand could be on holiday, out of the country or even away from home for a few days. Or he might refuse to see a low-level representative of the old firm even if he were at home. So it was with an unwonted tingling feeling that Staines dialled the Reigate number. He heard it ring and almost choked with relief when a quint-essentially military voice answered. Instinctively Staines knew that this was Durand, and that his luck was in.

"Colonel Durand?"

"Yes, what is it?" The voice was crisp, slightly irascible.

"I wonder if it would be possible for you to spare me a few moments of your time, sir. Staines, BISP section here. For obvious reasons the matter cannot be discussed on the telephone, but you may take it that I would not intrude on your retirement unless it was a matter of some importance."

"Oh, very well. I suppose I've had six years without a comeback; it was bound to happen some day. Perhaps it would even do me good to hear some Service gossip. Staines, you say. How about calling here at noon on Tuesday? We could have a drink and perhaps you might like to stay to lunch. Do you want me to meet you at the station?"

"No thank you, Colonel. I think I can find my own way. Midday on Tuesday, then."

On the day arranged Staines caught the train from Victoria, changing at Redhill. From the sleepy little railway station at Reigate he hired the one available taxi, which took him to Durand's address, about a mile away: a secluded house set in about an acre of its own grounds. He paid the taxi and advanced to the front door. Before he could ring the bell the door was opened and he was greeted by a man who seemed almost to have been born for a military role: it seemed inconceivable that such an individual could ever have done anything else.

Staines was shown into a shelf-lined study where his host immediately poured out two immense glasses of the finest malt.

"Now then, Mr Staines, what can I do for you?"

"This may be a bit difficult for you to remember, sir, but I am trying to clarify certain events that took place in Colombia in 1968."

Staines noticed a slight stiffening in Durand's bearing, almost as if he was cranking himself up to regain the alertness of his active Service days.

"Ah, that business. I often wondered if it would remain undetected for ever."

"What exactly do you mean, sir?"

"I mean that your presence here signifies that someone has realised that Sir Ian left a lot of loose ends untied."

"Sir Ian? That would be Sir Ian Crombie, Sir John's predecessor?"

"Yes. Died three years ago, you know. And I suspect that he took the answer you are seeking to the grave."

"I'm afraid you're way ahead of me, sir."

"Let me hazard an educated guess at what you're doing here. You're obviously one of BISP's bright young things. For some reason you've gone back over the Bogotá affair. I

231

can't be certain, of course, but I would surmise that it is not unconnected with the recent lamentable attack on the Pope. And you've discovered that one of our men was killed on active duty while investigating the rumour of a plot against an earlier pope. Am I right so far?"

"Uncannily so, Colonel. I can see why your reputation survives you in Sickle House."

"Nice of you to say so, young man. Now as to what really happened back there, you're probably as wise as I am. But I can perhaps fill in one or two clues for you, if that would help."

"That would be excellent. First of all, *was* there a genuine plot to kill the Pope in 1968?"

"Who knows? There was certainly something very strange going on in Bogotá then, but what the truth of it was God alone knows. Probably the only man who knew the full story was Sir Ian, and he has now gone to meet his maker."

"Then what do *you* think happened in Colombia, sir, and why did our man die?"

"Lancaster," said Durand suddenly.

"I beg your pardon, sir."

"David Lancaster. I've just remembered the name of the operative who bought it in Colombia. I'm sorry, you asked me what I thought happened to him. That depends very much on whether you think there was a plot against the Pope or not. You know, there was also a rumour going the rounds that Lancaster was not quite, well . . ."

"Not quite what, Colonel?"

"Not quite sound ideologically. It seemed that he'd got a lot closer to those Marxist guerilas out there than was considered proper."

"But surely if he'd done that it would merely prove his calibre as an agent?"

"That's what I said at the time; but Sir Ian seemed to think there was more to it than that. He said that just as a poacher can turn gamekeeper so can the gamekeeper turn poacher. Yes, and I think there was talk of a woman, too."

"What kind of a woman?"

"Some sort of Colombian Mata Hari, I believe. I forget the details."

"So what's your analysis of what really happened?"

"I read it like this. Either there was no plot against the Pope, in which case Lancaster was probably bumped off in some faction fighting among the Marxists. Or there really was a plot and either Lancaster learned who was behind it and they got to him – it could have been either KGB or CIA presumably – or . . ."

"Or what, Colonel?"

"Well, I do recall that when we got word of his death, Sir Ian seemed strangely unsurprised, almost as if he had expected it. I've often wondered about that. Perhaps Crombie sold Lancaster out to the Americans because he had crossed them. Or perhaps Lancaster found out something which meant he had to be silenced. I do know that Sir Ian ordered a blackout on all matters relating to Lancaster. His file was taken out of Personnel and incinerated."

"You know that for certain?"

"Of course. Crombie himself told me it was on the direct orders of the PM. And I do remember I got some mad letter from Lancaster, at my home address, written just before he died, full of the wildest accusations."

"What sort of accusations?"

"I really can't remember. Right-wing plots . . . Britain in danger . . . his own disgust with the Service . . . I mean, we none of us liked Crombie very much, but there's moderation in all things."

"Would you have kept the letter, Colonel?"

"Not a chance. No, young man, my advice to you is to forget the whole thing. Leave it in history's garbage bin as one more unsolved mystery. Life's too short."

It was time then to adjourn for lunch, after which Staines seized the first diplomatic opportunity to depart. Durand's remarks had left him even more curious about the events of 1968, but at something of a dead end.

Then, out of the blue, on the Friday following his visit to Durand, the phone rang in Staines' flat. The unmistakable voice of Colonel Durand was on the line.

"Look here, young Staines, I think I've found something

that might be of interest to you. Your visit sparked off a few lines of thought. I went through my papers last night and I found that letter . . . It's very much as I told you, a pretty incoherent piece, but there *is* one interesting thing. On the margin of the letter I seem to have made a note at the time: *See minutes of E.I./J committee*, seventeenth October 1968." Durand paused. "If you could get sight of those minutes you might be able to shed light in some dark corners."

Staines sighed. "Out of the question, I'm afraid, sir. The minutes of the E.I./J committee, as you may remember when you served on it, are not even to be released under the thirty-year rule. Even the historians at the turn of the century won't get a sight of them. And within the Service these minutes can only be released on an authorising signature from a member of the new Intelligence Cabinet."

Durand thought for a moment. "It's a long shot, but it might work. Who are the supremos nowadays?"

"Officially, nobody knows – but off the record it's an open secret. Apart from Sir John there's Lawrence, Taylor, Mackay, Gilbert and Humphreys."

"Aha. Sandy Mackay – there's my target. He owes me a few favours. Listen, Staines. I may as well admit I'm curious. I never checked on those minutes and I bloody well should have. Now I'd like to know what I was really involved in all those years ago. Besides, what else is there to interest an old man like me?"

There was a long pause. Staines could almost hear the old man's mind working. Finally Durand was ready.

"How about this for a scenario? I go to Sandy and tell him that I'm writing a book of memoirs which will include my time in the SIS. No startling revelations, you understand, just standard material showing how essential MI6 is and how much valuable work it does for the free world, that sort of thing . . . and of course I intend to send typescripts to the FO, Ministry of Defence and Sir John for vetting before I go anywhere near a publisher. Only the problem is my memory's letting me down a bit. Would Sandy object if I took a few trips down memory lane by consulting the files for some of the committees I worked on? Nothing specific, of course – I could go into that when I got to Archives. I'm sure that would swing it."

"Sounds marvellous. I'm very grateful to you, sir, for all the trouble you're taking," said Staines sincerely. "I can't explain why I'm so obsessed with this case, but I seem to have some kind of spiritual affinity with this man Lancaster. Does that sound far-fetched?"

"Not a bit. The good operative works on a ten per cent margin of inspiration anyway. And don't thank me either. I have my own reasons for doing what I'm doing. Too smooth, Crombie was. Too smooth by far."

It was two months before Staines heard again from Durand. Just when he had almost given up hope and concluded that the Colonel, having been unable to gain access to the relevant file, had from a sense of failure been unable to confess this to him, the mailbox produced one evening when he got home from work a bulky envelope from Reigate.

First there was Durand's covering note in a small, precise military hand. It seemed that all had gone to plan and nobody had suspected his motive for wishing to inspect the file. Having first perused the contents he had tried a bold stroke and requested a photocopy of the minutes of meetings from May–October 1968 from the Archives officer. With Sandy Mackay's imprimatur this request had been granted without question.

Eagerly Staines turned to the enclosed photocopy of the vital document itself.

17 October 1968 EI/J /I. Ref. 1936/7.
See also 1936/7/8/LA/C/8
Present: Sir Ian Crombie, Messrs Ledbury, Blakely, Hammond, Cameron. Apologies: Colonel Durand.

The committee learned with deep regret of the death of its agent in Bogotá. It seems clear that this agent's demise was not unconnected with his assignment there in connection with Operation Janos. The committee felt itself perplexed by various aspects of the case. In the first place, there was the issue of why agent 1936/7 ignored the cables from Sir Ian. Second, several members of the committee wanted to know why Sir Ian had ordered his withdrawal. On the second question, Sir Ian explained that he was acting out of consideration for overtures made to him by the Americans. It seems that the CIA had set a trap for the left in Colombia which was to be sprung on the occasion of the papal visit in August this year. Agent 1936/7 had somehow got his wires crossed and become convinced that there was a plot against the Pope emanating from the CIA. His intervention in Bogotá bade fair to ruin the Americans' carefully laid plans. CIA directorate then contacted London to have him recalled and hence Sir Ian's cable. Mr Blakely asked to see a copy of the cable from Washington. Sir Ian said that it had been unaccountably mislaid by his secretary. Mr Blakely seemed dissatisfied with this answer, but finally let the matter drop. The other members of the committee regretted that Sir Ian had been unable to produce documentary proof but were satisfied when he offered to produce affidavits from the registry clerk who received the cabled message.

The committee then moved on to the question of the motivation of the deceased agent. The circumstantial evidence, it was agreed, pointed to agent 1936/7's having become an apostate. It was doubted that he had actually thrown in his lot with Moscow, but his relationship with the female Colombian revolutionary denoted an abandonment of his professional integrity, which inference seemed proven by his refusal to answer Sir Ian's cable.

Sir Ian then explained that he had authorised the dispatch of a retrieval squad from section COM to Bogotá when 1936/7 disobeyed orders, but they too had failed to shed any light on the mystery of the aforesaid agent. They reported a large concentration of CIA men in the capital at that time, but this would be normal given the close monitoring of the papal visit.

Finally, the committee turned to the question of whether there had been a plot against Pope Paul VI. Mr Ledbury pointed out that the file on Operation Janos had now been closed. The informant code-named Janos had given information which was never specific enough to be related to particular cases. Whether Janos had had truly valuable information or not, events had by now passed him and his intelligence by.

Summing up, Sir Ian Crombie said that it would be extremely unfortunate if any link were ever to be assumed or made between the death of agent 1936/7 and rumours of a papal assassination plot. Mr Cameron then asked what our current representation in Bogotá was and its rationale. Sir Ian replied that we retained an operative under cover at the Embassy, mainly because FO intelligence indicated the possibility of oil strikes in the *llanos*, which could make Colombia a second Venezuela. It was therefore necessary to watch all covert developments which might jeopardise our future position, including the possibility that the Americans might steal a commercial march on us by secret deals with the National Front. The case of agent 1936/7 was declared closed.

The meeting ended at 4.30 p.m.

Staines returned, intrigued, to Colonel Durand's covering letter: "It is true that I was not at this crucial meeting, for if I had been Crombie would not have got away with his outrageous behaviour. I'm surprised there was not more protest at the time, for even the minutes suggest that something very peculiar was going on. It's true that Ledbury always did what Crombie did, but it *is* curious that the minutes show nothing from Hammond. Perhaps Crombie had found a way to silence him too. I know that's how he worked. He could never manage to pin anything on me, so I was always a thorn in his side.

"My own hunch, reading between the lines, is that Lancaster was right after all, and Crombie was deeply embroiled with the Yanks. It now seems clear that, while telling us on committee that he was playing for high stakes and trying to outwit the PM, he was in fact colluding with him all the time. Remember how the PM was the US President's poodle in those days. That would put the famous request from No. 10 to the CIA to investigate the British Secret Service itself in an entirely new and sinister light.

Now that I come to think of it, the department never did go into the details of that *cause célèbre*, did it? But as to definite proof about poor Lancaster's end, I'm afraid we're as much in the dark as ever."

There was more in the same vein, taking up detailed points in the minutes, but there was one particular passage in the Colonel's letter that stopped Staines dead. After rambling on about the general evils of the detested Sir Ian Crombie, Durand threw in the following: "By the way, did I tell you that Crombie's daughter is married to a John Johnson, now a member of the National Security Council in Washington but at that time head of Latin America division at the CIA? Amusing coincidence, wouldn't you say?"

It was midnight before Staines closed the file and got up from his desk. He lay down on his bed, but sleep was impossible. He believed he knew very well what had happened to agent 1936/7, David Lancaster. He had known too much. The details weren't important. What *was* important was that between them Crombie and this Johnson had been able to get rid of him and cover their tracks. Crombie had retired loaded with honours and tributes to his life in public service. Johnson, it seemed, like the poor, would always be with them.

Finally, as dawn was breaking, Staines slept. The world was a sick place, and he himself the member of a sick service. But sickness, if not always curable, could at least be ameliorated.

Colonel Durand tossed back a couple of brandies before going outside to stroll on his lawn and reflect. He took snuff, sneezed, paused to pinch some greenfly from his roses. He assumed that young Staines would have worked things out by now. But a fat lot of good that would do anybody . . . He sneezed again. A watchdog for the future? Perhaps. If Staines had the guts.

The Colonel's gardener shouted good day to him, which he acknowledged with a wave of his walking-stick. At the other end of the lawn he saw his wife Marion at work with the secateurs. This, after all, was the real world. Doubtless more and better Lancasters would be sacrificed on the bloody altar of national interest, but there was nothing he could do about it now. Who was it had said that the world would be a better place if people remained quietly in their rooms?

With a practised hand he lifted the latch on the side gate and walked out into the leafy lane beyond.

MORE FICTION FROM
HODDER AND STOUGHTON PAPERBACKS

ALAN JUDD
☐ 37986 3 Short of Glory   £2.50

DOUGLAS HURD & STEPHEN LAMPORT
☐ 39674 1 The Palace of Enchantment   £2.95

ELLIS DILLON
☐ 18802 2 Across the Bitter Sea   £3.95
☐ 40335 7 Citizen Burke   £2.95
☐ 32043 5 The Wild Geese   £1.95

DAVID BRIERLEY
☐ 39265 7 Skorpion's Death   £2.50
☐ 40569 4 Snowline   £2.50

All these books are available at your local bookshop or newsagent, or can be ordered direct from the publisher. Just tick the titles you want and fill in the form below.

Prices and availability subject to change without notice.

Hodder & Stoughton Paperbacks, P.O. Box 11, Falmouth, Cornwall.

Please send cheque or postal order, and allow the following for postage and packing:

U.K. – 55p for one book, plus 22p for the second book, and 14p for each additional book ordered up to a £1.75 maximum.

B.F.P.O. and EIRE – 55p for the first book, plus 22p for the second book, and 14p per copy for the next 7 books, 8p per book thereafter.

OTHER OVERSEAS CUSTOMERS – £1.00 for the first book, plus 25p per copy for each additional book.

Name ....

Address ....

....